RAZORBACK

Gripping crime fiction, full of suspense

Lou Holly

THE BOOK FOLKS

Published by The Book Folks

London, 2017

ISBN 978-1-9777-2884-5

www.thebookfolks.com

Special thanks to my wife, Liz

In life, every day is a new chapter

Chapter 1

"Son-of-a-bitch." Vint hit the ground hard and rolled a few times on the sharp stones. The train continued west, bathing him in flashes of mid-afternoon light as the box cars clamored over the tracks with a metallic squeal. He stood and inspected his clothes, noticing a tear in the elbow of his tweed jacket.

Vint brushed himself off and unzipped his light jacket by the rabbit foot hanging from the pull tab. He looked around. Another small town, like so many others. The tracks appeared to run right behind the main street. Good a place as any to spend his last two-bits on coffee and a burger.

Walking between two shingle-sided stores and onto the sidewalk, he looked one way down the street, then the other. A sign hanging over the sidewalk grabbed his attention, *Dewey's Diner*. On his way to the eatery, he paused to catch the date on the Arkansas Gazette in the window of the barbershop, *September 30, 1953*.

The wood-framed screen door chirped like a cricket as he walked into Dewey's. When he let go of the door, it snapped close with a bang. The waitress behind the counter, the two men to his left, sitting on counter stools, the older couple at a table to his right, all stopped and stared at him.

"Hey, fella, don't let the door slam," one of the burly guys at the counter mouthed off. "What's a matter with ya?"

Vint nodded and continued on toward the far end of the counter breathing in the enticing aroma of grilling onions. He removed his paperback copy of *Hell Hath No Fury* from the back pocket of his dirty dungarees and set it on the counter before sitting down.

A young waitress slowly approached, her blonde ponytail swung side to side like a pendulum. "Gonna be another hot one today." She held the steel pot toward the cup sitting in front of him. "Coffee?"

Glancing at the wall menu and locating the nickel price, he turned his cup over and slid it toward her.

"Getcha anything else, Tyrone Power?"

Vint smiled slightly. "Don't waste it on me, blondie. I'm afraid there won't be anything left over for a tip."

"Don't you worry your handsome mug over it. I'm just a friendly kinda girl." She tilted her head and put a hand on her hip. "You look hungry."

Doing his best to ignore the stares from the two guys guzzling their afternoon beer at the other end of the counter, he asked no louder than he had to, "That twenty-cent burger any good?"

"Any good? People drive all the way over from the banks of the Mississippi for our steakburgers."

"Give me one with everything, everything you can manage to fit on there." He stood. "Tell the cook to take his time. I'm going to get washed up."

Locking the men's room door, Vint removed his jacket and t-shirt, then hung them on a hook. He let the water get hot while he lathered his upper body and face. After scrubbing up and drying off, he took his straight razor from the right-side pocket of his jacket and flipped it open. He lathered his stubbles with bar soap and took his time getting a smooth shave. As he was trimming one of his earlobe-length black sideburns, someone pounded hard on the door, causing him to nick himself.

"Hey, what'd ya fall in?"

Vint recognized the voice of the loudmouth from the counter. "Be right out."

After rinsing off his razor, then putting it away, he placed a small piece of toilet paper on the nick. He redressed and went back to the counter. His tall burger, that he thought resembled one of Dagwood's, sat on a small white plate. He sat back down, pushed the buns together and took a bite, trying to recognize the mixture of condiments and dressings.

The waitress sauntered back, her breasts in her pointy bra bouncing slightly in her white uniform. "Hey, now. Look at you, handsome as a movie star." She watched him devour his meal. "Well, did I tell ya or did I tell ya?"

"That's a damn good sandwich, honey." He took another bite and wolfed it down. "Those mushrooms on there?"

"Yeah. We usually just put 'em on the butt steaks but I told Shadrack to throw some on for ya."

"Not bad." He took another big bite.

The guys down the way banged their empty beer bottles on the counter. One of them yelled, "Thirsty!"

She got them another round and chatted with them while Vint finished his sandwich. He pulled a lone crumpled cigarette from a jacket pocket, then rolled it on the counter in an attempt to straighten it. Removing a stick match from another pocket, he lit it off his hand calluses. He drew deeply on the stale cigarette and closed his eyes. Taking another drag, he let the smoke out slowly, thinking about a girl he knew years earlier, and the way her auburn hair smelled. A hard slap on the counter jarred him from his distant memories. His eyes popped open to find one of the beer drinkers plopping into the seat next to him.

"Hey, Yankee, ya gonna eat that pickle or what?" The big guy leaned in uncomfortably close, smelling of beer breath and body odor, his hand inching toward Vint's plate.

He pulled the plate to his right, away from the stubbly faced, bib-overall wearing man, who appeared to be in his late-twenties. Without looking directly at his antagonist, Vint answered, "Yeah."

"Well, see that ya do." The big guy stood with his round belly pushing into Vint's arm. "When I get back from the john, and that pickle's still settin' there, it's mine."

Finishing his cigarette, he looked at the pickle and wondered if it was worth the trouble. He sat and thought. If it wasn't the pickle, it would be something else.

The men's room door slammed and the man returned to the seat next to him. "What I tell ya?" He put his hand on the counter inches from Vint's plate.

Vint fingered the straight razor in his jacket pocket and opened it a little with one hand as he had practiced many times over. "You go for that pickle and you're liable to lose a hand."

"Is that so?" He pulled his head around to try and catch Vint's gaze. "I likes me some pickles a whole bunch. I mean I *really* likes me some pickles. I'd just about wrestle a bear for a good dill, believe I would."

"Then go buy one." Vint grabbed the pickle, took a big bite, then dropped what was left on the counter. "Here, you can have the rest."

The tall, portly guy shot to his feet as Vint remained seated. He pulled the razor from his right-side pocket out of view and snapped it all the way open.

"I'm gonna go back and finish my beer, ya bum. But, remember somethin', ya can't stay in here all day. Gotta come out sooner or later."

Vint closed the razor and put it back in his pocket. The last thing he wanted was trouble in this town. He had enough in the last one.

The waitress came back and smiled uneasily at Vint. "I hate those Skinner brothers. They've been starting trouble all their life." She pulled her order pad from her apron pocket and removed the pencil from behind her ear. "What else can I interest you in?"

"That'll be it." He fished his quarter from the pocket of his jeans and set it on the counter in front of her. He glanced over at the front door. Through the screen, he could see a horse-drawn cart rolling slowly down the street, carrying a homemade pine casket.

"What's your name?" She plopped her elbows on the counter, her lightly freckled face resting in her palms.

"Vinton."

"Anything else go with Vinton?"

"Mercurio."

"Is that Italian?" She picked the partially eaten pickle from the counter and dropped it in the ashtray.

"Guess so." He noticed the way her bright blue eyes twinkled. "Or French or something."

"You got a way about ya, the way you talk and stuff. Your clothes don't match your style. You're smooth. Not like guys around here."

"I don't always go around looking like this." Vint motioned toward his clothes. "It's a long story."

"Mind me asking how old ya are?"

"I was born sometime in 1922, to the best of my knowledge. So, I'm thirty or thirty-one, something like that."

"Where ya from?"

"Whoa, slow down, kid. What's with the third degree?" He paused, then smiled and patted her hand. "Let me ask you something. First off ... *your* name?"

"Lark." She leaned in closer on her elbows, exposing a bit of her cleavage. "Aren't you glad the war's over? Bet you're one of those guys just back from Korea."

"No." He glanced away. "The government had other ideas for me. Sent me to a different kind of camp."

Lark stared into Vint's light brown eyes, with a look of bewilderment.

"Prison, sister. Work camp."

5

"Goodness." Lark's eyes opened wide. "Did you kill someone?"

"No ... no, nothing like that. Got caught holding up a federal bank. Should have stuck to state banks." Vint smirked and shook his head. "So, you grow up around here?"

"Kinda. I moved to this town ..."

"Hey," one of the Skinner brothers called out. "How 'bout some service 'round here? Gonna spend all day talkin' to that hobo?"

The older couple, who were sitting at a table, got up, left a dollar bill and scooted out the door.

"Sorry. I better go over there and settle them down, they can get real nasty when they're drinking." Lark snatched a bag of peanuts from a rack and tossed them to Vint. "Don't go."

"Nothing to be sorry about. Go on ahead." He tore open the plastic bag and poured a handful onto the counter. While shelling and munching peanuts, he listened to the conversation down the way.

"We wanna shot of that Wild Turkey old Dewey keeps behind the counter. Pronto, little lady."

"I'm sorry boys but I can't sell you hard liquor. Dewey might lose his license."

"Who said anything 'bout buyin'? Just hand me the bottle and let us have a swig."

"I don't know. I could get fired. Dewey marks the bottle."

"Do I look like I'm askin'? Get your cute little ass over there and bring me the whiskey!" The brother threw his empty beer bottle on the floor, smashing it to bits.

Vint finally got a good look at Shadrack, the cook, when he peered out the kitchen counter window at the commotion. His coffee bean-colored face glistened with moisture and the shoulders of the big man were about as wide as Vint had seen.

"What are ya lookin' at, boy?" The brother slightly balder than the other shouted. "Get your big Alabama porch-monkey face outa that window 'fore I throw somethin' at ya!"

"Hey, I told ya to bring me that bottle, ya little twat." The other brother demanded. "Don't be a silly-ass bitch all your life. Dewey's not here, just make a new mark like he does or just add some water to make up the difference."

"I don't want any trouble." Lark began crying. "Please just go. I'll pay for your beers."

Vint stood and glared at the trouble makers.

Both brothers jumped to their feet. "Hey, ya better sit down, tramp, or we'll come over there and rip your arms off."

Vint pulled the razor from his pocket and flipped it open. "Time to move on down the line. I'm giving you boys one chance to leave right now."

Shadrack came out of the kitchen with a rolling pin in his huge hand but remained behind the counter.

"Ya don't want any of this, shine." The older brother spat in the direction of the cook. "Better get back in that kitchen. Ya know what happens to your kind if ya mess with a white person."

Shadrack didn't say a word. He just stood, tapping the rolling pin into his left hand while staring at the brothers.

"I said, get back in that kitchen where ya belong, coon." The brother closer to Shadrack picked up a steel napkin holder and flung it at him.

Shadrack batted it down with the rolling pin and remained silent.

Vint took three steps forward, then stopped. "I'll do what I have to. You can believe that like the sun's coming up tomorrow."

The brother to Vint's left, grabbed an ashtray and threw it at him. Vint put his left arm up and deflected it. The glass tray caught him on his forearm, next to his elbow. He yelled out in pain and shook his arm.

The younger brother broke the tip off his empty beer bottle and brandished it like a weapon. "Ya can't get us both." The other brother picked up a chair and they both charged at Vint.

As they ran past Shadrack, the big man stretched his tall muscular body over the counter and swatted the brother with the chair on the forehead, knocking him on his back. The brother with the bottle continued running at Vint. As soon as he was close enough, Vint side-stepped him and put his foot out, tripping him.

The drunken redneck fell on his face, knocking him out. His neck landed on the broken bottle, slashing his jugular vein. As he lay there unconscious, a pool of blood quickly formed around him.

Vint stared at the other brother who lay motionless with a gash on his forehead. "I have to get out of here. If the law shows up asking questions …"

"Go on, split, man." Shadrack finally spoke in a deep, booming voice. "We'll take care of this."

Vint looked to whimpering Lark, then back at Shadrack. "What will you say?"

"Let's see now." Shadrack glanced back and forth at the brothers. "These two drank themselves silly. They was racin' to see who could get to the washroom first and their legs got tangled up and … and they fell. This one bounced his head off the counter and the other landed on his bottle."

"When this guy wakes up." Vint motioned with his thumb toward the man Shadrack swatted. "He's going to have a different story."

Lark finally spoke up in a trembling voice. "It'll be our word against his."

"Yeah, but …" Vint looked at Shadrack. "Will they take his word over a white man's?"

"I cook for the marshal and deputy. Save 'em the best steaks. Throw an extra egg in their omelets. They don't wanna lose their favorite cook. These river rats." Shadrack

8

motioned toward the prone brothers. "The man's gonna be glad at least one of 'em's gone."

"I'll get the tip of the bottle Lester knocked off on the bar and put it by him," Lark said.

"I owe you." Vint put his hand out toward Shadrack. "I owe both of you."

Shadrack took Vint's hand in his and shook it gently. "You scram now. I gotta call for the doc."

Vint grabbed his book from the counter, waved goodbye to Lark, then ran out the backdoor of Dewey's.

Racing toward a freight train that was pulling away, he caught up to a car with the slide-door open, grabbed hold and swung his body up into it. He lumbered into a dark corner and flopped down onto some loose hay. Catching his breath, he thought about Lark and her friendly smile. He liked how she didn't judge him, even after finding out he was an ex-con. But he knew he couldn't go back there again. Chalk Lark up to another memory from the long, long road.

After a few minutes of traveling slowly, the screech of brakes shook Vint from his thoughts. Before he had a chance to see what was going on, a railway inspector shined a flashlight into the car, locating Vint.

"All right." He aimed a pistol. "Get out of there. Right now."

Standing and raising his hands, Vint answered back, "OK, don't shoot. I'm coming." He lowered his weight onto one hand by the door and hopped to the ground.

A deputy marshal, accompanying the inspector, kept his hand on his holstered pistol. "What's your name, boy?"

"I look like a boy to you?" Vint kept his hands raised as he looked down on the short, stocky young man.

The deputy drew his sidearm and aimed it at Vint. "Take that bass outa your voice. What's your name?"

"Smith." He looked away, avoided eye contact.

"Another Smith, huh? How many of you damn Smiths are there ridin' the rails?" The deputy nodded toward Main Street. "OK, start walkin'."

* * *

"Empty your pockets." The deputy shoved Vint toward the desk where the town's marshal sat.

Vint set a comb, toothbrush, handkerchief, can opener, paperback book, his razor, and a billfold on the old wooden desk.

"Sit down, son," the broad shouldered, beefy marshal ordered. "What kind of business you got here in Logan County?"

"Just passing through." Vint read the nameplate on the man's tan-starched uniform as he lowered himself onto the chair across the desk.

Gilstrap studied Vint's face. "You read right, *Marshal Gilstrap*. I'm in charge around here," he said, tapping a wooden baton on his desk. "Name?"

"Smith," he answered, "Vinton Smith."

"Got any identification there, Mr. *Smith?*" Gilstrap dragged out the name out with a sarcastic tone as he rubbed his long square chin.

"No." Vint knew not to say any more than he had to.

Gilstrap picked up Vint's razor and opened it. "Ever kill anyone with this?"

Vint shook his head.

"Lucky you don't have a gun on you. Carrying a gun on your person in this town'll git you a year in my jail." Emptying the contents of the billfold onto his desk, Gilstrap fingered through scraps of paper containing addresses and phone numbers. He held up an old photo and asked an unspoken question.

"Parents. Only picture I got. Please be careful with it."

Carelessly shoving the contents back into the billfold, the marshal looked at Vint with piercing blue eyes that were set too close together. "You over at Dewey's today? Just a little while ago?"

Vint cleared his throat and shifted his weight on the hard steel chair. "I ... yes. Stopped in for coffee."

"Tell me what you know about the Skinner brothers." Gilstrap flipped through the paperback as though he was looking for something hidden between the pages.

"Don't know anyone by that name."

The marshal picked up a small stack of wanted posters from his desk and thumbed through them, glancing at Vint while he studied the photos and information. "What do you go, about one-seventy, one-eighty? Six-foot?"

"Yeah, around that."

"You can take back everything except the razor and opener." Gilstrap turned his head. "Deputy Anfield, put Mr. Smith in cell one. We're going to have him as a guest a while."

"Am I being charged with something?" Vint slowly stood up.

"No. Not yet anyways." Gilstrap pushed his hat back revealing a forehead filled with rows of creases. "We're holding you on vagrancy."

Anfield walked behind Vint down the short hallway that had two cells next to each other. He unlocked the cell door with a large steel key and swung it open. "Maybe your memory will improve while your here with us, Smith."

Vint walked in, sat on the one narrow bed that was bolted to the wall and pulled off his well-worn engineer boots. He spread his handkerchief on the filthy looking pillowcase, turned his jacket collar up and lay down. He opened his book and read until he dozed off.

Chapter 2

"Mr. and Mrs. Harrell, is this the man you saw at Dewey's yesterday?"

Vint woke from an afternoon nap to see Deputy Anfield standing outside his cell with the older couple who had been at the diner.

Neither of them said a word, they just nodded yes.

He opened his book, thankful that he had something to keep his mind occupied. He hated waiting. But waiting and not knowing what was coming next was much worse.

* * *

Vint rubbed his palms together after doing a few sets of pushups on the dirty floor, then sat on the edge of the uncomfortable bed.

A man walked up to the bars of his cell and removed his homburg hat, revealing thick, wavy, salt and pepper hair. "Vinton Smith, I presume."

"Yeah." Vint stood and studied the man's expensive looking but well-worn three-piece suit. "Who's asking?"

"The name's Edric Randall, Counselor at Law." He put his hat back on and handed Vint a business card through the tan paint-chipped bars.

As soon as Vint took the card, Edric's hand pulled back.

"Well, Mr. Randall, Counselor at Law." He stood eye-to-eye with the man who appeared to be roughly forty-five years old. "Long way from home, aren't you?" Vint examined the card. "Sound English."

"I hail from London." He ran a finger under one side of his neatly trimmed graying moustache.

"London." Vint held the card in his right hand and flicked it against his left. "What are you doing in a nowhere little town like this, talking to a nobody guy like me?"

"I'm here to represent you. If you'll have me."

"I can't afford to be fussy." Vint stuck the card in his pocket. "I'm flat broke, dad."

"There are other ways of paying a debt besides money, Mr. Smith."

"I see." Vint looked him up and down, noticing the green alligator briefcase clutched in his left hand. "First of all, let's do away with the formalities. Call me Vint." He put his hand out through the bars.

"All right then." They shook briefly, then Edric wiped his hand on his pant leg. "You can call me by my given name, Edric."

"Who sent you?"

"Why, no one. I came on my own accord."

"Have your own accord, do you?" Vint smirked. "Always wanted one of those."

Edric stared at Vint for a moment, then replied, "Let's get down to business. Would you like to tell me about this diner matter?"

"As a matter of fact, I wouldn't."

"You can trust me, Vint."

"I love it when people tell me that. It fills me with confidence."

"Seriously. I'm here to help you."

"Could be." Vint looked at him stone-faced. "Only thing I know for sure is you're here to help someone."

"All right then. Regardless of your distrust, I'll see what I can do about getting you released as soon as possible."

"That would be grand, Edric, Counselor at Law." Vint made a motion of tipping a cup with his pinkie finger out. "Perhaps we can get together over a spot of tea."

Edric looked at Vint sternly. "You're a curious type."

"I get curiouser all the time. Just wait till I do card tricks."

"What are you jabbering about?"

Vint's tone turned serious. "That's just what I want to know."

"I told you, I'm here to assist you. Are you normally in the habit of biting the hand that feeds you?"

"You haven't fed me anything yet except a line. Got a feeling I'm going to be the one helping you."

"One hand washes the other, Vint." Edric glanced to the side when he heard footsteps around the corner. "I no longer feel comfortable talking here. I have an office of sorts, the apartment above the bakery on Main. We'll talk more there after you're released. Good day." Edric tipped his hat, pivoted and strode away.

Chapter 3

After spending two nights in jail, Anfield unlocked Vint's cell door about 9:00 am. "OK, Smith, you're outa here."

Vint sat up, stuffed his handkerchief into his pocket and pulled his engineer boots on over socks that he had washed in the sink. "Did that English lawyer spring me?"

"What English lawyer?"

"Oh, it's going to be like that, huh?" Vint stood. "You got some kind of shower here? I'd like to get cleaned up."

"Oh, a shower." The deputy smiled and nodded. "Maybe you'd like me to draw you a bubble bath. Did ya git the mint I left on your pillow?" He slammed the cell door behind Vint with a loud clang. "Git the hell outa here."

Gilstrap put his leg out, blocking Vint's path as he tried leaving. "There's gonna be a hearing on this Skinner business. Don't even think about leaving town." The marshal put his leg back down. "I put in calls to all the surrounding counties. Gave them your description. We're keeping an eye on the freight trains too."

Vint stood with his hands in his jacket pockets. "Anything else?"

"You better find yourself a job real quick or you're gonna be right back in here eating stale bread and cold gravy three times a day."

"Can you point me in the right direction?"

"Try down by the river, over at Hurst Lumber. They usually have some kind of labor that needs getting done."

"What about the rest of my things?" Vint pulled a hand from his pocket and held it out.

Gilstrap opened a desk drawer and took out Vint's items. "You can have the church-key." He tossed it on the edge of the desk where it slid off onto the floor. "I'll hold onto this for a while." He held up the straight razor.

Grabbing his opener off the floor and walking out, Vint stopped when the marshal called out. "One more thing, Smith. Lark Stookey from over at Dewey's came in asking how much your bail was. I told her there wasn't any. Why is it you think she did that?"

Vint didn't turn around, he just shrugged and kept going.

Stepping down the two wooden slat steps to the concrete sidewalk that had tufts of grass growing between the cracks, he felt the morning sunlight on his face. He paused for a moment and listened to the call of a freight train moving along the tracks in the distance. Breathing in the rich air, filled with the scent of pines, he gazed around at the lush country surrounding him in the river valley. In the distance to the south, the majestic rock-covered plateau of Mount Magazine jutted into the blue horizon, to the north, lay the Ozark Mountains, decorated in a palette of nature's fall colors.

Making his way up Main Street, Vint spotted a hardware store and walked in. "Say, where can I find Hurst Lumber?" he asked the old-timer behind the counter.

The old guy in a tattered shirt-collar and polka-dot bowtie pulled the corncob pipe from his thin lips. "Does it look like all I got to do in this world is hang around here and give directions to someone who probably doesn't know the difference between cornpone and cornhole?"

"What?" Vint's eyes narrowed. "Looks like you're just standing there doing nothing to me."

"May look that way to you, sonny britches. But I'm solvin' the world's problems," the frail man said, tapping a boney finger to his temple, "right here in my head."

Vint let out a big breath. "Can you just tell me where it is?"

"All right. Don't get impatient. Everybody's in a dang hurry." He cleared his gravely sounding voice. "Go up Main here." He motioned with a veiny hand. "Turn left at Adams and follow it all the way down. Tell Widow Hurst that Jacob sent ya and I could use a couple dozen two-by-fours."

Vint ventured east on Main, past the one restaurant in town, past the one diner, the one bar, the one grocery, the one bank. Looking up at the second floor over Krause Bakery, Vint read *Edric Randall - Counselor at Law* spelled out in one of the facing windows. He turned left when he saw a small rusty street sign reading *Adams*.

As he traveled on, the houses, at first large with spacious yards and plenty of white oak, shagbark hickory and shortleaf pine trees, became smaller and less appointed, until after several blocks they became little more than shacks. The paved street was replaced by loose stones as he reluctantly put one foot in front of the other, wondering whether he should make a run for it. A little further on, the road that continually sloped downward was nothing more than a wide dirt path that took him closer to the sounds of the nearby rushing Arkansas River.

Peering through the high weeds, he spotted a towering two-story building. The front of the timeworn frame structure was adorned with large red-painted letters spelling out *HURST LUMBER*.

Noticing, but not looking directly at the men carrying lumber and loading planks onto an old flatbed truck, Vint passed by them and went straight to the office entrance. He was struck by the strong smell of fresh cut lumber when he walked in the open door.

"Can I help you?" A slightly plump, middle-aged woman peered at Vint through silvery cat's-eye reading glasses.

"I'm looking for work. Jacob over at the hardware sent me." Vint stood straight with his shoulders squared. "Said he needs a couple dozen two-by-fours."

"You a friend of Jacob?" She sat back in her chair and looked him up and down.

Vint read the nameplate sitting on the desk, *Mrs. Margaret Cooms*. "Wouldn't go that far." He smoothed back his straight black hair with both hands. "We're on friendly terms. Good old boy, that Jacob."

"Good old boy? Really. Jacob?" She put her pen in her mouth, closed red-painted lips around it and stared at him through half-closed eyes.

"Well, do you have any work for me?"

"Mrs. Hurst," the secretary called out over sporadic muffled sounds of electric saws. "You have time to come in here and take a look at something?"

"What is it Margie?" A strong smooth voice replied from an adjoining office. "You know I'm busy." A tall, beautiful woman with brilliant, dark-red hair appeared in the doorway of the side office. Her high cheekbones, creamy taut skin and expressionless face gave her a mannequin-like appearance. She smoothed her tight-fitting emerald linen dress over her narrow waist and shapely hips.

"This guy's looking for work." Margaret leaned back and laced her fingers behind her head. "He remind you of anyone?"

"Margie. I don't have time for your games." Mrs. Hurst turned her attention to Vint. "What kind of work you looking for? Can you run a table saw?"

"Never have but I'm a quick learner."

"Forget it. We're not here to teach you. Besides, I don't need your blood all over my lumber. Go out and ask for the foreman, Gerald. Tell him I said to put you to work loading." Mrs. Hurst disappeared back into her office.

"Here. You'll need these." Margaret pulled a new pair of canvas work gloves with pigskin grips from a drawer and handed them to Vint.

Taking the blue and white striped gloves, he nodded to Margaret, then headed out to find the foreman.

After asking around, he located Gerald in the upper loft with pencil and paper in hand, looking up at bundles of planks stacked twice as high as himself.

"Mrs. Hurst told me to find you." Vint walked up to the medium-height man dressed in dark green work clothes. "I'm supposed to help load."

"God damn it." The paunchy guy turned to Vint and threw his pencil down. "Couldn't you tell I was countin'?"

"I'm not a mind reader." Vint noticed a couple food crumbs in Gerald's bushy, graying moustache.

"Holy hot shit. Now I gotta start over." Gerald picked up the pencil from the floor, looked at the broken tip, then shook his head. "Over here." The foreman walked to the open second-story door and waved Vint over. "Go and help Pete down there." He pointed. "One with the hat brim pushed up in front."

As Vint walked away, he heard Gerald grumbling, "I swear …"

* * *

"Say, Pete." Vint looked down the stack of long planks at the wiry man who was carrying the other end. "Anyone by the name Skinner work here?"

"Yer new in town. Maybe ya didn't hear." They both set the planks down on a hand trolley. "Two of the Skinners worked here until a couple of days ago. Lester got hisself killed over at the diner, kinda suspicious like. By a stranger … like you, matter of fact." Pete squinted in the bright midday sun and rolled his long sleeves high on his thin arms. "Merk Skinner's been off work since. Suspect he'll be back any day, now that they got his brother in the ground."

"Two of the Skinners?" Vint asked over the clanging of train cars coupling about twenty yards behind the lumberyard. "There's more?"

"Yeah. There's Polk Skinner, the oldest and the meanest of the bunch. He's in prison for manslaughter." Pete pushed his beat-up fedora back and wiped his brow with a dirt-smudged handkerchief. "Now that ya mention it, Polk oughta be gettin' out soon."

Vint looked around at the tall stacks of planks covered in huge tarps, hiding any reaction.

"Why ya wanna know 'bout the Skinners? I know yer no friends of theirs, not many are. Want me to tell Merk you was askin' 'bout him?"

"Just as soon you didn't. Forget I asked."

* * *

Working under the hot afternoon sun later that day, Vint removed his jacket and t-shirt. He hung them on a stack of skids as he separated straight boards from warped ones in the area in front of the office. A short while later, he observed Margaret, then Mrs. Hurst watching him from the office window. When Mrs. Hurst saw that he noticed her, she disappeared out of view.

Gerald came out of the office and straight up to Vint. "Hey, you. Put your damn shirt on. Where d'ya think you are?"

Pulling his t-shirt back on, he noticed Margaret retreating from the window.

* * *

When the 5:00 pm whistle finally blew, everyone dropped what they were doing. Vint slipped into his jacket and quickly headed into the office, ahead of a few dozen men doing the same. He walked up to Margaret's desk and stuck his hand out as a line rapidly formed behind him.

"Don't blow it all at the bar, handsome." She handed him an envelope. "There's just about enough there to keep you fed 'til Monday."

Vint glanced at the calendar on the wall. *Friday, October 2.* Then he noticed Mrs. Hurst standing in her doorway. She slowly turned, giving him a good view of her tall, curvy body, then closed the door behind her.

Having missed lunch because he was flat broke, Vint started heading straight to Dewey's Diner.

As he walked up the sloping road, a car pulled up. "Hey, wanna lift?" Pete slowed down and called through the open window of his Plymouth sedan that was full of passengers. "Hop on the runnin' board."

Vint caught up and jumped on, holding onto the window post. The men in the car hooted and hollered all the way to Cooper's Bar on Main Street. He hopped off as the Plymouth slowed to a stop.

"Comin' in?" Pete got out and called out over the top of the sedan.

"No. You guys go ahead. I've got to get something in my belly before I pass out." Vint walked the short distance up the block, past Sally's Restaurant and straight to Dewey's. He stepped in and carefully closed the screen door behind him so it didn't slam.

"Welcome to Dewey's, stranger." Hopping to his feet off a stool, Dewey appeared shorter than he did sitting down. The potbellied owner, who looked to be in his fifties, tipped his white Navy cap. "Sit anywhere you'd like." Holding a few menus, he spread the other hand out toward a row of six empty tables.

Looking at Lark's welcoming smile, Vint answered, "Then I'll sit at the counter." He walked back to the same stool near the end where he'd sat before, nodding to Shadrack through the kitchen counter window on the way. Pulling his book from his back pocket and setting it on the counter, Vint eased onto the stool with a sigh.

"Hi, Vinton." Lark smiled nervously. "I heard they had you in jail."

"And I heard you tried to help me."

"Didn't do much good. But I'm glad you're out. Will you be sticking around?"

"Lark, I'll be happy to answer all your questions after you put my order in. Tell Shadrack I'd like another burger just like that last one, mashed potatoes, bowl of beef-barley soup and a cup of joe."

She put in the order, returned with a glass of ice-water and poured him a steaming cup of coffee.

"Looks like I'm here whether I want to be or not." Vint looked over at Dewey sitting on a stool half-way down the counter and wondered how good his hearing was. "Going to be a hearing about you-know-what."

"The marshal questioned me and Shadrack, over and over, separately," she said quietly, "like he was trying to trip us up."

"Once they caught up to me, it didn't really matter anymore. If I could have, I'd have told you both to tell the truth." He glanced over at Dewey again, who was now working on a newspaper crossword puzzle. "Hate to see either one of you involved."

"I'm glad we stuck to our story. You know they could charge you with manslaughter or maybe murder?" Lark raised her eyebrows. "That's not right. You were minding your business until the Skinners started getting rough. You were just trying to help me."

"One thing's for sure, they don't give an ex-con an even break. They figure, once a con always a con."

"I'm worried. I don't want anything to happen to you."

"Get me my soup, kid." Vint patted her hand. "And a pack of Old Gold."

By the time he finished his meal, more than a half-dozen teenagers crowded by the juke box, jitterbugging and slow dancing to pop and country songs. The girls bounced about in their bobby sox and saddle shoes, twirling their skirts. The boys looked like they all went to the barbershop together for their flattop haircuts.

Lark set the cigarettes in front of him. "Here, Vinton. Got some matches for you too."

"Why don't you call me Vint?" He unwrapped the pack, put one in his mouth and lit it.

"I like that ... Vint."

He held the pack toward her. "Told the marshal my last name's Smith."

Glancing at the cigarettes, Lark shook her head. She leaned in close. "All of us have to stick to our story. If the marshal finds out me and Shadrack lied, he could make a lot of trouble for us. What did you tell them?"

"No more than I had to. I admitted being here, said I stopped in for coffee. When I was asked about the Skinners, I played dumb." He knocked his ash into the square glass tray. "We're all going to be sworn in for the hearing and there'll be plenty more questions, can be sure of that. They're designed to trip you up. Just keep your head."

"What should we tell Shadrack?"

"He invented the story, seems smart enough. He'll do OK. It's you I'm worried about. They're going to try their best to rattle you." He took a deep drag. "What're you, about eighteen?"

"No. I'm almost twenty ... in a couple weeks."

Neither of them saw Dewey approach. "Lark, honey, who's your friend?"

"This is Vint ... Smith."

Dewey ignored Vint's extended hand. "So, you're the one that was here Wednesday, when Lester Skinner died. See that floor? I had to get on my hands and knees and scrub up all that blood. Took me over two hours. I bleached those tiles four times and there's still a stain." Dewey's face turned red as he ranted, his arms waving about. "What really happened here that day? The marshal and his deputy keep coming in asking a lot of questions."

"Why ask me?" Vint looked directly at Dewey. "I wasn't even here."

"Marshal Gilstrap found out from the Harrells that just before they left, the Skinners were threatening you."

"I left right after the Harrells did. Went out the back door."

"Marshal said you don't seem the type to run from trouble and the Skinners ain't the kind to let someone walk away from a fight."

"Well." Vint took a drag and blew smoke out the side of his mouth. "Gilstrap can speculate all he wants."

"Lark, pay attention." Dewey motioned with his thumb. "You got other customers." Dewey stood squinting at Vint for a moment, then walked away.

Without enough money to go to the bar or anywhere else, Vint sat at the counter reading his book, smoking and listening to the jukebox. When 9:00 pm finally rolled around, Dewey shut off the outside lights.

Strolling up to Vint with a wiggle in her walk, Lark removed her apron and flung it over her shoulder. "Got a place to stay tonight?"

"Don't worry about me." He stood. "I made it this far in life."

"I live with my Grannie. She's got a little house not far from here. She'll be in bed by the time I get through. I'm sure she won't mind if you sleep on the couch 'til you find something better."

Vint thought about the two dollars he had left. He was going to have to stretch his meager funds. "I appreciate that." He studied Lark's curvy, trim body in her tight-fitting uniform. "Sure that's a good idea, young lady? You hardly know me."

"I know enough." She rested her hand on his. "You're a good man."

"Don't kid yourself." He looked down at her fair hand on his. "Nobody's that good."

Vint walked out the front door and sat on Dewey's windowsill. He gazed at the stars and waning crescent moon, waiting for Lark to finish up.

Minutes later, she flew out the front door with a big smile. "Glad ya waited."

Walking close with their hands grazing one another's, Lark said, "I didn't always live here. I grew up in a bigger town a few hours away, in Kansas. I came here because I lost my parents in an accident. A train they were on derailed. Lot of people died or got hurt."

"I'm sorry. How old were you?"

"Fourteen. Summer before my freshman year."

"You weren't on the train?" Vint pulled a small, low hanging branch off a tree as they walked along the cracked concrete sidewalk.

"No. I was at camp. They were coming to see me."

"That's horrible."

"Yes. It was. I felt so guilty ... still do."

"It was an accident." He pulled leaves from the branch, dropping them as they slowly walked along. "You didn't cause it."

"No, but if they weren't coming to see me ..." Lark turned her head to catch Vint's gaze.

"You shouldn't think like that."

"I had nowhere to go so Grannie took me in. I went to high school here. It was a big adjustment. Losing my mom and dad, and then leaving all my friends. The school here is a lot smaller than the one back home."

"Must have been rough."

"I did my best to fit in, became a cheerleader and had a boyfriend. He was captain of the football team. I was in love but he left me."

"Left you? A beautiful young lady like you?"

"He joined the Merchant Marines. Said he wanted to see the world before he settled down."

"Expect him back?" Vint slightly slapped the bare branch into his palm.

"I wrote him a bunch of times but never heard back. Before he left, he said I was too clingy. I thought I'd go crazy when he went away. Losing my parents and then him. Sometimes I think I am going nuts. But I'm happy again, now that you're here."

"Whoa. Don't get too used to me being around. If it wasn't for this Skinner business, I'd be gone."

"I'm sorry you're stuck here because of me. Well, maybe I'm not sorry." Lark stopped and took his hand. "I don't know what would've happened if you weren't there when those drunken rednecks started getting rough. I just hope everything turns out all right at the hearing."

"Well, I appreciate you lying to the marshal for me. You could get in trouble for helping me too."

"I guess, in a way, we're kinda stuck with each other." Her demeanor suddenly turned from sad to giddy. "I'm happy things turned out the way they did."

When they approached her house, Lark giggled as she opened the creaking unlocked door. "Grannie can sleep through a tornado."

Entering the front room, Vint breathed in a combination of aged wood, fried chicken and liniment. Lark disappeared for a minute, leaving him standing in the dark. She returned, flipped on a light switch and held a pair of long-johns up in front of her. "These belonged to Gramps. They're clean. You can sleep in them."

"Mind if I take a shower before changing?"

"We have a bath. That OK?"

"More than OK."

Lark led Vint to the bathroom and handed him a clean towel from the linen closet. "I'm getting in here right after you."

Vint brushed his teeth while the tub filled, then settled down in the hot water. He quickly and thoroughly washed up, let the water out and filled it again with clean rinse water. After toweling off, he slipped into the cotton long-johns and carried his clothes out with him.

"My turn." She brushed past him holding a *Movie Stars* magazine with Marilyn Monroe on the cover.

Vint noticed the couch was now covered in a sheet and Lark had a pillow and blanket set out for him. He grabbed his cigarettes, matches and a saucer from the kitchen table and got comfortable on the couch. Adjusting the pillow and pulling the blanket up to his waist, he lay back and lit a smoke as he thought about Lark in the next room, naked in the bathtub.

When the bathroom door opened, she stood backlit by a bare lightbulb hanging from a long cord, showing the shape of her body through her thin nightie. She walked up next to the couch and purred, "Can I get you anything else?"

"That's a loaded question."

Lark leaned over him and said, "Good night, handsome."

She kissed him lightly on the lips and began straightening up. Vint kicked the blanket off, grabbed her around the waist and pulled her down on top of him. They kissed furiously, then she pulled away. He reached up, grabbed the back of her hair, pulled her close and kissed her some more. She squirmed and ground her hips into him until she stiffened, lightly bit his earlobe and let out a loud moan. Breathing heavily, she jumped to her feet. "Sorry."

"You got nothing to be sorry about." Vint folded his hands behind his head. "But you are old enough to know what a good looking young lady like you can do to a man. Maybe we should skip the goodnight kiss unless you're ready to get to know me a whole lot better."

"I, I didn't mean for anything to ...," she stammered, looking at the rise in his long-johns. She backed into her bedroom and closed the door behind her.

He heard the click of the lock.

Chapter 4

Vint slept as he hadn't in weeks, dreaming on and off about making love to Lark. Rolling away from the back of the couch to the smell of bacon frying, he saw his clothes, clean and folded on a nearby chair.

"Good Morning." Lark appeared before him. "Hope you slept all right after you-know-what last night. Sorry again."

"If you don't quit saying I'm sorry, I'm going to put you over my knee, young lady."

"Oh, big man." She giggled. "Ready for some breakfast, Mr. Smith?"

Standing and grabbing his clothes, he asked, "You have a razor in there somewhere?" He nodded his head toward the bathroom.

"Gramps' old straight razor's in the medicine cabinet. You can use that."

Vint carried his clothes into the bathroom that was filled with the aroma of a lit lavender candle. Lathering up with a bowl and brush, he was glad to see a razor strop attached to the sink. After sharpening the vintage razor and getting a close shave, he dressed. Walking into the kitchen, he nodded to Grannie.

"Grannie," Lark spoke loudly, "this is Vint Smith. He might be staying with us for a few days." She gave Vint a sly smile and added more quietly, "If I don't drive him too crazy."

* * *

"What do people do in this town on a Saturday afternoon?" Vint nudged Lark as he sat next to her on the paint-peeled front porch.

"You're looking at it," she said with a sigh. "Sometimes people drive over to the next town and see a movie. Men around here go to the bar and get drunk, then sleep it off Sunday before work. Of course, if you're married…" She leaned into him. "There's always indoor sports."

"Don't get me started again. Maybe I should go for a walk."

"It's not that I don't want to. You know I like you. I like you a whole lot." Lark rested her head on Vint's arm. "Grannie hardly ever leaves the house. Except for Sunday, when she goes to church …"

She tilted her head back and their eyes met.

"Praise the Lord." He couldn't hold back a smile.

Chapter 5

"Bye, Grannie." Lark waved from the front door to her cane-carrying grandmother as she slowly hobbled along the sidewalk to the church down the block. "And hello, Mr. Smith." She turned to Vint, who walked out of the bathroom with a towel around his waist.

"Get your ass over here." He brushed his thick hair back with his fingers.

Lark slowly sauntered across the living room up to Vint.

He grabbed her by the front waist of her Levi's and yanked her hips up against his. "You've been driving me crazy since I first laid eyes on you." He kissed her open mouth and softly caressed her breast. Smacking her on the ass, he said, "Get in the bedroom."

Vint followed close behind, then flopped back onto her chenille blanket-covered bed. "Stand there." He laced his fingers behind his head. "Take off all your clothes."

"What? You mean strip? Vint ... I never done anything like that ... undressed in front of a guy." She locked her hands behind her waist and turned her body side to side. "I'm kinda shy that way."

As rain began tapping the roof, he said in a soft voice, "Get them off."

Lark's face turned red as she unbuttoned her white blouse. "You're not the romantic type, are ya?"

"Keep going." He watched as she untucked her top. She slowly took it off and dropped it on the floor.

Undoing her button-fly jeans, Lark had a tremble in her voice. "Am I doing it right?"

"There's no wrong way." He gazed at her flat stomach. "Get them down."

Lark bent over and pushed her pants to her ankles, then stepped her bare feet out of them. She stood before him in her bra and panties. "More?"

"Your brassiere."

Breathing heavily, she reached behind her back and undid her bra. She held it to her breasts, taking down one shoulder strap, then the other. She watched the rise under Vint's damp towel grow and let her bra drop to the floor.

"You're beautiful. Now, take off your panties."

Lark turned around and slowly pulled her white cotton underwear down. She looked at Vint over her shoulder.

Vint said in a breathy voice, "Turn around, gorgeous."

"Am I? Really?" She put her hand over her pounding heart.

"Come here." He pulled his towel open.

* * *

"You don't sound like anyone I know." Lark lay on top of Vint, her lips close to his. "You sound like ... I don't know ... like sophisticated or something."

"Most people grow up mimicking their parents and siblings. Never had that luxury." Vint turned on his side, depositing Lark on the bed next to him. "I grew up mostly alone. The orphanage was full of other kids, but when I wasn't fighting, I was by myself. Reading. I learned proper grammar listening to the radio, sneaking into movies every chance I got. Ronald Colman, Errol Flynn, Douglas Fairbank, Jr. That's who taught me how to talk, walk, eat in a restaurant, take a lady's arm." He gestured with his hand. "They were my mentors. Otherwise, I'd have been like any other mug who grows up poor."

She traced his full lips with a fingertip. "Well, you're the classiest hobo I ever met."

31

Grabbing her hand, he shot back, "I'm not a hobo. Had to make a quick get-away from the last town I was in." He released her hand. "I don't like to stay in one spot too long, that's all."

"I'm sorry. Just joking." Lark ran her fingers lightly over Vint's nipple. "Was it a girl?"

"Some of it was. It got all jumbled up. Had to get out of there fast. What little I had got left behind." He pointed a thumb at his chest. "But I'm not a bum."

"OK, OK." She rolled onto her stomach.

Vint patted her leg. "I ran away from that orphanage when I was thirteen. Hopped a freight train. Been on the move ever since."

"Does anyone else here know your name's really Mercurio?"

"Marshal suspects my name's not Smith. He doesn't know anything for sure yet."

"Why'd you tell me?"

"You seemed nice. Made me feel welcome." He sat upright and ran his hand up the back of her thigh. "I was passing through. Never thought I'd see you again."

Lark gazed up at him as she lay on her belly. "I'd never say anything to anyone."

"I know. How about heating me up some of that corned beef hash?" He lightly slapped her bare ass. "Fry an egg and lay it on top."

"We better get dressed." She rolled over and sat up. "Grannie will be back soon."

Vint watched Lark stand, then pull up her panties. He asked, "You know anything about an English lawyer in town by the name Randall?"

"This town?"

"Yes, this town. Where do you think I mean, Poughkeepsie?"

"Randall, hmm."

"Edric Randall. Middle-aged guy, gray suit and hat, refined looking, about six-foot. Has an office over the bakery."

"Nope. I know just about everyone in this town." Lark stretched, then began putting her bra on. "You say he's English, like from England?"

"Forget it." Vint hung the damp towel around his neck and stood. "I'm going to borrow that old straight razor of Gramps'."

* * *

"G'night Grannie." Lark dried and put away the last dinner plate while Vint sat at the kitchen table smoking an Old Gold.

"Got anything to drink around here?" He stubbed the cigarette out in a vintage *Marion Hotel* ashtray.

"Well, sure. We got milk, root beer, apple cider. I can make some more lemonade."

"No, kid." He waved his hand to the side. "I mean do you have anything to *drink*?"

"Oh … you mean."

"Yeah, I mean."

"Let's see." Lark went to the cabinet beneath the sink. She bent over and put her hands on her knees. Coming up with a half-empty fifth of whiskey, she asked, "You mean like this?"

"Get me a glass and bring the bottle over."

"It was Gramps'." She set the bottle and a glass in front of him. "Said it was for Arthur."

"Arthur?"

"That's what he called his arthritis."

Vint poured himself a few fingers of the blended whiskey. "Join me?"

"I'm not much of a drinker. I get a little silly."

"Then I insist. Get another glass."

"I don't know." She put a hand to her cheek. "I never had the hard stuff, just beer. And some champagne at a

33

wedding a couple years ago. Then I jitterbugged like crazy all night."

"Life is for living. Get a glass."

"OK … I guess."

Lark removed a clean glass from the cupboard and set it next to his. He poured her a couple shots, then pulled her onto his lap. He raised his glass and she lifted hers. Vint clinked them together. "To your pretty little ass."

They both took a sip and Lark shot to her feet coughing. "Oh … oh my." She went to the refrigerator, opened the freezer door and took out a metal ice tray. Pulling up on the tray handle, she loosened the cubes, then dropped a few into her glass. She grabbed a bottle of ginger ale from the refrigerator, popped the cap with an opener and poured some in with her whiskey.

"Get over here." Vint reached out, grabbed her hand and pulled her back onto his lap. "Drink up."

She swirled her glass. "How long you gonna stay?"

"In town?"

"Here." Lark made a sweeping motion with her hand.

"I have to stick around at least until the hearing's over. Not sure how long I can sleep on your couch. The looks your Grannie gives me. She's old but she's not stupid."

"When she goes, this house is mine. All I'll need to come up with is the taxes and utilities. This town's not a bad little place to settle down." She ran a fingertip along the rim of her glass. "Raise a family."

"Are you proposing to me?" He tried not to smile.

Pushing her drink away, she blushed. "I told you I get silly."

"I don't think you're silly." He pushed her half-empty glass back in front of her. "I think you're cute."

"Cute." Lark made a sour face and moved to the chair next to him. "My boyfriend thought I was cute. He took my virginity … two months later joined the service. Guess I didn't have what it took to make him stay."

"You shouldn't look at it like that." He finished his drink and poured himself some more. "Can't blame the young man for wanting to see the world a little. See what's outside this small town. There's a lot to experience, a lot of other girls too."

"Are you talking about him or you?"

"You're a fine young lady, Lark. You're good looking, bright, devoted. You'll make some very lucky guy a great wife."

"You never really answered my question." She took a sip.

"I don't know how long I'll stick around, depends. Let's not get ahead of ourselves." Vint patted her hand and smiled, showing his straight white teeth. "Take it slow, doll. We'll see how it goes."

* * *

After Lark went to bed, Vint lay half-covered on the couch, bathed in the dim glow of light coming from the kitchen. Dressed only in his boxers, he crossed his feet, thinking about his conversation with Lark. He heard something and looked over to see her tip-toeing barefoot out of her bedroom, toward him.

"Hi, Vint." She giggled, holding onto the bottom of her nightie with both hands. "I'm kinda tipsy."

"I can see that. Maybe you should go back to bed."

"I don't wanna go to bed." She raised her nightie a little, revealing her pale upper thighs.

"You look a little wobbly." He pointed to her room. "Go on now."

She walked next to the couch and lifted it some more. "You look so good laying there." She pulled the hem up to her hips, showing she had nothing on underneath.

He pushed his boxers and cover down to his knees. She straddled him and they had sex the second time that day.

* * *

Lark lay on top of Vint, catching her breath. "I really hope you'll stick around."

"I better get some rubbers."

"It's my safe time of the month. I just finished … you know." Her face turned red. "My period," she said in a whisper.

"Still, I should go to the drug store tomorrow."

"No. I don't want everyone to know. The way they gossip around here." Lark made a hand gesture like a mouth gabbing. "Go to the filling station on the edge of town. There's a machine in the men's room. That's where my boyfriend used to get them."

"I get the impression he was the only guy you were with," Vint asked casually.

"Yes." She looked away and put her head on his chest. "He was."

Chapter 6

Vint glanced around Hurst Lumber Monday morning as he worked alongside Pete.

"A little on edge today, ain't ya?" Pete smirked. "Whatcha keep lookin' 'round at?"

"Oh, nothing."

"I heard 'bout that business at the diner. Merk Skinner's been goin' 'round tellin' everyone who'll listen that he's gonna getcha."

"So where is he then?" Vint stopped working and looked Pete in the eye.

"Merk was in the bar last night, tyin' one on. 'Spect he didn't make it in today 'cause he's hungover. Probably be in tomorrow."

Vint shrugged, keeping his thoughts to himself. "It's a free country."

"Maybe you should get outa town and explore some of that free country. Word is, Merk Skinner's killed before and he wouldn't hesitate to do it again."

* * *

That afternoon, stacking eight-foot studs onto skids out front by himself, Vint got a bad feeling as he watched Deputy Anfield pull up. The deputy walked straight up to Vint and threw a set of handcuffs at him, landing by his feet.

"Put those on and make 'em tight."

Vint picked up the cuffs and put them on. It wasn't his first time.

Anfield kept his right hand on his holstered sidearm. "All right, walk ahead of me and get in the backseat."

* * *

"Just stand there, Smith." Marshal Gilstrap sat back with his boots on his desk, holding a sheet of paper in his hand. "Or should I call you Mercurio?"

Vint showed no reaction.

"Says here, a con by the name Vinton Mercurio violated his parole when he left Knox County, Ohio." Gilstrap looked Vint up and down. "Six-foot tall. Hundred-seventy-five pounds. Black hair, light brown eyes." Gilstrap set the paper on his desk. "How many guys you suppose there are with the first name Vinton who fit that description this part of the country?"

Vint just shrugged, looking at the floor.

"We're gonna get your fingerprints and take a picture of you. Anfield, take care of that, will you?"

* * *

Anfield skidded to a stop in front of Hurst Lumber, let Vint out, then pulled away, leaving him in a cloud of road dust.

Gerald immediately approached Vint. "Go see Mrs. Hurst, right now."

Vint walked into the outer office rubbing his wrists and examining the ink stains on his fingertips.

"She's in there." Margaret pointed a long red fingernail toward the private office.

Stepping in and looking around the spacious office, he inspected framed photos on the walls. There were a few of Mrs. Hurst with the late Mr. Hurst, and another of her alone, a glamour shot from her bare shoulders up that must have been taken a good ten years earlier. The print on the bottom of the photo read *Adelle Amour*.

Mrs. Hurst looked up from the papers she was signing. "Damn it. If I have to read over one more contract." She threw her pen on the desk. "You were gone from your job forty-eight minutes. That means you'll be docked one hour. What was that all about anyway?"

"Just a misunderstanding." He tried not to stare at her ample bosom in her tight, mint-green sweater. "Case of mistaken identity."

"This is a small town. There isn't much that doesn't get gossiped about around here, including me. Either I find out from you or I find out through the local grapevine."

"You hear about Lester Skinner croaking in the diner?"

"Of course." She remained expressionless. "He was one of my employees."

"Seems the marshal suspects me of being involved somehow."

"One laborer more or less around here doesn't mean much to me." Adelle rolled her office chair back away from her desk and slowly crossed one leg over the other, bringing her knee up high before setting it back down. "Are you going to be sticking around or are you going bye-bye?"

"Prison? Always a possibility." He shrugged. "A little too early in the game."

"It's a game to you?" Her left eyebrow raised slightly.

"Everything's a game, lady."

"I've got some pull around here. Come see me if the noose gets too tight." Adelle motioned with her hand like she was shooing away a fly. "Get back to work."

* * *

When the workday ended, Vint hitched a ride to Main Street. Standing in front of Cooper's bar, he looked to his right toward Dewey's. It was after 5:00 and he was hungry, but he turned left instead and walked over to the bakery. When he got to the outside wooden stairs, he hesitated. Something didn't feel right about Edric Randall, but he decided that listening to what the man had to say couldn't hurt.

After climbing the creaky stairway, he knocked on the side door. He heard shuffling, then what sounded like something falling over. He knocked again.

After a minute, Edric opened the door and straightened his tie. "Forgive me. I wasn't expecting anyone just now." He stepped back with a wave of his hand. "Welcome."

Even the delicious aromas filtering up from the bakery below couldn't mask the musty odors of molding wood and aging linoleum. Vint detected alcohol on Edric's breath too. He got a closer look at the sign in the window and realized it was made of carefully constructed electrician's tape.

"Come and sit." Edric led him to a kitchen table that looked as old as both of them put together. "May I offer you a drink?"

"What've you got?"

Edric opened the vintage icebox and pulled out a bottle of gin. He held it up and raised his eyebrows.

"That'll do."

"So, I see you're out. No need to thank me," Edric said, waving the bottle about.

"Why would I thank you?"

"For God's sake, Vint." He set the bottle on the table. "For getting you released from that miserable jail last Friday."

"How do I know you got me out? You have release papers or a receipt of some kind?"

"Things don't work that way in these backward little burgs." Edric removed a glass from a cupboard and set it next to one on the table that looked used. "It's all done quietly, behind closed doors. The fact that you're out is all the proof you need." He poured them both a small amount of spirits.

"Why don't we get down to brass tacks?" Vint took a sip and found it very palatable. "Let's say it was you that got me sprung from that cracker-box. I appreciate it, but it's not worth much in trade."

"Forget it. That was a gift." Edric took a big gulp. "Besides, you're worth more to me on the outside."

Vint slowly sipped his cold gin and thought carefully about what he was going to say next. He set his glass down. "Just what is it you want me to do for you?"

Pushing a bakery box toward Vint and opening the top, Edric asked, "Would you like a cruller? They're really very good."

Peering into the box and lifting his glass, Vint shook his head. "Gin and sweets? I'll pass."

"I have a business relationship with the people downstairs who own the bakery, a Mr. and Mrs. Krause. Helping with their affairs ... taxes and such." Edric added a bit more gin to his own glass. "Hard working lot, highly uneducated. Unbeknownst to them, I've uncovered information that is of particular value. It turns out that the grandfather of the wife was worth a lot of money."

Vint pushed his glass forward. Edric added another splash.

"The Krauses never had children," Edric continued. "Although they tried for years. Now that they're pushing fifty, it's highly unlikely that will ever happen. Their house is past its prime, but at one time it was the finest structure in these parts."

Becoming annoyed with the constant dripping from the ice box, Vint noticed that the tray underneath was close to overflowing. "Why don't you cut to the chase?" He downed his glass and set it hard on the table.

"The grandfather didn't believe in banks. Didn't trust them." Edric waved a hand around. "With bank robbers like yourself running around and such."

"So, you think I'm a bank robber, do you?" Vint's expression turned hard. "OK, I can see where this is going." He tapped his glass for a refill. "Where did he stash the dough?"

"It's somewhere in the house." Edric poured him a bit more gin. "I haven't been able to ascertain the exact location yet, but hopefully that information will be forthcoming."

"Who's feeding you info? And why would they tell you?"

"That I cannot say," Edric said without expression.

"I get it. You don't want me doing an end-around."

"Precisely."

"Why don't you just go in and get it yourself? You wouldn't be trying to shoehorn me into a tight squeeze, would you?"

"Of course not, dear boy." Edric stood and wobbled a bit. "Why, I think highly of you. Heard about some of your capers. Good show … Mercurio." He threw his head back and laughed. "You make Dillinger look like an amateur."

"What have you heard?" Vint slammed his empty glass down and stood. "From who?"

"I must lie down now." Edric loosened his tie and stumbled toward the sofa near the front window. "There's nothing here of value. Check if you'd like." When he flopped on the sofa, a puff of dust sprang up.

Vint looked around for the alligator briefcase. After searching every conceivable spot, he gave up. He went back to the table, took a swig from the bottle and returned what little was left to the ice box.

Chapter 7

Vint fingered the straight razor in his jacket pocket as he walked up to Hurst Lumber on Tuesday. He spotted Gerald out front and went straight to him. "Where do you want me today?"

"Go 'round back and help get that load of logs in for cuttin'."

With no sign of Merk, Vint continued working until the lunch whistle blew. He removed his work gloves and picked up the paper sack he had set on a stack of skids earlier. Peering inside, he inspected what Lark had put together for him and decided to eat his lunch back there by himself. After he finished his meatloaf sandwich, hard-boiled egg and apple, Vint lit a cigarette. He sat on the ground, leaning up against the wooden building and sipped coffee from a thermos.

"So ... this is where ya been hidin'."

Vint shot to his feet when he saw Merk round the corner some twenty feet away. He pitched his cigarette and removed the razor from his pocket. Flipping it open, he held it behind his leg.

Merk, with a square of dirty white gauze taped to his forehead, walked up chewing tobacco. He stopped when he was about five feet from Vint. "I'm gonna kill ya."

"Trying and doing are two different things." Vint held tightly onto the steel handle of the razor that began to feel slippery in his sweating hand.

"Last thing I remember, my brother was comin' atcha. When I woke up with my head bleedin', Lester was dead

43

on the floor and you was gone. I know ya done murdered 'im. And now I'm gonna do you in."

"You're wrong. I didn't kill your brother. It was an accident."

"I'm gonna get you and that spade, Shadrack."

"OK, let's get this over with, right here and now." Vint held the razor out in front of him.

"We ain't doin' this now, you ape." Merk looked at the razor and laughed. "My brother Polk's gettin' outa jail in a week and a half. He wants a piece of you for killin' his baby brother too. So's as much as I wanna rip your eyes out and stomp on your throat, I gotta wait for Polk." Merk spit tobacco juice on the ground between them. "See ya then, pretty boy."

Vint watched Merk lumber away, then disappear around the corner. He closed the razor, put it away and dried his hand on his pant leg.

* * *

Vint finished out the afternoon working in the area in front of the office, separating straight boards from warped ones. He looked up to see Adelle sashaying directly toward him.

"Mr. Smith." Adelle stood with her hips cocked to one side, a manicured hand on her waist. "I'd like you to come to this address tonight. Around eight?"

Without looking at the printed information, he stuck it in his pocket. "Sure."

When Vint immediately went back to work without another word, Adelle gave him a cross look. She turned and walked back to her office muttering something he couldn't make out.

* * *

It was getting dark as Vint walked toward the west end of town, smoking and kicking at stones on the crack-filled concrete of Main Street. Other men at work often talked about Adelle's luxurious home. A handful of them had worked on the construction of it a few years back. He ventured beyond the two-block downtown area with stores and shops lining both sides of the road, most of them closed for the evening. He kept moving and went beyond the large, old wooden framed homes, painted in tans and grays with lights in the windows. When he got to the edge of town, where the trees became denser, he looked up at a street sign that looked out of place. Unlike the rust-tinged metal ones that were attached to leaning, paint-chipped poles, this sign was fashioned out of walnut wood. In the moonlight, he read a carved-out name, *HURST BOULEVARD*. It was perched high on a sturdy, tooled, wooden pole pointing straight to the heavens.

Vint turned north on the private road, toward the river, and followed it up about a quarter-mile until he got to the Hurst manor. Under the deep-blue, star-filled sky, the house, constructed of meticulously arranged natural stone, was illuminated with spotlights of purple and gold.

As he walked up the circular driveway, he could see Adelle standing in the open doorway, smoking.

She glanced at her diamond-encrusted watch. "You're late."

"Don't have a car."

"Obviously." She pitched her cigarillo. "Come in."

Vint stepped in, glanced around at the crystal chandelier, marble floored entranceway, and luxurious appointments. He nodded and said, "Swanky joint you got here."

"Yes," she said, with a blank expression. "I'm aware of that. This way."

Vint followed Adelle across the foyer, then the spacious great room. As he walked directly behind her, up the wide marble staircase, he got a good look at her shapely derriere in her clingy silk robe.

She led him to a large bedroom to the left at the top of the stairs. "This was Mr. Hurst's private bedroom. I'd like these boxes carried down to the basement." She looked at Vint over her shoulder. "Think you can handle that?"

Vint took his jacket off and threw it over the back of a chair. "No problem."

Adelle looked surprised when he picked up boxes two at a time and easily carried them down the marble flight.

"The basement stairs are off the kitchen," she called out after him.

After three trips, up and down, he returned to the bedroom where she was waiting.

She had spread a few of her late husband's suits on his bed while he was carrying boxes.

"Aren't you getting tired of that t-shirt and those blue jeans?" She shook her head.

Adelle bent at the waist, pushing her derriere out seductively. Pausing as if deciding which suit to choose, she picked one up and said, "Try this one on." She turned around and removed a suitcoat from a wooden hanger, then handed it to Vint.

He slipped the jacket on and walked to a full-length mirror.

Adelle gazed at Vint's broad shoulders. "Very nice." She walked up close behind him and tucked excess material into her hands at the waist. "A little altering."

He made a side motion with his head. "Not bad."

"Not bad? That's a hand-crafted suit."

"You think I never owned a custom-made suit?" He looked at her through the mirror. "I had a closet full of bespoke suits, silk shirts and ties. When things were good, they were real good." He turned around face to face with Adelle. "I smoked the finest cigars, drank only top shelf liquor. Had my share of beautiful women too." Vint looked down at Adelle's full lips, just inches away.

She backed up a step. "Don't forget why you're here."

"Look, sister. You could've got any one of those monkeys down at the plant to move that junk. You brought me up here because I make you curious." He took a step closer. "I think your curiosity has given you an itch."

"I can scratch my own itch, Mr. Smith." Adelle raised her chin. "I think you better go now. And leave the jacket."

* * *

Vint walked in the unlocked front door of Grannie's house. The living room was dimly lit and soft music was playing on the radio. He could see Lark sitting on the couch with her bare legs crossed.

"Where were you?" She stared straight ahead at the blank wall.

"Did a little work for Mrs. Hurst. Over at her house."

"Adelle Hurst?" Lark shot Vint a concerned look. "You were in her house?"

"Yeah." He got a whiff of her light perfume. "She needed some boxes moved."

"And she asked *you*."

Vint hesitated, then asked, "What's your problem, girl?"

"I want to know what else you did over there besides move boxes."

"I don't like this third degree. Maybe it's time I move out of here."

Lark folded her arms in an exaggerated manner. "Thought you'd stop by the diner tonight."

"Came straight here from work, napped in your bed, then took a bath. I made myself a sandwich and headed out." He noticed a dinner plate covered in tinfoil sitting on the kitchen table.

"Adelle." She frowned and shook her head.

"You know her … personally?"

"Yeah. I know her." Lark stood in her nightie facing Vint. "Merk Skinner and some goon rode by here a few times tonight. They were hollering stuff, bad stuff. Threw empty beer bottles in the front yard."

"I need to know what they said." He pointed a finger at her. "Exactly."

"Couldn't make all of it out. Said he was gonna cut your balls off and feed them to his pigs. Said, I'm gonna getcha, yank."

"For your safety, I think I should find another place to stay."

"Adelle's?" The name caught in her throat.

"Don't be silly." Vint could tell Lark wasn't wearing a bra under her pink nightie. "I barely know her."

"Please don't leave me." She grabbed his arm and held on tight. "I shouldn't have said anything about Merk."

"No. It's a good thing you told me. But you're going to have to stay off my back, girl. I don't like answering to anyone. Had enough of that in prison."

"Come to bed with me." Lark tugged on his arm as she walked backward. "I'll make you feel good," she said in a whisper as they passed Grannie's room.

Chapter 8

"Margaret wants to see you, Smith." Gerald motioned with his thumb. "That is, unless you have some other pressin' engagement."

Pulling off his work gloves, Vint walked into the office and up to Margaret's desk. "Yeah?"

"Mrs. Hurst isn't in for the rest of the day. She told me to give you this." She handed him a sealed envelope. "I don't know what's in there, but when I hold it up to the light it looks like cash."

Vint snatched the envelope from her hand. "You know what your problem is? You need a man to take a hand to your ass and give you a good hard roll in the hay."

"You say when, handsome." Margaret studied Vint walking out the door.

Tearing open the envelope, he looked around, then peeked inside. A crisp twenty-dollar bill was waiting for him, nearly as much as he made working four days. He assumed it was for moving boxes for Adelle the night before. Not bad for ten minutes work, plus the time it took to walk to her house and back. Then he noticed a small folded piece of paper in the envelope. He opened it.

Vinton, There is a private matter I would like to discuss with you, Adelle.

* * *

With a little jingle in his pocket, Vint headed straight to the one place he wanted to visit since he stumbled into this tiny corner of God's earth. He walked into the shop that smelled of hair tonics and witch hazel. "Haircut and shave."

"Hello." The lone barber in the small storefront jumped up from a chair and dropped his newspaper on the floor. "You must be Mr. Smith. The one the ladies say looks like that actor feller."

Vint didn't answer. He hung his jacket on a hook, then sat in the only barber chair.

"I'm Ned." His smile drew back, revealing a smattering of well water-browned teeth.

"Don't try anything cute." Vint looked straight ahead. "I just want a normal haircut. Trim it up on the sides and back. Leave it a little longer on top."

"Yes, sir. I'm the best barber in this town." Ned laughed and slapped his leg. "OK. I'm the only barber in town." He chuckled some more.

"Cut out the funny business and get to it. I don't want to be here all day."

"Of course, sir." Ned spread a clean white barber cloth over Vint.

Ned remained quiet throughout the haircut, then asked, "Shorten up them sideburns for ya?"

"Shorten them and I'll shorten you."

"I-I'll just brush ya off 'fore I shave ya then."

Ned sharpened his razor on his leather strop, then began applying shaving cream to the right side of Vint's cheek.

The front door flew open, ringing the bell hanging over the top. A guy in his early-twenties stepped in and pushed his western style hat back. He took the toothpick from his mouth and dropped it on the floor. "Didn't know ya shaved pigs, Ned."

Vint briefly glanced at the medium-height young man dressed in a checkered cowboy shirt.

"Got nothin' to say, tough guy?" The man bent over, lifted the leg of blue jeans and pulled a small .22 caliber revolver from a cowboy boot. "Uh huh. Gettin' scared now, ain'tcha?"

Vint looked at him again, smiled and shook his head.

"Say somethin'!" The slim guy stepped within a few feet from Vint. "Lester Skinner was my best friend!"

"Put that popgun away before I take it from you and put a new hole in your ass."

"I'm a damn killer, mister. I know what it's like to kill. I'll kill a man for lookin' at me wrong. Damn it. You're lookin' at a real, true killer."

"Anyone who talks about it that much never did it." Vint looked him in the eye. "Go away, sonny boy. Before I blow on you and knock you over."

"Say your prayers, smart guy."

"You watch too many John Wayne movies, kid." Vint grabbed the edge of the barber cloth with his left hand. "Go home and pop your pimples."

The guy cocked his pistol and moved closer. "Nobody talks to me like that!"

In a split-second, Vint sliced through the white cotton, bringing his razor up to the underside of the young man's nose. "Put that gun back in your pocket real calm like or I'll take your nose off. It won't be my first time. A nose comes off like popping a dandelion."

"I'll shoot ya, mister." His voice trembled and his hand shook as he pointed the pistol at Vint's chest. "Don't think I won't."

"Go ahead then." Vint grabbed the man's shirt and pressed the blade a little harder against his nostrils. "Shoot and quit talking about it."

"Wait a minute now," the young man appealed, as a bit of his blood appeared on Vint's silvery blade.

"I said shoot! You pimple-puss cowboy. It takes a lot of bullets to kill me. Either way I'm taking your nose."

"OK. OK. I-I'm gonna put my g-gun back in my pocket. So ya can take that blade away."

"When the gun's put away, I'll take the razor from your nose."

"Wait. Wait now. If I put my gun away, how do I know you're not gonna cut me?"

Vint pulled the young guys face closer to his, holding the blade in place. "Put it away now before I change my mind and cut you for fun."

"All right now. You win. I'm puttin' it away." The man's movements were slow and deliberate. "See?"

"Let's see that empty hand." Vint pointed with his chin.

"They're empty." The guy held both hands up. "You said you'd take the knife from my nose."

"First, I want you to apologize to Ned here. The man has piss running down his pant leg."

"OK. I'll do it. Ned?" He kept his eyes on Vint. "I'm sorry, Ned."

"It's all right, Grover." Ned's voice wavered. "Please don't cut him, Mr. Smith. Blood makes me kind of ill." Ned crumpled to the floor.

"See all the trouble you caused, Grover." Vint shoved him back and jumped out of the chair with the blade out in front of him. "Back out that door and keep your hands up. If you ever see me in town, I'd suggest you walk on the other side of the street." Vint followed Grover as he backed away. "Tell all your little buddies that the next person who crosses me is going to be buried out where the pines get heavy."

Grover reached behind his back.

"Careful, boy." Vint moved in closer with his razor.

"I'm j-just gettin' the door." Grover's chest heaved as he opened the door behind him. "Don't cut me. Please don't cut me."

"Go on now. Get!"

Grover flew out the door and ran.

Vint wiped his blade on the damaged barber cloth, then put it away. He took the cloth off, walked up next to

Ned and nudged him with his boot. "Come on, get up." Vint bent over and shook him as he lay on the hair-covered floor.

"W-what happened?" Ned's eyes fluttered.

"You fainted like a little girl at the thought of blood. Stand up." Vint extended his hand and helped him to his feet. "You're in no shape to shave anyone. You probably *would* cut someone's nose off. Give me some shaving cream."

Ned shook a can of Barbasol and handed it to him.

Vint lathered his face, then used Ned's strop to sharpen his razor. He stood in front of a mirror and took his time getting a close shave.

"How much for the cut?" Vint reached into his pocket.

"Go right on ahead, Mr. Smith. You don't owe me nothin'." Ned's head bobbed up and down like a parakeet. "I'm startin' a new policy as of right now. First haircut's on old Ned here. Sure is."

"Better go home and change your pants." Vint grabbed his jacket and walked out the door.

* * *

"Nice haircut." Lark winked at Vint, then poured him some coffee.

Vint glanced to his left as he did every time Dewey's front door opened. Edric Randall strolled in with his shoulders back and his head held high. It was the second time Vint had seen him in public.

"Thought I'd find you here." Edric took the stool to Vint's left.

"You again." Vint looked straight ahead and spoke in low tones to Edric without eye contact. "What makes you think my name's Mercurio?"

"Unlike that bumbling marshal, I have my ways of finding things out. What he suspects, I *know*."

"OK … for now." Vint took a drag off his cigarette and blew smoke out slowly. "How serious were you about what we discussed? You were three sheets to the wind."

Edric removed his homburg. "Very serious." He went to set his hat on the counter, then put it on his lap instead.

Vint dropped his half-finished smoke into his empty soup bowl. "You remember everything we covered?"

Edric looked around and said softly, "Of course. I recall everything that was said. I was more tired than inebriated. We need to discuss this matter further. But, I do better with appointments. When are you free to come by my apartment again? Providing it is no later than 8:00 pm."

"How about tomorrow? I can come right after work if you're going to have something else to eat besides stale donuts."

"Why don't you go ahead and eat dinner first, then swing by."

"Sure." Vint grinned and shook his head. "Why not?"

"Can you please do me the courtesy to look at me when I'm speaking to you?"

"Sure, governor." Vint turned on his stool. "That the only suit you own?"

"The rest of my things were held up in transport. This must suffice for now."

"Held up, huh? The clothes that got *held up* must be out of style by now, judging from the frayed edges of that flannel."

"It's a long story." Edric looked around again. "After we accomplish the plan I have set in place, we'll both be buying plenty of new suits at the finest haberdasheries in the world."

"Think you might be overselling this deal a little?"

"There are three things I never do. I never speak badly of the Queen. I never sleep with a woman with hairy arms." Edric plopped his hat back on his head. "And I never exaggerate." He stood, turned on his heel and walked out of Dewey's in long strides.

Lark had a quizzical look on her face as she slowly approached Vint with the coffee pot. "That the one you asked me about, the English lawyer?"

"Well, he seems to be the only limey barrister in this tiny town, so my answer would be yes."

"You don't have to get so smart-alecky with me. Just 'cause I'm younger than you, doesn't mean I'm dumb. I made real good grades in school."

"Don't mind me. I'm not used to talking to a real lady. Been a while."

"It's OK. I'm kinda sorry for getting on your back about Adelle last night. I baked you a cake before I came in for my shift today. You know, to make up."

"Cake? Haven't had a homemade cake in years. What kind?"

"Chocolate with coffee icing. Since you like coffee so much, I figured …"

"You shouldn't be so nice to me. I really don't deserve it."

"Stick around. I'll be off in less than an hour. It's a slow night."

Vint pulled out his paperback and flipped through the pages until he got to his torn matchbook cover marker. He became so engrossed in the story that he didn't notice the broad-shouldered, six-foot-three marshal walk up.

"Mercurio."

Stopping mid-sentence, Vince stared at the page and tried to hide any reaction.

"Smith."

Vint slowly turned, looked up at the big man and nodded. "Marshal."

"Cup of coffee, Lark." Gilstrap took the seat next to him. "Keeping your nose clean?"

"I mind my business."

"What kind of company you been keeping … besides Lark here?"

Vint closed his book. "Like I said, I mind my own business."

Lark poured Gilstrap a cup, read the faces of the two, then walked away.

"Would that business be bank robbery?" The marshal poured a little sugar into his cup from a glass dispenser.

"If I had a lawyer, I think he'd advise me not to answer any questions without him present."

"What about Edric Randall? He might qualify as a lawyer." The lawman stirred his coffee. "Saw you through the window. Y'all seem pretty chummy."

Vint pulled his cigarettes out, turned the pack sideways and tapped one out. He lit a stick match on the side of his engineer boot and held it under the tip of his Old Gold. "Am I under arrest?"

"Not yet. But that day could come sooner'n you think." Gilstrap leaned in closer. "All of us in this town are fond of Lark. She's like a flower growing in the desert. What the hell she sees in a pisser like you …"

"Far as I know, there's no law against keeping company with a lady. She's over eighteen. Old enough to choose who she wants to see."

"Try getting out of line one time … hell … I'll arrest you for farting inside town limits." The marshal poked Vint's arm. "We got our eye on you, boy." He stood, put a dime on the counter and walked out without touching his coffee.

* * *

Lark had a bounce in her step as she held Vint's hand, practically dancing around him on their way to her house. *"Your cheatin' heart, will tell on you,"* she sang in a clear, melodic voice.

"Can you sing something else besides Hank Williams?"

"Oh, sure." She cleared her throat and sang out in perfect pitch, *"Don't let the stars get in your eyes …"*

Vint interrupted her. "Say, you have a beautiful voice. Why are you hanging around this backwoods town? Don't you have any ambition?"

"I was thinking about joining the church choir."

"That's not what I had in mind. With your looks and that voice, you could go places."

"Oh, there's girls prettier'n me, ones that can sing too."

"Ever think about entering a beauty contest?"

"How am I going to do that, working at the diner? Me and Grannie just get by. You need money to take off work … travel."

"You need a sponsor. If I had the dough …"

Lark stood in front of Vint, stopping him in his tracks. "The only ambition I have tonight is feeding you some cake … then feeding you something else … if you know what I mean."

* * *

After their baths, Vint sat at the kitchen table in his boxers with a glass of bourbon in front of him.

Straddling his lap, facing him in her white bra and panties, Lark said, "Open up, daddy," and put another forkful of cake in his mouth. She giggled and brushed a crumb from his full lips. "That a boy, eat up. You're gonna need lots of energy."

"I just hope Grannie doesn't come out here."

"She never gets up at night, not even to pee." Lark smiled and fed him another bite. "It would take an earthquake to rouse her."

Vint washed the confection down with a sip of bourbon. "That's good cake. You make that all by yourself?"

"That's right. Little ole me. How'd ya like this kinda treatment every night?"

"Mmm, tempting, doll."

Lark put the last bite in his mouth, then ran her finger along the plate, wiping up icing. She stuck her finger in her mouth and sucked it off. "OK, big boy." She lightly slapped his cheek. "Ready for your dessert?"

Vint took a slug of bourbon. "Aren't you afraid someone's going to look in a window?"

Reaching back and setting the plate and fork on the table, she answered, "You don't know this town. It's after 10:00." She took a small sip of his bourbon, then kissed him deeply and passionately. Slipping one bra strap down, then the other, she leaned forward, pressing one of her pinkish nipples to his mouth.

After Vint licked and sucked her nipples, Lark stood with her legs apart, still straddling him. "Now that you've had your cake, you can have a little pie." She slid her panties down around her upper thighs, then grabbed the sides of his hair and pushed her hips forward.

As he pleasured her, she ground herself into his mouth harder and harder until she climaxed with a loud moan.

He looked up at her. "What happened to that girl who was shy about undressing in front of me a few days ago?"

"There's a lot you don't know about me."

Vint shoved his chair back and scooped Lark in his arms. He carried her into the bedroom and tossed her onto her bed. He pulled her panties off, then his boxers and gazed at her in the dimly lit room.

She put her hands behind her head and spread her legs. "I belong to you now … every part of me."

"Damn, you look beautiful laying there." He lay on top of Lark, kissed her once, then entered her. Their passion rose with every thrust, but he stopped abruptly and got to his feet.

"Why did you stop? Did I do something wrong?"

"No." Vint walked into the living room nude and went for his jacket that was hanging on a chair. He reached into a pocket and pulled out a condom. Walking back into the bedroom and removing the protection from its wrapper, he said, "Last thing I need right now is a baby holding me back." He rolled it on and lay on top of Lark again, entering her with one thrust.

* * *

As they lay panting, Lark said in a breathy voice, "A baby wouldn't be such a bad thing. I love babies." She stroked the black hair on Vint's hand. "I wanna have a bunch of 'em."

He pulled his hand from her stomach. "Babies don't fit into my picture."

"What's this picture look like? Who's in it?"

"Been the same for a long time. Me with a lot of dough. Owning a successful business, in a real city with upscale restaurants, night clubs. I want to walk into a joint in an expensive suit, gold watch, diamond ring. I want to shove a door open like I own the place and have my pick of beautiful women."

"You don't need all that. Those things aren't important." She lay on her side, poking his chest. "And you don't need a lot of beautiful women. Just one that loves you."

"There you go again." Vint put his hands behind his head as he lay on his back. "Don't you want to get out of this town and see the world?"

"I'd like to travel some. But having a home to come back to, family, that's what matters. All that other stuff just makes you feel good for a little while. What are you gonna do when you get older? Don't you want someone to take care of you?"

"Older? I don't think that far ahead. I want to live now while I'm young enough to enjoy it. If I play my cards right, I'll be busting out of this burg soon."

Lark rolled onto her stomach. "Oh, go on. Go sleep on the couch. I've heard enough of your big dreams for one night." She shoved at him. "Get out of my bed and leave me alone, Mr. Big Shot."

Vint grabbed his boxers from the floor and stood. "You and me are like oil and vinegar. We go together, really tasty on a salad, but we don't mix."

"You're just a dreamer. How are you gonna get all those things unless you rob banks? You'll just end up back in prison again." She threw her panties at him, hitting his face.

Catching the panties before they fell to the ground, he brought them to his nose and breathed in looking into her eyes.

"Yeah, that's all you care about. Get out of here. Now."

Vint tossed her underwear back and left the room. He looked at the made-up couch, then got dressed. He grabbed his cigarettes and walked out the front door. Lighting an Old Gold, he continued on, weighing his options.

After pacing up and down the street a couple times, he went back to Lark's and slowly opened the door, quietly as he could. He found her sitting cross-legged on the couch in her pajamas.

"Didn't think you were coming back." Lark folded her arms under her breasts, pushing them up.

"Where am I going to go?" He took off his jacket and threw it at the coatrack, where it rested on top of the pole.

"I'm glad you decided to stay." She unfolded her arms and legs.

"I may be stubborn but I'm not stupid. You've been good to me. I've got it made here."

"Sorry I pressured you." She stood and touched his arm. "I know you don't like it."

"You didn't say anything wrong. You said all the right things, just to the wrong guy." Vint sat on the couch and pushed his boots off. "You're a good kid. I don't want to hurt you."

"That's just it, I'm not a kid. By the time my mom was my age, I was three years old."

"Bet your mom was good looking." He stood and pulled his jeans off, then lay on the couch.

"She was gorgeous." Lark kneeled next to him. "Her and my dad never had much but they were happy."

"Let's not go down that road again."

"I'm just saying …"

"I know exactly what you're saying." He adjusted his pillow. "I don't want to rehash the same conversation."

"OK, OK. Can I lay next to you?"

"Sure, blondie."

Lark settled next to him with her ass pressing against his boxers. "Nothing's ever settled between us. And it's driving me crazy."

"Don't fall asleep out here. I don't need Grannie waking up screaming at me."

Chapter 9

"C'mon. Follow me, Smith." Gerald motioned and walked ahead of Vint. He led him back behind Hurst Lumber and they continued on to the train tracks. When they got there, Vint found Merk Skinner sneering at him in one of the open boxcars.

"You're workin' with Merk today. Y'all gonna be loadin' these fence posts into that there train car."

Merk smiled, showing his greenish teeth. "Hey now. This is gonna be fun." He laughed in a hiccupy manner, then jumped to the ground.

Gerald walked away without another word, leaving Vint and Merk alone together next to a tall pile of posts, all sharpened on one end.

Vint stared at Merk a moment. "OK, let's get this over with. Sooner the better."

"These posts is pretty sharp there, boy. Don't wanna rush. Ya might have a deadly accident."

Shooting Merk a stern look, Vint said, "One of us is going to have to be on the ground handing up posts. The other is going to block and stack them. We can switch off after a while."

"You get up in there, ya Yankee shit-head. I'm gonna hand 'em up to ya."

Vint reluctantly climbed into the car, watching his back. "OK, let's get going. I don't want to be here with you any more than you want to be with me."

Merk picked up a post and laughed. "I asked Gerald for you to be my partner on this detail, you stupid fuck." He heaved a post at Vint, sharp end first.

"Watch it!" Vint jumped out of the way. "You try that again and I'll throw it right back at you."

"Ha." Merk slapped his leg. "Shoulda seen the look on your face." He laughed some more.

"I'm telling you, I'll kill you if you try anything stupid."

Merk started throwing posts into the car faster than Vint could stack and band them. To Vint's surprise, the big guy went through the whole pile in about twenty minutes.

While Vint was busy with his end of the job, Merk climbed up into the car and found Vint behind the stack of posts, securing them. He walked up to Vint, out of view of the open door, and picked up a post from the top of the pile. Vint stood against the inside wall and pulled his razor. Merk lunged forward with the wooden pole, shoving the unsharpened end into Vint's solar plexus. Vint gasped as air was forced from his lungs. He stood helpless, holding his razor while Merk put his weight into the post. Vint tried moving side to side but he was pinned against the wall by the powerful young man. He struggled to breathe and felt faint. Drawing his razor back to throw it, Vint stopped when he heard something.

"How y'all comin' along in there?" Gerald's voice called just outside.

Merk dropped the post and stepped back. Vint fell to one knee, gasping.

Gerald poked his head into the boxcar. "Good job, boys. Y'all got 'er done quick."

Breathing heavily, Vint put his razor away, grabbed onto the neatly stacked posts and pulled himself to his feet.

"You OK back there, Smith?"

"Yeah … yeah." Vint waved his hand, catching his breath.

"Good." Gerald looked at Merk and laughed. "Sometimes there's a little accident 'round here but I don't like anyone dyin' on my watch."

"We's just havin' a little fun." Merk chuckled.

"Well, why don't ya go help on the sawmill, Merk," Gerald said. "Smith can finish this up by himself."

"All righty then, boss." Merk stared at Vint a moment. "You and me's gonna have more fun tomorrow, ain't we, polecat?"

* * *

Vint stood in the center of Main Street after work. He looked east up the road, then west. A green Model A Ford with dented black fenders turned onto Main a block away and slowly chugged toward him. He stood, watching the old car approach, then stepped out of the way when it got within fifteen feet. The old guy behind the wheel tipped his straw hat expressionlessly and kept going. As he watched the dog-tracking Ford drive away, he stood there contemplating some way to end his increasing boredom.

He hadn't had anything to eat since lunch but he wasn't hungry, he just felt empty. Reluctantly, he walked up to the entrance of Dewey's and stopped outside. He looked through the dirty screen of the door and saw the same sights he'd seen over and over since he came to be stuck in this town. Dewey sat on a stool with his back to the counter, leaning on his elbows, staring off. The usual crowd sat at the counter and first two tables making small talk. He'd only been in town a short time and was already tired of the same stories being rehashed about someone having a baby, someone getting sick, or someone dying – probably of boredom, he thought. Lark walked around with a pot of coffee, smiling that smile. It was an empty smile that seemed to hide her inner feelings.

Vint pushed the door open and cringed at the metallic squeak. "Damn it, Dewey. Don't you have an oil can around here somewhere?" He let the door snap closed.

"Oil can? For what?"

"For this squeaky door." Vint motioned with both hands.

Dewey shrugged. "I didn't hear nothin'."

"Well, do you have some oil?"

"Don't reckon so."

Lark walked up to Vint. "Why the sour look?"

"Doesn't that noisy door bother you?"

"Oh. Guess I just got used to it. Don't even notice it anymore. You'll get used to it too."

"No, I won't. Go to the kitchen and bring me a bottle of vegetable oil."

"OK, grumpy." She disappeared into the kitchen and came back with a bottle of Wesson Oil. "Here you go, bossy pants."

Vint carefully dripped oil onto the hinges of the screen door.

"Just what do you think you're doing to my door there, mister?" Dewey protested. "You wanna attract flies?"

"There." Vint opened and closed the door a couple times. "See. No more of that annoying squeak."

"Somehow, it just ain't the same." An old guy sitting at a nearby table in a beat-up *Bathers* baseball cap spoke up.

A freckly, middle-aged lady sat at the counter sipping a root beer float. The buttons looked close to popping on the white cotton dress with yellow flowers that she had squeezed into. "Doesn't sound right," she said, in a voice that climbed the scales.

"What've you done to my door?" Dewey whined. "I miss that squeak."

Vint walked up to the counter, set the bottle down hard, then headed back to the last stool.

Lark followed him and touched his arm when he stopped. "People don't like things to change around here. Shouldn't mess with stuff like that."

"Good Lord." Vint sat on the red, cracked, Naugahyde covered seat. "Is everybody in this town buggy?"

"Yep." Lark crossed her eyes and stuck out her tongue. "Including me."

"I don't know how you can take it, year after year. I've only been here a week and it's already driving me nuts."

"Well, there. See? That's how it starts." She pulled out her order pad and pencil. "Get ya anything? Another one of those burgers ya like so much?"

"No. Please. Not another burger. Just surprise me. All right?"

"You got it. One surprise plate coming up."

Vint lit a cigarette as he watched Dewey and others gather around the screen door, opening and closing it, muttering. He turned his back to them and opened his book.

* * *

After filling up on pork chops with apple sauce and hash brown potatoes, Vint stepped out of Dewey's to an orange and purple sunset. The thought of sitting on that stool the next few hours waiting for Lark to get off work depressed him. He pulled Adelle's note from his pocket and reread it.

Walking west on Main in the direction of Adelle's house, Vint lit a cigarette and thought back on the good times in his life. After a big bank score, he would always celebrate with a new suit of clothes and dinner at an expensive restaurant with some doll. He knew he couldn't stand still too long. He had to make a move, had to get back in the chips again. Turning onto the private road, Hurst Boulevard, Vint breathed in the October air, heavy with the scents of fragrant sumac and a variety of shrubs and trees. As he got closer to Adelle's home on the far outskirts of town, he could hear the sounds of the flowing river through the dense trees.

He walked up the long driveway of neatly arranged brick, pressed the lighted doorbell button, then knocked loudly on the oversized double doorway.

A curtain pulled back in the large picture window and Adelle's face appeared. A few moments later, the door opened.

"Yes?" Adelle stood halfway behind the door dressed in a long, lavender robe, trimmed in matching dyed ostrich fur.

Pulling the note from his pocket, he held it up in the cool, early evening air.

"I thought we'd discuss it in my office."

"Well, you weren't there again today, so I thought I'd drop by."

"I was out of town, delayed on business. I'll be back at the plant tomorrow."

"If you don't want to do this now I can turn around and walk back." He motioned over his shoulder with his thumb.

Adelle glanced down at Vint's dusty boots. "Wipe your feet." She opened the door wider and stepped aside. "Follow me to the study."

Vint brushed his soles on the outside mat and noticed that it did not say *Welcome*. He stepped in and glanced around at the luxurious white carpet and French provincial furniture. "I'm going to have a pad like this one of these days." He trailed close behind as Adelle led him through large rooms with high cathedral ceilings.

"Have a seat." She motioned toward a burgundy-colored, leather armchair.

"You live in this big joint all by yourself?" He sat down and crossed his legs.

"Since my husband died, yes. I have a cook, housekeeper, gardener. But they're off duty in the evening. My maid leaves right after she serves me dinner."

Vint inspected the rich, reddish-brown wall paneling. "Nice setup."

"Can I get you a brandy?"

"Sure. That'd be swell."

Adelle opened an ornate, cherrywood liquor cabinet with lattice windows and produced two snifters and a bottle of cognac. She poured them both a generous amount of spirits, then set Vint's glass on a sturdy mahogany end table next to him. Gliding around the room in high-heeled slippers, she returned with a humidor. She stood in front of him and opened it. "Cigar?"

"Why not?"

She removed a cigar cutter from the case and snipped the tip of his Habana.

"Thanks." Vint took the cigar and lit it from the pedestal lighter standing next to his chair. He motioned toward his clothes. "Sorry I'm not dressed for the occasion."

Adelle rolled her eyes. "You already know what I think of that getup. Who do you think you are, Brando?"

Knowing she didn't expect an answer, he puffed on his cigar and ignored the question.

"There're rumors floating around about you." She stood with her feet apart. "You been in prison?"

"Don't believe everything you hear." Changing the subject, he remarked, "Saw that picture of you on your office wall, *Adelle Amour*. That some kind of stage name?"

"I was a dancer ... of the exotic nature." She sat across from Vint on an overstuffed sofa. "Didn't think Agnes Glumb would look very enticing on a marquee."

"See what you mean. Trying to raise a man's spirits not dampen them. That what you were doing when you met Mr. Hurst?" He smirked. "You raise his?"

"Obviously." Adelle looked around the spacious room and motioned with her left hand. "I'd say it worked very well."

"How much older was your husband than you?"

"Eighteen years."

"I get the picture." Vint watched flames from the fireplace dance in reflection on his glass. "How *did* the dearly departed depart?"

She swirled the brandy in her snifter. "Mr. Hurst, God bless him, died in the saddle."

"He rode horseback?"

"No. He rode me. Doctor warned him, but Mr. Hurst couldn't seem to resist my charms."

"Got it." Vint rubbed his five-o'clock shadow, noticing how Adelle's blank expression never changed while talking about her late husband. "Guess that's enough getting-to-know-you jabber. Let's get down to business. The note said you wanted to talk to me about something."

"I didn't envision what my life would be like once my husband died." She stood and paced. "Didn't know that there wasn't much in the bank. He was in hock up to his eyeballs after he built this place, and he built it just to impress me. How was I to know? He played it like he had millions. I have money coming in from the lumber business but it's just enough to support me and this house. One bad year and it all goes under."

Vint glanced around at various animal heads mounted on the walls. "Maybe you can sell this place."

"I've tried. It's a white elephant. People who can afford a place like this don't want to live around here. Nothing but trees and that joke of a town. We're over an hour to a decent restaurant, for God's sake."

"Have much equity tied up in it?"

"Not as much as you'd think. Mr. Hurst went overboard on everything. He borrowed and borrowed some more."

"I see." He took a sip of brandy. "Doomed in paradise."

"I never realized what monotonous work it would be running that damn wooden jail of a business. If I don't get out of there soon, I'm going to kill someone." Adelle raised one eyebrow. "Just an expression."

"I suppose you've tried selling the lumber business."

"Without any luck. Investors consider it too big a risk. Could you imagine if we had a forest fire around here?"

"Yeah. See what you mean." He studied her hard-to-read face. "You have insurance on that timber yard?"

"Of course." She stopped pacing and took a sip. "You're on the right track."

Vint blew a smoke ring in her direction. "Fire insurance?"

"You're getting warmer." She sat back down. "Yes, and it's expensive. Takes a gouge out of my profits every month. Don't think I haven't thought about it. I dream about it. But these insurance investigators aren't stupid. They go through every ounce of ash looking for incriminating evidence."

"Suppose … yeah." He tapped his temple with an index finger. "That could work."

"What?"

Vint drained his glass. "I have an idea that could solve your problems."

"Well?"

"Sometimes ideas are worth money." He set his snifter down and stood. "Thanks for the brandy. I'll let myself out."

Adelle shot to her feet. "When are we going to talk again?" The desperation in her voice told Vint that he had her hooked.

"I'll contact you." He walked away, then stopped and turned. "One more thing, I want you to tell that Gerald to never pair me up with Merk Skinner again. Bastard did it just to spite me. In fact, make sure me and that big galoot are working in opposite parts of that mill from now on."

* * *

Vint walked back to town and over to the bakery. He avoided touching the splintered handrail as he climbed the stairs to Edric's apartment. After knocking, the door quickly swung open.

"Come in." Edric made an exaggerated sweeping gesture. "Come in." He walked straight and tall to the kitchen table.

Vint followed him, pulled out one of the sturdy ancient chairs and sat down.

"May I offer you a cup of tea?" Edric struck a match, turned on the gas under his kettle, and lit the stove.

"What? No gin this evening?"

"Alas, my supply ran out." Edric took the lid from a sugar bowl and pulled out a tea bag. "I must make do with my old friend, *Earl Grey*." He put the bag into a cup on the table and sat down.

Tapping the tabletop with his index finger, Vint said, "OK, let's get to it."

"I've just learned that the cash in the Krauses' home totals over a half-million dollars."

Vint whistled. "Damn. That's a lot more than I ever got from any bank."

"And even better, it's not in a safe." Edric opened a bakery box and tilted it toward Vint, this time revealing three bismarcks, one half-eaten. "That I'm sure of."

Vint made a sour look and waved the box away. "There's two things about this set up that bothers me. First of all, if the Krauses have all this dough, why do they slave away in the bakery six days a week?"

"Since they've never had children, the bakery is all they really have. They adore seeing their regular customers every week and hearing about their children and grandchildren. The Krauses seem to live a family life vicariously through their patrons."

"I walked past their house. It's a grand old place but needs some repairs and a coat of paint. If they do have money, you'd think they'd spruce it up."

"They're a peculiar lot. Who knows why people do the things they do?" Edric went to the stove, turned off the flame and poured steaming water into his cup. "I knew a man in London, was worth a small fortune. A miserly old coot. If you saw the way he lived. Didn't make sense." He stirred his tea. "This I *can* tell you, the Krauses simply don't care about money and the things it can buy."

"I don't know." Vint shook his head. "The other thing. Why do you need me to go in and get the cash? This isn't a bank we're talking about. It's just a house."

"Why, I would be the first person the authorities looked at. I am in the process of establishing an airtight alibi. As soon as I find out exactly where the money is hidden, I'll set the alibi in place and we'll move ahead with the plan."

Vint rubbed his chin, then lit a cigarette. "Something else doesn't quite fit. It doesn't make sense that someone would tell you about this money and not take it themselves."

"I'm sorry but that end will have to remain a mystery. If you knew the whole story, it would make perfect sense to you."

"Hmm." Vint took a deep drag and let it out slowly. "You banging the wife?"

"Preposterous." Edric took a small, careful sip.

"You're not a bad looking guy, sophisticated, especially compared to Mr. Krause. Some broads go for a guy with an English accent."

"No. You're way off base." Edric scooted his chair back making a scraping sound and stood with his head held high. "That will conclude tonight's meeting." He went to the door and opened it.

Vint blew smoke out the side of his mouth, then dropped his cigarette into Edric's teacup making a hissing sound. He walked to the open door and smirked. "Cheerio, pip-pip, and all that other malarkey."

Edric scowled. "I could have given you an ashtray."

"All right, don't get pissy." Vint tapped the back of his hand on Edric's vest. "I'm just taking the mickey out of you a little."

"There are some things you shouldn't trifle with," Edric huffed.

"You guys and your tea." Vint smiled, then started out the door.

"One more thing, Vint, my good man, would you please be so kind as to bring me a good bottle of gin next time we talk?"

"I don't know, squire. I think I like you better sober." Vint walked down the rickety stairs into the cool evening air.

Chapter 10

Adelle tore a contract in half as Gerald entered her office. "Go get Vint Smith," she ordered.

"Yes ma'am." Gerald bowed. "Should I say what for?"

"Just get him." She pointed at her door. "Now."

Gerald looked around Hurst Lumber and finally located Vint sitting in the loft above the storage area, smoking.

"What the hell ya think you're doin'?" Gerald waved his arms about. "Loafin' son-of-a-bitch. You know there's no smokin' in this buildin'. You're fired!"

"I doubt it." Vint stood, dropped his lit cigarette on the sawdust-covered floor and stubbed it out with his boot.

"Get over and see Mrs. Hurst right away." A wisp of Gerald's graying hair fell across his forehead as he motioned frantically with his hands.

"Adelle wants me?" Vint dusted his pants off. "Guess I got time for her."

"You done lost what little sense God gave you?"

Vint strolled down the stairs and took his time walking over to Adelle's office. As he strutted into the outer office, Margaret said, "Let me see if she's available."

Vint went right past Margaret. "She's available." He opened Adelle's door and walked in.

"Close that door." Adelle shot to her feet. "Just when did you plan to contact me? We have important business to discuss."

Vint shut the door behind his back. "You can't rush genius." He plopped into the seat across her desk and put his feet up. "I'm working out the fine details in my head."

She put her hands on her hips. "And just how long do you think that'll take?"

"I don't know." He didn't try to hide his gaze at her ample breasts. "Maybe I just need a little inspiration."

Adelle sat down and stared at Vint with a cross look on her otherwise hard to read face. "Come over to my house tonight at nine. We'll talk more then."

* * *

Vint went straight to Lark's house after work while she pulled her shift at the diner. He walked in, immediately went back to the kitchen and opened the refrigerator.

Grannie was sitting at the kitchen table making a grocery list. "You got a good appetite."

"I get paid tomorrow." He closed the refrigerator door, then washed his hands at the kitchen sink with a lavender-scented bar of soap. "I'll give you some money for food."

"Well, go ahead and eat. Never turned down a hungry person in my life." Grannie looked at him over wire-rimmed bifocals. "There's still some fried chicken from last night."

Vint went to the refrigerator again and pulled out a covered plate. He sat at the table, removed the aluminum foil and chose a leg from the assortment.

Grannie got up, went to the cupboard and took down a clean dish. She grabbed a paper napkin and set them in front of Vint. Looking down on him, she asked, "What are your intentions with my granddaughter?"

"Mmm," he said, chewing. "I don't have any intentions."

"You're intendin' somethin'. Either good or bad, but you got somethin' on your mind."

"Look, ma'am." He swallowed. "I appreciate the hospitality you and Lark have shown me but if you think I'm taking advantage of the situation …"

"I'm concerned about you taking advantage of Lark, not some situation." She walked to the refrigerator. "What would you like to drink?" she asked, holding the door open.

"Some of that sweet tea would be fine." He took another bite of chicken.

Grannie poured Vint a glass of cold tea and set it in front of him. "You're a good lookin' boy. Probably had your share of girls like Lark."

"Well, I wouldn't say …"

"Haven't you?" She sat back down. "This is a Christian home. Please don't lie."

He swallowed and looked down at his plate. "Guess I have."

"Don't suppose it took much guessin'." Grannie pulled a lace hankie from the pocket of her flowered house dress and fidgeted with it. "I worry so about that girl."

"I wouldn't fret too much. Lark's nice looking, smart, talented." He dropped his half-finished chicken leg on his plate. "Some nice boy is going to marry her. She'll do OK."

"What kind of reputation you think she's gonna have after you been stayin' with her under one roof?"

"Yes, but you're here too." Vint wiped his hands on the napkin.

"It's what people are thinkin'. You know what I mean. You two keepin' house."

"I never paid much mind to wagging tongues."

"Well, you should care what they say about Lark. If you care about her at all."

Vint balled the napkin in his fist. "I do care about her."

"She's gonna be twenty years old in six days. In my time, bein' unmarried at twenty was considered an old maid. Every other girl from her class is hitched already. Even that chubby, little cross-eyed gal workin' over at the feed store got herself a man."

Vint suppressed a smile.

"I may be up in years but I can still hear things. I hear you two makin' noise doin' one thing or another after I go to bed. I don't even wanna know. Breaks my heart."

"I'm sorry."

"Haven't you noticed anything off about that girl?"

"You mean?"

Grannie tapped a finger to the side of her head. "A little tetched."

"Well. I've noticed how her moods can change like the breeze. Real sad one minute, unusually happy the next."

"It's more than just that. Did she tell you about goin' in the hospital after that boy, Danny, left her?"

"No." Vint continually squeezed the balled-up napkin in his fist. "She told me about him but ..."

"Doctors called it a nervous breakdown. Said she had separation anxiety resultin' from losin' her mom and dad in that accident. Gave her shock treatments."

"I had no idea."

"I'm worried the same thing's gonna happen all over again once you've lit out of here."

Vint folded his arms across his chest and didn't say anything for a few moments. "I was concerned when she got so attached to me so fast. I've tried discouraging her."

"Got yourself in a pickle. Whatcha gonna do about it?"

"I don't know." He pushed his plate away. "Right now, I'd like to shave and take a bath. OK if I get in there?"

"Go ahead. I don't need to use the facilities. I got a strong bladder."

After Vint got ready, he put the same clothes on that he worked in that day, not having anything else to wear.

He splashed a little of Gramp's Old Spice aftershave on his neck and walked into the living room where Grannie sat listening to *Lum and Abner* on the radio.

She looked up from her knitting. "You think more about what I said?"

"That's all I've been thinking about. Your granddaughter is a peach of a girl and I don't want to hurt her."

"Seems like you got two choices … marry the girl or make a clean break."

"Good night, ma'am." Vint grabbed his jacket and walked out the front door.

*　*　*

The note on Adelle's door read, *Vint, come in and make yourself a drink.* He walked in and looked around. The house smelled of rose water and the lights were low except for the glow of an antique ceiling lamp hanging over the bar. He walked under the soft shaft of light and sat on one of the velvet tufted stools. Picking up a few cubes from the ice bucket, then dropping them into a crystal rock glass, he poured a few fingers of expensive bourbon over them. While listening to soft swing music coming from the bedroom at the top of the wide ornate staircase, he swirled the ice in his glass and considered the situation. The whole set-up seemed familiar to him somehow. He sat sipping his drink until he heard what he expected.

"Vint. Come up here, please. There's something I'd like to show you."

After pouring some more whiskey, Vint climbed the staircase. When he got to the top, he could see Adelle standing in the doorway of her bedroom in red, stiletto-heeled shoes and a red, see-through negligee with nothing underneath except a black garter belt and stockings.

"Follow me." She turned, walked to the bed and bent over. "Here, take a look."

Vint gazed at Adelle's backside as she stood with her feet apart and her hands on her knees.

As he walked up close behind her, she motioned with her hand. "These are the floorplans to the plant. I don't have blueprints. My husband's father built the place himself."

He took a sip of bourbon, then threw the glass into the fireplace, shattering it to bits. With one sweeping motion, Vint shoved the floorplans to the thick carpet. He dropped his pants, pulled Adelle's negligee up and took her.

* * *

"You don't talk like anyone from these parts." Adelle lay next to Vint with her head on his shoulder, running her fingernails through his thick, black chest hair. "Where are you from?"

"All over."

"Where did you spend most of your time as a kid?"

"Back east. I grew up in orphanages."

"Why's that?"

"Not sure." He shrugged. "That was a long time ago."

"Is that the way it's going to be?" She grabbed the hair on his chest. "Getting information out of you is like pulling taffy."

"OK. What in the hell is it that you want to know?" Vint raised his leg and pushed the cover down with his foot, revealing their nudity except for Adelle's garter belt and stockings. "I vaguely remember my parents. Heard my mother died when I was young. The old man ... I don't know, supposedly a hobo, rides the rails."

He rolled on top of Adelle, shoved her long shapely legs open by spreading his knees, then entered her again.

* * *

Over an hour later, Vint said between breaths, "Damn. You wore me out." He rolled onto his back with his chest heaving. "Don't climax very easily do you?"

"You're pretty good, but ... let's just say you're not my type."

He rubbed his forehead and squinted at her. "Not your *type*? Just what is it you like? That husband of yours wasn't much to look at."

"He was less my preference than you. But he understood my needs and let me have what I wanted once in a while without kicking." She looked him in the eye. "Oh, just drop it."

Vint studied her, trying to make sense of what she said. "I'm really tired. You think I could sleep in one of these beds tonight?"

"Absolutely not. My cleaning lady will be here first thing in the morning. I don't want anyone seeing you coming or going around here. Why do you think I always have you come over so late?"

"All right. Just that it's a long way and I worked all day." He got up and put on his clothes.

"Have a good walk."

"Don't suppose you could tear yourself out of bed and drive me?"

"No. I couldn't." Adelle yawned in an exaggerated manner. "Make sure the door's locked on your way out."

Vint walked over the floorplans, then down the staircase in the dim light and over to the bar. He took a slug of bourbon from the bottle, then set it down. Walking toward the front door, he hesitated, went back for the bottle and took it with him. He opened the front door to the breezy night air and sound of the river rushing past about sixty yards to the north. Turning the lock button, then pulling the front door shut, he tucked the bottle in his half-zipped jacket and started the journey back to Lark's.

Stepping into his moon shadow along the private road, Vint pulled the bottle of whiskey out and tilted it to the stars as he gulped the strong, smooth spirits. "One of them has to work, even if the other fails," he mumbled to himself as he thought about the dirty deals with Edric and Adelle. "Then you get your ass out of here. Quick. Get the money and go. This place is trouble." He looked over at a skunk alongside the road. "You hear me? Trouble. With a capital T, that rhymes with bubble, and it's going to pop soon." The skunk slunk away into the thicket.

Walking in the night to the sounds of crickets all around and coyotes in the distance, Vint kept moving along, drinking and smoking until he got to Lark's house. He took a leak on the old cottonwood in the front yard, then sat on the front porch. "Goodbye, my friend." He drank the last of the bourbon and tossed the empty bottle behind the shrubs lining the front of the house. Lying back and looking up at the stars, he folded his arms behind his head.

* * *

"Wake up." Lark shook Vint as he lay on her porch. "What are you doing out here?"

"Let me be." He rolled onto his side.

"You can't sleep out here." She looked east at the sun's first hint of daylight. "What are the neighbors gonna think?"

"Fuck the neighbors." Vint slapped a mosquito on his cheek.

"You smell like a bar rag. Come on." She tugged on his arm. "It's only about ten steps to the couch."

"All right, damn it." He sat up. "Why didn't you tell me you were in the hospital?"

"We'll talk about it after you sleep it off." She tried helping him to his feet.

"Get off me." Vint pulled his arm from her grip. "I can stand up by myself. What do you think? I can't handle my liquor?"

Lark held the front door open as he staggered in, then flopped back on the couch. She unzipped his jacket, then pulled his boots off.

"Why didn't you tell me you were in the cuckoo house?" Vint's eyes closed and he drifted back to sleep.

Chapter 11

Vint woke up on the couch close to 9:00 am with a dull headache and dry mouth. He sat up, put his stocking feet on the living room floor and slipped his jacket off.

"He has risen," Grannie said, walking past on her way to the kitchen.

Lark approached Vint in a terrycloth robe, drying her hair with a bath towel. "I was just about to get you up. We have to be at the hearing in two hours."

"It's Saturday already?" He pulled a pack of Old Gold from his jacket pocket.

"Yes, mister." She stood with one thigh showing. "Want me to make you some eggs and bacon?"

"How about after I get cleaned up?" Vint stood and walked out the front door. He leaned against a porch rail and lit a cigarette.

Lark came out a moment later, still in her baby-blue robe, brushing her shoulder-length hair. "You asked me about being in the hospital." She stopped brushing and frowned. "I suppose Grannie told you."

"She's worried about you ending up back in there, because of me."

"That's not gonna happen. I'm a stronger person now."

"Should have told me." He blew smoke from his nostrils.

"It's embarrassing. I didn't want you to think of me that way." Lark ran the brush through her hair with a hard stroke. "I could just kill Grannie."

"You didn't think I'd hear something eventually?" Vint tapped his ash into the bushes. "In a town like this?"

"Guess I wanted you to get to know me better, before you heard the gossip ... and decided I was damaged goods."

"You seem perfectly all right, most of the time. But I got to tell you, you worry me once in a while."

"I'm fine. Seriously." She touched his arm. "I'll be OK."

Vint spoke with the cigarette in the corner of his mouth and winked. "I got my eye on you."

Lark smiled. "Of the two of us, I think you're the crazy one."

"How's that?"

"Oh, I don't know." She rolled her eyes. "Robbing banks, getting into fights, walking around with a straight razor, getting involved with a floozy like Adelle ... you can't seem to stay out of trouble."

"Hmm." He took a drag, then pitched his Old Gold off his thumb. "You might have a point there."

"Where were you last night?" She brushed her bangs down.

"Adelle's."

Lark threw her hands up. "Speak of the devil."

Vint clenched his teeth and rubbed his aching forehead. "There were things we had to go over."

"Yeah. I bet."

"I got to take a leak and I'm bone dry."

"Better watch it, Romeo." She wagged a finger at him. "I might use that razor on you."

"That's what I'm talking about. I'm watching my back around you."

"Grannie says, you reap what you sow."

He pushed off the railing and opened the door. "See if there's a white dress shirt in Gramps' closet that'll fit me, maybe a tie. I'm getting in the tub."

* * *

Vint walked into the church that doubled as a courthouse with Lark at his side. They took a seat in the second pew near the other witnesses. "Well, this is it. The rest of my life is in the hands of these possum eaters," he said quietly to Lark. He felt someone's stare and looked to his left. Merk Skinner glared at him from the other end of the first pew.

Lark took Vint's hand. "Judge Chester is a fair man."

"Yeah, but I'm an outsider."

Mrs. Sinks, the librarian, who also served as volunteer bailiff, stood next to the pulpit. She fidgeted with a black, soft-covered bible, then glanced at her watch.

Judge Chester entered from the back of the church at 11:00 am sharp, adjusting his black robe over faded denim overalls. He set his fishing pole in a corner and walked up to the desk that was routinely pushed in place for legal proceedings.

Mrs. Sinks called out loud enough for gatherers in the last row of pews to hear. "All rise for the honorable Judge Henry Chester."

Everyone stood except Merk. When the judge sat down, everyone resumed their seats.

"This is not a trial," the bailiff stated. "It's an informal hearing to determine if there is enough evidence to warrant charges."

Judge Chester cleared his throat and spoke directly to Mrs. Sinks. "Let's get started. You can call the first witness."

"Shadrack Jones," her voice echoed. "Please approach the bench."

Carrying his beefy frame up front, Shadrack stepped up onto the raised level of the altar and put his left hand on the bible.

"Raise your right hand. Shadrack Jones, do you solemnly swear to tell the truth, the whole truth, and nothing but the truth, so help you God?"

"Yes, ma'am." The wooden chair next to the desk squeaked when he sat down. "I don't mess around when it comes to our Lord."

A few people in attendance laughed.

"Mr. Jones," Judge Chester instructed, "please tell us, in your own words, the sequence of events that took place at Dewey's Diner on Wednesday, September 30th, concerning the death of Lester Skinner."

"Well, your honor, that afternoon, the Skinner brothers was settin' at the counter in Dewey's drinkin' lots of beer. And that day they was gettin' a snoot full. They liked to come in and ogle Miss Lark."

A young man, with an *I Like Ike* button on his St. Louis Browns baseball cap, called out, "Hubba-hubba."

Lark's face turned red. Vint turned around and gave the guy a dirty look.

"So … after they got a belly full," Shadrack continued, "they decided they was gonna race to the men's room to see who could get there first. I saw the whole thing. They was runnin', Lester had his beer bottle in his hand, and their legs got kinda tangled up. Merk tripped and bumped his head on the counter real hard, then landed flat on his back. Lester, God bless his soul, fell on his bottle. There was nothin' Doc could do. Said it cut his juggler vein."

"You mean his jugular vein?" Judge interjected.

"Yes, sir. That's what I said." The audience giggled some more. "The one on the side of his neck."

"Shadrack." Judge Chester tapped his gavel into his hand silently. "You can cut the simple, cornpone act with me. I know you're smart as a whip … you read half the books in the library." Judge held up a sheet of paper. "Homer and Mary Harrell signed an affidavit testifying that Merk and Lester were giving Vinton Smith, over here, a hard time." The judge pointed with his gavel. "Now you tell me some cock and bull story about a foot race in the diner. You have any reason to protect Mr. Smith?"

"I don't know what you're talkin' 'bout, your honor. It happened just like I said."

"Shadrack, do you understand the penalty for lying under oath in a court of law?"

"Well, I don't rightly know ... but I'm guessin' it's bad."

"You can step down." Judge pointed his gavel at Lark.

"Lark Stookey," Mrs. Sinks called out. "Will you please come up and be sworn in."

Lark squeezed Vint's hand, then slowly stood. She went up to the witness chair like she was walking on ice. After agreeing to tell the truth, Lark took the stand.

"Miss Stookey." Judge smiled at Lark and glanced at her knees as she sat and crossed her legs in her plaid skirt. "Please tell us, to the best of your knowledge, how Lester Skinner died September 30th."

"It happened just like Shadrack said."

"What did Mr. Smith order at Dewey's?"

"Coffee and a burger." She folded her hands in her lap.

"What time did you put his order in?"

"I ... I'm not sure." Lark hesitated. "I don't keep track of those kinda things."

"To the best of your recollection, what time do you think it might have been?"

"If I had to guess, it would've been between 2:30 and 3:00."

"Did Mr. Smith finish his meal?" the judge asked, then bit at a hangnail.

"Yes." She nodded. "I believe he did."

"Did he eat his pickle?"

"Eat his pickle?" She raised her eyebrows. "I guess so."

"The Harrells both swore that the Skinners were threatening Mr. Smith. Is that true?"

"Well ... I did hear the boys say a couple things. They were always doing things like that with people they didn't like ... or strangers passing through."

"Did the Harrells leave before or after Mr. Smith finished his meal?"

"I'm not sure. I don't think I noticed what time they left."

"What I want to know, young lady, was Vinton Smith in the diner when Lester died?"

"No, he already left."

"Lyin' bitch," Merk muttered.

Lark gasped and looked to Vint.

"Quiet!" Judge glared at Merk. He returned his attention to Lark. "It's common knowledge that Mr. Smith has been staying with you at your grandmother's. Do you have reason to protect him? Enough to face jail time for perjuring yourself?"

"It's true that he's been sleeping on my grandmother's couch." People in the pews murmured and whispered. "He was out of money and Marshal Gilstrap insisted he stay here in town until this hearing. It seemed the Christian thing to do."

A middle-aged woman, clutching a cross hanging from her neck, shouted, "Shacking up with a stranger isn't Christian in my book!"

Lark buried her face in her hands.

Judge Chester pounded his gavel on the round wooden block. "I've been very patient so far, but the next person who interrupts is going to find themselves in contempt of this court, and will spend the night in jail, Christian or not!"

The rustling of people shifting in their seats filled the otherwise quiet courtroom.

"Murder and manslaughter are very serious matters. There's nothing amusing about a man dying. These proceedings are not for your entertainment." He banged his gavel once more. "Step down, Miss Stookey."

When Lark sat next to Vint again, he remarked, "What kind of kangaroo court are they running here? I've been in hearings and trials but I've never seen anything like this. Where's the prosecutor?"

"I don't know about stuff like that." She shrugged. "This is the way they usually do things around here."

"Bailiff, call the next witness." Judge Chester smoothed down the long lock of hair covering his bald spot.

"Merk Skinner, please approach the bench." Mrs. Sinks scowled at Merk as he lumbered up. "Do you promise …"

"Yeah," Merk interrupted. "I promise to speak the truth. But I ain't puttin' my hand on no damn bible and ya can't make me." He flopped into the chair next to the judge's desk. "Shoot."

"If I wanted your hand on that bible, you can bet that river shack you live in, it would be on there." The judge's face turned red. "I could lock your sorry ass up until you decided to cooperate. But I've got better things to do with my time."

"Yeah, yeah." Merk slumped down in the chair and crossed his legs with his knees wide apart.

"I want to know what happened September 30th." Judge shook his gavel at Merk. "Get to it."

Vint nudged Lark and whispered, "This'll be interesting. Merk can't admit that him and Lester were charging at me because it would obviously be self-defense on my part."

Merk sat there as if still deciding what he was going to say. "Guess it happen like they said. But the last thing I remember before I got knocked out was, this Smith character comin' at Lester with a straight razor. Probably cut 'im. Yeah, that's what happen. I remember now. The hobo said he wanted his money and slashed his neck. Then my brother went down."

"Mr. Skinner, what you're telling us doesn't make sense. Did he cut Lester after you both tripped? I thought the fall knocked you out."

"Well, it's fuzzy but I think we tripped. I went down and Lester got up. That's when Smith attacked him. Then I passed out."

Judge scowled and shook his head. "Get off that chair. Mrs. Sinks, call Doc up here."

After Doctor Harris was sworn in, Judge Chester asked him, "To the best of your knowledge, did Lester Skinner die from a razor wound anywhere on his body?"

"It didn't appear that way to me." Doc adjusted his vest down over his round belly. "I examined Mr. Skinner thoroughly. He died from a single laceration to his jugular vein. From the width and depth of the incision, it was obviously made from the broken beer bottle that was lodged in his neck. There were no other marks on his body."

The judge stared steely-eyed at Merk. "Skinner, I should lock you up for lying in this hearing. But, I'm not going to waste taxpayer money feeding your big moose ass." Judge stood and turned to Vint. "Smith, you're free to go." He pounded his gavel twice. "These proceedings are over. Time for lunch."

Vint and Lark shot to their feet. She threw her arms around him, then let them slip off. "I guess this means you're free to go now."

"I'm not going anywhere." He loosened his tie and unbuttoned his top button. "Not just yet."

Vint watched the marshal exit the building ahead of him, then he walked out with Lark by his side.

Gilstrap grabbed Vint by the arm as he passed by on the sidewalk. "I want a word with you, son."

"Give me a minute." Vint squeezed Lark's shoulder.

Vint followed Gilstrap to his police vehicle. "Looks like you're in the clear, Smith. So, the sooner you get out of town, the better."

"I've come to like it here." Vint thought about the nefarious deals lined up with Adelle and Edric. "Might just stick around a bit."

"At this point, I don't care if your name's Smith, Mercurio or Dwight D. Eisenhower. Polk Skinner's getting out of prison next week and I want you long gone before then." The lawman leaned against his car. "Since you've been in town, a man's dead under suspicious circumstances, and I heard that you threatened Grover Strunke with a straight razor."

"That pipsqueak pulled a gun on me. You ought to lock him up for carrying a concealed weapon," Vint complained. "Am I being charged with anything?"

"No. But, you bet your hide I could come up with something real quick if you decide to stick around." The marshal poked Vint's chest. "Don't be stupid. Git while you got the chance." He got in his car, scowled at Vint through the windshield for a few moments, then pulled away.

Lark approached Vint and touched his arm. "What did he want?"

"Told me to get out of town."

"Are you?"

"Not yet."

Lark tugged on his sleeve. "If you go, please take me with."

"Let's not talk about anything like that right now. Let me enjoy getting that noose from my neck, will you?"

"Sure, sure. I won't bug you." Lark's face brightened and her mood changed suddenly. "Let's do something fun to celebrate."

"Like what?"

"How about I ask Dewey if we can borrow his car?" She played with his tie. "Take a ride over to Booneville and have lunch, maybe see a movie."

"A movie? Sure. As long as it isn't one of those sappy romantic films."

"What kind of stories you like?"

"Ones about bank heists, armored car robberies. You know, stuff like that. Crime. Or a good Western."

"I bet you root for the bad guy." She smirked.

"I root for the guys who have the balls to go after what they want. The risk takers that don't live a humdrum life. The ones who do things in a big way, even if they have to step on a couple toes to get there."

* * *

"Well, what do you think?" Lark locked her arm through Vint's on the way out of the Savage Theatre.

"I liked it." He put an Old Gold in his mouth. "For a short guy, Alan Ladd pulled it off."

"He's so handsome."

"The guy's 5' 6"."

"He's dreamy. And the one who played Van Heflin's wife …"

"Jean Arthur," Vint said as people milled out of the theater past them.

"Yeah. She was in love with both men, her husband and Shane."

"Shane did the right thing. He left in the end. He could see she was falling for him."

"Because he was being noble." She sighed. "I think he loved her too. He stepped aside because she was married."

"You would look at it like that. That part didn't interest me so much. I like the way Shane stood up to the cattle baron and his guys. The Jack Palance character, I've known guys like that. Met a few in the joint."

"What was it like for you in there?"

Vint stood silent on the sidewalk for a moment. "You're on the other side of a fence. You can walk right up to the chain-link, grab hold of it, look through it. Everywhere is the same air, the same sky, same grass. Except you're on the other side. I don't know how to explain it. It's just a feeling you have."

"I think I understand."

"I don't ever want to go back. It's like lying in a coffin the whole time you're there. You're dead to the world, it moves on, you don't." He patted her hand. "Don't ask me again. Just as soon not think about it."

"What do you want to do now?"

"Let's stop for a quick drink." He pointed to the tavern across the street with a neon sign spelling out, *Tee-Pee Lounge.*

Vint took Lark's arm and guided her across Broadway Avenue. He pushed the door open to loud up-tempo pop music coming from the jukebox. They walked up to the bar through a haze of cigarette smoke.

The bartender's watery eyes lit up and he flashed a smarmy smile as he gleamed at Lark. "What'll you have, doll face?"

"I'll just have a Coca-Cola, thank you." She sat on a stool.

"I'm Woodrow Wilson." He reached across the bar to shake her hand. "Just like the president."

Lark took Woodrow's fingers in her hand briefly. "Pleased to meet you, sir."

Woodrow stood grinning at Lark, pulling on the ends of his striped bowtie. "One Coke coming right up, gorgeous."

"Going to ask me what I want, Woodrow?" Vint squinted at him.

"Sure." His smile dropped. "What'll ya have?"

"Bring me a bottle of Goldcrest." Vint took a seat next to Lark. His brow furrowed as he watched the bartender walk away to get their drinks. "I don't like this place. Let's drink up and get out of here."

"Fine with me." She shrugged and tilted her head to the side. "Whatever you want."

As they sat drinking, Vint became aware of three tall, broad-shouldered, young men dressed in matching burgundy cardigan sweaters with a large white 'A' over their hearts. They stood in front of the jukebox, singing

92

and snapping their fingers to an Eddie Fisher record. He became irritated watching them give Lark the eye. She noticed their antics and swiveled her stool so her back was to them.

"It's a long ride back. I'm going to hit the head." Vint nodded toward the rear of the bar. "Then we'll split."

On the way to the men's room, Vint shot the three beefy lettermen a deadly look. He shoved the toilet door open, then stood at the urinal, fuming about the gall of the young collegiates and the way they outwardly flirted with Lark right in front of him. He thought about being in prison and what you had to do when someone disrespected you in front of others. Trying to calm down, he reminded himself that he was no longer incarcerated. He went to the sink and splashed cold water on his face. Combing his black hair back, the fire in his eyes looking back from the mirror told him he better settle down.

Vint came out of the men's room wanting nothing more than to have a last swig of beer, then get out of the Tee-Pee. As he pushed his way through the crowd, he saw Lark surrounded by the three young men from the jukebox. As he moved closer, he saw one of the guys, with a blond crew-cut, standing with his face close to Lark's, his brown loafer resting on the rung of her stool.

When Vint was within earshot, he heard the guy say to Lark, "I've got scouts from all over the country coming to watch me play."

"Excuse me, boys." Vint tried to move in next to Lark but the men refused to give him any room.

"Hey, quit shovin'." The largest of the young men, a couple inches taller than Vint and a lot wider, turned around to face Vint and puffed up his chest.

"Let me get to my stool, bub." Vint looked the man in the eye, steely faced.

"Can't you see we're talking to the lady?" the crew-cut man said. "Go find another seat."

"The lady's with me. That's my stool and that's my beer. I suggest you boys find another girl to try and impress with your football stories."

"I am with him," she pleaded. "We don't want any trouble."

She tried to stand but the crew-cut footballer put his hand on her shoulder and held her down. "Relax, toots. Let me buy you another drink."

The three men turned their backs on Vint and crowded around Lark, not letting him near her.

"I'm not going to tell you boys again, get away from the lady. Now."

"I don't see a ring on her finger." One of the guys, with a face full of freckles, pointed at her left hand. "She's fair game."

Vint hesitated a moment, then asked, "You boys like playing football?"

"What? You still here?" the biggest one said. "Go away, ole boy."

"Do we like to *play*?" The crew-cut guy smirked. "We're the best there is. We'll all go pro after college."

"Reason I ask is, if you don't leave now I'm going to end your careers."

"OK, buddy." The biggest of the three turned to face Vint. "Shove off or you're gettin' your ass kicked." He shoved Vint to the dirty floor.

Vint jumped to his feet and grabbed a bar stool. He busted the big guy over the head with it, knocking him to the ground.

The freckly guy charged at Vint. "I'll kill you!"

Vint flipped the stool in the air, grabbed the padded seat and shoved one of the legs into the man's eye. He threw the stool to the floor as customers backed away.

The man screamed, "My eye! My eye!"

"I'm gonna fuck you up." The blond man put his fists up and came at Vint swinging.

Jabbing at the young man while circling to his right, Vint bobbed and ducked punches, but stumbled slightly when he slipped on a cigar in a puddle of beer. The crew-cut guy caught him on the jaw, jarring him. The man threw a wild right-cross but Vint weaved to the side avoiding the punch. Vint came up with a left uppercut to the man's chin, shattering his teeth together, then punched the crew-cut guy as hard as he could with his right. He felt the man's nose crush under his knuckles. The blond guy went down with a thud, his head bouncing off the floor.

"Let's go." Vint grabbed his bottle of beer from the bar and took a swig. He took Lark by the arm and threw harsh looks into the eyes of those gathering around them.

She shot to her feet and they pushed their way through the crowd. When they got to the door, Vint looked back to see the biggest guy stumble to his feet with blood running down his face.

"Stop that guy," he shouted and wiped blood from his eyes.

Vint and Lark tried leaving but two men in motorcycle jackets blocked the exit. One sneered at Vint and said, "Where d'ya think yer goin', puke."

"Let the lady through," Vint demanded.

The big guy, wiping blood from his face, and the freckly guy, covering his eye with one hand, came at Vint yelling. The crew-cut guy still lay in a heap where Vint tagged him.

The two at the door stepped aside just enough to let Lark squeeze past.

Vint tossed her the car keys. "Get out of here, now."

She caught the keys and shouted, "Vint, no. What's going to happen?"

"Get the car! Go on!"

Lark raced down the sidewalk just as the two injured men approached. "Grab him!" the big guy shouted. "We're gonna fuck you up bad!"

Vint pulled his straight razor and lashed out in front of him as he circled around. "First one that lays a hand on me is going to lose it!" He lunged with the blade and the four men backed off. "Get away from that door."

The big guy grabbed a barstool and came at Vint with it, legs first. Vint backed out the door and the man threw it at him. The glass door shattered when Vint ducked the flying chair. Lark flew up in front of the bar in Dewey's car and Vint hopped on the running board. "Go!" he yelled through the open window. As she raced away, Vint hung onto the window post with one hand and waved the razor at the men chasing him just a few feet away. Vint ducked a beer bottle and it shattered on the top edge of the car door, inches from his head. When they were a safe distance from the crowd, he snapped the razor closed, opened the front passenger door of the speeding car, and swung into the seat.

"Are you OK?" Lark's voice quavered with fear and excitement.

"Yeah." Vint rubbed his aching jaw. "That guy can hit."

"I get the feeling things like that happen to you a lot."

"Trouble has a way of finding me." He pulled out a smoke. "Guess I got the Indian sign on me."

"If I had a gun, I would've shot them." She looked in the rearview mirror.

"You serious?" He studied her wild-eyed expression.

"Before I let anyone hurt you, I would." She turned to Vint. "You'd do the same for me, wouldn't you?"

"Shoot somebody?" He lit his cigarette.

"Kill for me if I was in danger. Do whatever you had to ... to protect me."

"Sure, baby." Vint blew smoke out the side of his mouth toward the open window. "I'd take a bullet for you."

"That's the way I feel about *you*."

"Slow it down, baby." He waved his hand down and looked around. "We don't want to get a speeding ticket."

Lark looked at Vint with glazed eyes. "Let's pull over somewhere."

"Pull over? Where?"

"Anywhere. Down one of these country roads."

He pitched his Old Gold out the window. "Better not. I don't have any protection with me."

She turned right on a narrow, bumpy dirt road. "Just pull out. You know."

After driving a short distance, Lark steered onto the side of the road under a gnarled, reaching tree. She turned off the headlights and engine.

Vint looked around in the dusk at the flat land surrounding them. He saw a farmhouse in the distance with no lights in the windows.

Lark took off her panties, then undid Vint's jeans. She took him in her hand and stroked him. Straddling Vint, she eased down onto him, then bucked against him wildly.

"Slow down, honey." He grabbed her ponytail. "Wait."

She moved her hips back and forth faster and climaxed the same time as Vint. Her body went limp and she breathed heavily with her cheek next to his.

"You didn't give me a chance to pull out."

"Don't worry." She pulled her head back so she was face to face with him. "What are the chances?"

"I don't know, doll. I wouldn't want to make book on it."

Lark kissed Vint. "We better get Dewey's car back before he closes up." She got off him and put her panties back on.

He zipped up his jeans. "You're one crazy kid."

In an instant Lark's mood changed. "Don't ever say that to me!" she screamed. "Ever!"

Chapter 12

"What is it, Vint?" Lark poured him a cup of coffee as he sat by himself at a table in the rear corner of the diner. "It's a beautiful day today. Why are you sitting there scowling?"

"Don't bug me." Vint's body was tense as he faced the wall. "I'm in no mood."

"Is it something I did?"

"No," he answered without looking at her.

"If you tell me what's bothering you, maybe I can help."

"What did I tell you?" He spoke harshly, "Get off my back."

Lark set the coffeepot on the table, stood behind Vint and tried massaging his shoulders, but he stiffened up. "I've seen you in black moods before but you look like you could kill somebody."

"At least you knew what it was like to have parents, people who loved you. Even though they died on you, consider yourself lucky for having them as long as you did. It's a better deal than some people get."

Her face turned sad. "I miss mom and dad every day."

"You don't know what it was like, growing up in an orphanage. There were some sadistic sons-a-bitches there. There were these three kids, a few years older than me. Made my life a living hell."

"I'm sorry."

"What the fuck are you sorry about? You didn't do anything."

"I just ..." She looked around the nearly empty diner and sat at the small square table next to him.

"They used to torture me and taunt me. They used to keep it up, and keep it up until I lost my temper. Then I'd tear into them with everything I had. I didn't want to beat them up, I wanted to kill them."

"Oh, Vint." She rubbed his tense arm.

"One night, after the lights were out, these goons thought they'd have their way with me. You know?" He looked at her and nodded. "Have their *way* with me? I was only about eleven years old."

She tried to caress his cheek but he pulled his face away.

"I fought those bastards, and I fought them. They were finally too tired to do anything and let me alone. The next day when I showed up at breakfast with two blackeyes, a busted lip and scrapes all over, I got in trouble for fighting. A week with no supper."

Vint slammed his fist on the table, causing the cup full of coffee to jump and spill some of the hot, dark liquid on the table. "I'd like to know where those three are now. No wonder no one ever adopted them. Ugly mother fuckers."

"I'm surprised no one adopted you." She ran her fingertips along the side of his slicked back hair. "I bet you were a little cutie."

"Lady that ran the place, said, 'No one's ever gonna take a brat like you home. Not with that attitude. You'll be here until you're eighteen.' Lousy bitch."

"That's not a good thing to tell a kid. It's not right."

"Always telling me that if I smiled more and followed the rules ... she didn't know what it was like being an unwanted kid. That piece of shit was always making an example of me. Singling me out. Made me her 'whipping boy.' Encouraging the other kids to laugh at me in class."

"I don't get it." She gently placed her hand on his. "Why would she do that?"

"Trying to break my spirit." Vint turned his palms up. "Sick bitch. She had no business being in charge of kids."

"I never heard you talk like this before. You go around with this stuff bottled up in you?"

"I don't blame my mother. She couldn't help it. She died." His eyes remained on the wall in front of him. "But that no good prick that brought me into the world … I don't know how a father could abandon his son. Leave him alone to grow up in a hell hole like that. It was like being raised in a looney bin."

"Maybe he thought you'd be better off. Maybe he wasn't equipped to raise a kid."

"Don't make excuses for him. You don't even know him."

"I just mean …"

He put his hand up between them. "This one little brat at the home told me my dad was a jailbird. She said everyone knew about it except me."

"Vint, I don't know what to say."

"I guess when he wasn't in jail, he was riding the rails. That's what I heard. I used to dream he'd show up at my window one night and say, 'Come on, boy. You're coming with me.' And we'd ride in boxcars and eat beans out of a can over a fire."

A tear dropped from Lark's eye onto the table. "You know, I was in a good mood. Now you got me feeling sad too."

Vint swept his hand across the table knocking his cup against the wall, smashing it to bits and splattering coffee. He stood and said, "I'm going for a walk."

Storming out the front entrance, he ignored Dewey calling after him, "You're gonna pay for that cup."

He walked down the sidewalk several doors, then stopped. The late nineteenth-century building tugged at something deep inside him. Every time he went near the one-story structure, his heart beat faster. This time, he couldn't resist its allure. Stepping into the bank, Vint's mouth went dry. He looked around, wall to wall, floor to ceiling. His anger turned to excitement as he cased the savings and loan. With a gleam in his eyes, he imagined how he would rob the place. He studied the one teller, a middle-aged lady with thinning hair, dyed bright orange. As the late afternoon sunlight cast its rays onto her, he could see the shape of her scalp. She reminded him of the thin-haired bitch from the orphanage. He imagined going up to her, telling her that he had a gun and what he would do with it if she didn't follow orders.

A hard slap on the back of his neck broke the trance. "You interested in banks, Mercurio ... I mean, Smith?" The six-foot-three Marshal Gilstrap held onto the back of Vint's neck.

"Just the architecture." Vint stepped forward, breaking the marshal's tight grip, then turned to face him.

Gilstrap put a hand on his holster. "You gonna be opening up an account here today?"

"No, not today. Wanted to see how secure it looked first."

"Bet you did, old boy. Bet you did." Gilstrap looked around. "This bank has never been robbed, not once. I'm very proud of that. Guess you could say that the safety record of this bank is my pride and joy. Got me?"

Vint stuffed his hands into his jacket pockets. "Understand perfectly."

"Well, unless you got some business here, I suggest you leave, you smooth talking son-of-a-bitch."

* * *

A few hours later, with nothing better to do, Vint was back at the same table in Dewey's with his feet propped on a chair, reading his worn paperback. He glanced up to see Deputy Anfield walking in his direction, then went back to his spot on the page. His boots slammed to the floor when Anfield kicked the chair from under his feet.

"Git up," the deputy ordered. "I'm takin' you in."

"What for?" Vint grimaced at Anfield.

Anfield pulled his pistol from its holster. "Try askin' another question. I'll bust your teeth out." He raised his revolver inches from Vint's face. "On your feet."

Vint stood and put his paperback in the pocket of his dungarees.

"Turn around with your hands behind you."

"Am I being charged with something?" Vint asked as he turned around and complied.

"What'd I say about questions, boy?" Anfield yelled in Vint's ear and handcuffed him.

"Son-of-a-bitch." Vint winced. "They're too tight."

"Tell it to someone who gives a hoot." The deputy grabbed the chain between the cuffs and yanked Vint's arms up behind him.

"You lousy bastard." Bent forward, Vint stumbled toward the front door of Dewey's while Anfield chuckled, walking behind him with the chain between the cuffs held high.

"Anfield!" Lark yelled from behind the counter. "If you hurt him, I'll kill you!"

The deputy stopped and glanced around at the handful of customers. "You just threatened an officer of the law in front of witnesses."

She grabbed a steak knife off the counter and shook it at Anfield. "I swear to God."

Dewey ran behind the counter and up to her. "Lark, calm down." A look of shock came over his pasty face. "Please, drop it."

Glaring at Anfield, Lark flung the knife to the floor.

The deputy marched Vint to the screen door and pushed it open with Vint's head. When they got to the patrol car, Anfield opened the back door, put his boot to Vint's ass and shoved him in.

Vint flew onto the backseat on his stomach, knocking the wind from him. He got himself to a seated position and slowly caught his breath. When they got to the west end of the row of old wood-framed buildings, they stopped.

Hopping out and opening the back door of the patrol car, Anfield ordered, "Git out before I drag you by your slicked-up hair."

With the deputy right behind him, Vint walked up the steps and into the open door of the marshal's office.

"Over here." Gilstrap motioned toward the chair across from his desk. "Take a seat."

"Tell this Nazi to loosen up these cuffs. They're cutting off my circulation."

"Anfield." Gilstrap nodded toward Vint. "Get those cuffs off him." He looked at the deputy disapprovingly, shaking his head. "Sometimes I think you enjoy this job too much."

"All right, ya damn baby," Anfield said to Vint, uncuffing him.

"What're you running me in for this time?" Vint rubbed his wrists.

"Got the paperwork back on you, Mercurio." Holding a sheet of paper in front of him, Gilstrap raised his eyebrows, wrinkling his brow. "Might as well fess up, boy."

"I don't know what you're talking about, Marshal."

"Admit it!" Gilstrap stood, shaking the piece of paper that Vint could only see the backside of. "You're Vinton Mercurio, bank robber! Wanted for parole violation!"

Vint shrugged and looked away. "Name's Smith."

Gilstrap slapped the information onto his desk and plopped into his chair. "Damn mimeograph bullshit." He looked at his deputy. "Anfield, this might as well be your picture and prints."

Anfield walked up behind Gilstrap and looked over his shoulder. "Kinda looks like my Uncle Clem."

"You think this is funny?" The marshal elbowed Anfield in the belly.

"Oww, that smarts," Anfield protested, doubling over.

Vint remained silent and smiled.

"Look at those prints." Gilstrap shook his head. "Just smudges."

"Yeah, boss, smudges." The deputy said, straightening up.

Vint leaned forward and inspected the poor-quality copy. "Well, can I go now?"

"Since you won't leave town on your own, looks like I'll have to find some charges on you and ship you out."

"What kind of charges?"

Gilstrap ignored the question and looked at Anfield. "Put him in cell one, his favorite."

Anfield grabbed the back of Vint's collar and pulled him to his feet.

"I asked you, why are you locking me up?" Vint raised his voice at the marshal as Anfield yanked at him.

"Because I don't like your smug attitude," Gilstrap growled. "Because I don't like you keeping company with Lark." The marshal jumped to his feet and slammed his fist on his desk. "Because I don't like you in my town, you show-boating prick."

"That's no cause to jail someone."

"I already told you but you didn't listen. I want you gone before Polk Skinner gets back in town and more people die." Gilstrap motioned with a large veiny hand. "Empty your pockets, boy."

Vint placed his contents onto the desk.

"OK, Anfield. Lock him up."

"What about my cigarettes?"

"We don't want you accidently starting any fires." Gilstrap picked up the pack of Old Gold and smiled. "I'll hold onto them for you, for your own safety."

Vint reached toward the desk. "Let me have my book."

"New rule. No reading material in the cells. We're just going to let you stew awhile." The marshal picked up the paperback. "Maybe I'll read this. See what's so interesting."

"Thanks for nothing."

Anfield shoved Vint toward the cells. "Git!"

Vint turned back to the marshal. "How long you keeping me here?"

"I don't know. Maybe a few days. Maybe a few years."

"Think you're God around here?" Vint said to Gilstrap as Anfield shoved him along.

"I'm God in this here marshal's office."

* * *

Close to an hour later, with Anfield out on patrol, Adelle walked into the marshal's office with a look of determination in her eyes.

"Adelle." Gilstrap put his marshal's hat on over his thinning hair and jumped to his feet. "So good to see you again."

"I understand you have a Vinton Smith locked up here?"

"Yes. The man's a danger to the community."

"I need all the good hands I can get right now. And unless Smith is being charged with something serious, I'd like him released to my custody."

"Adelle." The marshal jerked a thumb toward the cells down the hall. "That buzzard's a blight on our town. He's suspected of being a dangerous criminal, a damn bank robber on the lam."

"Has he robbed our bank?"

"No ... of course not but ..."

"Then I'd like him released right away. I need him back on the job tomorrow." Adelle crossed her arms under her full bosom.

"Well, if you say you're responsible for him, I guess ..."

"Now, please."

"Sure." Gilstrap took the keys from his top drawer. "I'll let him out right away." He walked back to cell one and found Vint sitting on the edge of his bed.

"I heard." Vint stood up and stared at Gilstrap. "Who did you say was God here?"

"Don't say another word." The marshal unlocked the door of bars and swung it open. "Not a fuckin' word."

Vint smirked at him, then strutted around the corner and up to Adelle. He nodded to her. "Thanks."

Gilstrap walked behind his desk. "You're lucky this time. Lucky this fine woman helped you out, but don't count on that in the future. Once I get proof who you really are, no one can help you." He tipped his hat to Adelle. "Ma'am."

Vint stood staring at Gilstrap.

Leaning forward on his knuckles, the marshal stared back at him. "Well, go on. Git outa here."

"My things?"

Gilstrap sighed, sat down and opened a drawer. He tossed Vint's book and other belongings onto his desk. All except the razor which he held up. "Think I'll hold onto this."

Adelle spoke up, "Oh for God's sake, don't be petty, Amos. Give the man his razor. How do you expect him to shave?"

The lawman tossed the razor onto the desk with the other items. Vint smiled smugly at him and scooped up his things.

Following Adelle out front to her white Cadillac, Vint said, "You really *do* have some pull around here."

She opened the passenger door and said, "Get in."

He slid in on the smooth red leather. "Always liked Caddys. Had me a brand new black '48 convertible."

"Where is it now?" She started her car and backed into the street.

"Who knows? I sold it to come up with bond money and a lawyer. Lot of good that did me." He let out a deep breath and put a cigarette in his mouth.

"Don't you dare light that in my car."

He put the smoke behind his ear. "Got something on the marshal?"

"Yes." She put it in drive and headed west on Main. "But that's not my only power over him. He knows damn well if I close the doors on that lumber mill, this town will dry up and blow away. And he'll be out of his cushy job."

"How did you know I was locked up?"

"Got a call from someone over at the diner." Adelle looked straight ahead as she spoke.

"It wasn't Dewey?"

"No. A girl."

"That's what I thought." Vint eased back into the soft leather and crossed his leg. "Ever been in the diner?"

"I was there one time with my husband when he first brought me here. I told him to never drag me into that menagerie of local kooks again."

Vint nodded and smiled. "Ever eat at Sally's?"

Adelle turned her head and looked at him sullenly. "Please."

"It's not that bad. Like home cooking."

"Yes. If you like cabbage rolls and dumplings. I'd rather starve."

"So, you eat most of your meals at home?"

"I have an excellent cook. And when I get tired of eating at home, I drive over to one of the bigger towns and dine in an actual restaurant."

"Where we heading?"

"My place." She turned right on Hurst Boulevard. "Speaking of food, you're probably famished."

"Starving. I decided to skip the shit-on-a-shingle they brought me back there." He rubbed his stubble. "Hmm. It was after business hours when I got hauled in. You never stay at the plant after 5:00. How did Lark get ahold of you? I know your home number's not listed."

Adelle pulled in the circular driveway to her home and stopped near the front door. "Do you want to play detective or do you want to come in for something to eat?"

"I was just curious."

"Don't ask me questions about my personal life." She turned the engine off and removed the key from the ignition. "I'll offer you the same courtesy."

* * *

Lying nude in bed after a rigorous go with Vint, Adelle propped herself on one elbow and pulled the sheet up to her waist. With her chest heaving, she said, "It's about time you fill me in on your plan."

"What plan is that?" He rolled onto his back and folded his hands behind his head.

"What *plan*? Are you serious?" She waved a hand about. "You know what plan ... burning my lumber plant down."

"I just wanted to hear you say it ... out loud."

"Well?"

"If I told you my plan you could pull it off without me. No offence, but I'll keep the details to myself." Vint looked at Adelle sideways. "What I want to know is, how much are you going to pay me?"

"I figured $1,000 should be enough."

"Oh, you did, did you? Forget about it. If that's all you can afford, find someone else."

"I suppose I could manage $2,000 but that's as high as I can go."

"I may as well leave now." He propped himself up on his elbows. "We're not even in the same ballpark."

"Look. If I scrounge together everything I have, I can make it $2,500. That's it. *Finito.*"

"How much are you going to make if I pull this off?"

"Well ... I'm not sure."

"Don't give me that malarkey." He wagged a finger at her. "I bet you know exactly what the insurance company will pay out, right to the penny. Double your last offer and we got a deal."

"*5,000*? Are you crazy? I could get just about anyone to do it for a fraction of that."

"Well go ahead then. Get caught, lose your business, your home, and spend a few years in prison. It's up to you."

"Your plan is that good?"

"It's that good."

"I don't know." Adelle fidgeted with the sheet. "Where do you expect me to lay my hands on that kind of money?"

"Sell something. I don't care how you come up with it. That's my price. Take it or leave it."

"All right, all right." She sighed mournfully. "$5,000."

"Good. Now that we got that settled, when are we going to do this thing? The sooner the better."

"It'll be at least two more weeks."

"What?" Vint shot up to a sitting position. "That's no good. Things are getting too hot for me in this town. I got to move on."

"I need time. It's business."

"*We* have business, toots."

"We'll do it right after I get my yearly big shipment out of the way."

"I can't believe this." He flopped on his back.

"This is important. The commerce we do all year round is worth my while, enough to keep us going. But once a year we do one large delivery. We've been gearing up for it for months. It's big money. I can't turn it down."

"You saw what Gilstrap's up to. He's leaning heavy on me to get out of town. If he levels charges against me for one thing or another we're both screwed."

"You really who he thinks you are?"

Vint reached for his pack of Old Gold on the end table. He lit one and let the smoke out slowly. "My name's not Smith. That I can tell you."

"What is it?"

"What did you say about not asking personal questions?"

"All right all ready," she huffed. "I'll keep him off your back. I'll tell him you'll leave town once we get the big load out."

"You better know what you're talking about. My freedom's on the line here."

"I can handle Amos."

"He's not my only concern."

"Why don't you try laying low?" Adelle shook her head. "Stay out of trouble for God's sake."

* * *

Vint walked into Lark's house and found her lying on the couch with a candle glowing on an end table. She opened her robe revealing nothing underneath, her fair skin shimmering from the flame. "Welcome home, Vint."

"You got over your shyness quick." He began undressing.

"There's a lot about me you don't know." She twirled a blonde lock of hair around her finger.

Dropping his clothes on the large area rug that covered the hardwood floor, he replied, "Let me take a quick bath."

"Aren't you going to kiss me hello first." Lark put one leg on top of the back cushion.

"Give me a few minutes, OK?"

Vint quickly filled the tub and washed off the scent of Adelle's perfume. Toweling off, he walked out of the bathroom, reached into the pocket of his jeans on the floor and pulled out a condom. Kissing Lark's thighs and working his way up, he became hard again. He unwrapped the condom, rolled it on and entered her. She moaned with pleasure, getting louder as he thrust into her.

"Shhh. We don't want to wake Grannie." He put a finger across her lips.

Breathing heavily, Lark took his finger in her teeth and moaned louder. After a few minutes, her body stiffened. She bucked against him hard and let out a cry.

Vint felt a blow to the back of his head. "Oww." He felt it again, then turned to see Grannie whacking him with her cane. He jumped off Lark, still erect, and shielded himself from her blows.

"You ... you, devil! I let you in my house and you fornicate on my granddaughter!" She kept swinging. "Get out of here, right now! And don't ever come back!"

Scooping up his clothes as quickly as he could, Vint ran out the door naked, except for the condom, with Grannie pursuing him.

"If I see your face around here again, I'm calling the marshal!" She slammed the door and locked it.

Vint peeled the condom off his shrinking member and tossed it behind the bushes lining the front of the house. He pulled his boxers on, sat on the porch, then put the rest of his clothes on. With nowhere to go, he walked and thought, finally deciding he would try to sneak into Hurst Lumber for the night.

When he got to the plant, he searched for a way in. Every door and window was locked except the second-story loft doors. They were hanging open but out of reach by several feet. Vint looked around and found a long rope lying in a pile like a snake. He scaled the tall elm tree near the loft doors and tied the rope to a high branch. After a few attempts, he was able to swing in through the open doors. He landed on his feet, then fell over and rolled in.

Vint sat back against a pile of four-by-fours not far from the open doors, smoking and reading by the quarter-moon. When he got sleepy, he laid his head on his arm, curled up with his jacket over his upper body and slept.

Chapter 13

"What in Sam Hill you think you're doin'? Get up, ya bum!" Gerald stood over Vint and kicked the bottom of his foot. "This time you're outa here, for good."

Vint sat up, pulled his boots on and jumped to his feet. He grabbed Gerald by his collar with both hands and shoved him back by the open second-story doors. "You ever kick me again, I'll kill you." He dangled Gerald over the edge of the doorway, where the foreman's arms flailed about as he stood leaning backward.

"Don't drop me! Please!"

Vint threw him to the floor. Gerald scrambled to his feet and ran down the stairs. "You're fired! You're fired!"

Picking up his cigarette butts, then tossing them out the doorway, Vint knew he better go to Adelle's office and wait for her. As he ambled down the stairs, the 8:00 am whistle blew.

Gerald stood by a group of workers. "He tried to kill me." He shook a finger at Vint. "You'll never work here again."

Vint walked into the office combing his hair back. "She in yet?"

Margaret leaned back in her chair and licked her lips. "She's never here before 9:00."

"I'll wait in her office."

Margaret stood. "She doesn't like anyone but me in there."

"So, fire me." He walked in, sat behind her desk and checked the drawers but they were all locked. He sat back and read his book until he reached the half-way spot in the lurid tale.

* * *

"Smith's in there." Vint heard Margaret informing Adelle.

Adelle walked in and slammed the door behind her. "Get out of my chair."

Vint stood, then took the seat across from her. He leaned back and crossed his boots on the edge of the spacious, mahogany desk.

"Are you *trying* to blow this?" She raised both hands. "Do you understand what's at stake with the insurance claim? It's not just this old building. It's the loss of business. The cost to rebuild. It's everything." She waved her arms about.

Vint yawned. "Except you're not going to rebuild. You're taking the money and never coming back."

"Gerald told me he found you sleeping up in the main loft. He's the only one with a key besides me. Said you broke in."

"I wouldn't call it breaking in. The upstairs doors were hanging open like an invitation. I sort of swung in."

"Swung in? Who do you think you are, Tarzan?" She looked at him scornfully. "He said you were smoking up there too. You realize how dangerous that is? I told you, it's too soon to pull this thing off. I need more time to get things in order. If you fell asleep with a lit cigarette …"

"But I didn't, did I? Don't talk down to me, lady. I'm not stupid. Don't confuse being down on one's luck with intelligence."

"Yeah, real smart. You're not exactly setting the world on fire so far, Einstein."

Vint squinted at her. "I've been up there before and I'll be up there again. With or without your insurance scam."

"Gerald is screaming for me to fire you. What do you expect me to do? I can't lose him. He's too valuable around here. He works his ass off and he's loyal like a puppy dog."

"Do what you got to do. I'm not going to be working here much longer anyway. This place'll be a pile of ashes soon."

"With you fired, it'll make things that much harder for me to keep Gilstrap off your back." Adelle removed a set of keys from her purse and unlocked her top desk drawer. She took out an envelope and removed four twenty dollar bills. "Here, get lost for a while." She held the money out. "That comes out of your $5,000."

He stood and took the eighty dollars.

"Maybe I can settle Gerald down and you can come back next week."

"I can't wait." Vint stuffed the cash in his pocket.

"Why don't you come by tomorrow night around 7:15? I have something I'd like you to do for me."

* * *

Walking back to town, Vint remembered seeing an old sedan for sale at the service station where he bought his condoms. He put his thumb out and walked backward alongside the road.

Several minutes later, a Model AA flatbed truck slowed down and the old guy behind the wheel called out from the open passenger-side window. "Where ya headin'?"

Vint nodded east. "Other side of town … service station."

"Hop on back with the chickens. Ya kin jump out wherever ya want."

Vint grabbed hold of the wooden gate on the back of the flatbed and hoisted himself over. He sat down between cages of squawking hens and flying feathers. After sneezing several times, he tied his handkerchief over the bottom half of his face, resembling a bandit.

When the pickup stopped at the intersection by the filling station, Vint climbed out and slapped the side of the truck. After taking the hanky off his face and brushing off chicken down, he went into the station. He negotiated a deal and drove to Dewey's with a full tank of gas in his 1936 Nash Ambassador sedan.

Parking out front, Vint walked in the front door and saw Lark behind the counter. She followed along as he walked to the far end of the counter out of earshot of the few customers there. He asked her, "What're you doing here so early?"

"I had to get out of the house." She rolled her eyes. "Couldn't take any more of Grannie's preaching, so I came here. Figured I might as well pick up a little extra cash."

"Speaking of cash." Vint pulled out his billfold and gave Lark a five-dollar bill. "For groceries. Tell Grannie I said thanks."

"I appreciate it. But I'm not going to tell Grannie I saw you. She'll start up all over again. Screaming at me that I'm a sinner and I'm going to Hell if I don't change my ways."

"Sorry I got you in trouble."

"I think we both know it was more my fault than yours." She sighed. "I got carried away."

"We'll call it even." He brushed his palms together. "How about a few scrambled eggs, some bacon and rye toast?"

Lark put in his order and came back with a pot of coffee. "It's fresh." She poured him a cup. "Why aren't you at work?"

"I'm on paid vacation."

"What? You only worked there about a week."

"Boss has a soft spot for me." He turned his hand over and splayed his fingers.

"Yeah, I bet she does. That horny old Margie too, no doubt."

He shrugged slightly. "Women always came easy to me."

"Hmm." She shot him a harsh look, then shook her head and smiled. "Where are you going to stay?"

He motioned toward the front window with his coffee cup in hand. "See that sedan out front?"

Lark stood on her toes and looked out the front window. "That old green one?"

"Hotel Mercurio. At least for now."

"Does it have a big back seat?" She had a twinkle in her eyes.

"The seats fold down into a bed." He shook his head, smirking. "I created a monster."

Lark giggled. "Well, what did you expect?" She leaned on her elbows, gazing at him.

Vint finished his breakfast, then read for a while. He looked at the clock on the wall and stubbed out his cigarette. "What time does the tavern open?"

She glanced at her Timex. "About now."

He left his car in front of Dewey's and walked down a few doors to the bar. He was the first customer in the door.

"What'll it be this fine morning?" The bartender spread his big hands out wide on the bar in front of Vint. "Name's Lee."

"Well, Lee." Vint set a dollar bill on the bar. "It's a little early for whiskey, so how about a cold bottle of beer?"

Lee set a cardboard coaster in front of Vint, then placed a frosty bottle on it. "Never saw you in here before. New in town?"

Vint took out his book. "Just passing through." He opened his paperback to the dog-eared page. "I'm going to read a while, Lee."

"A reader, huh? Don't get many of those in here. Matter of fact, you're the first. We get a couple guys in here that read the paper but I don't recall anyone ever come into this place to read a damn book."

Vint looked up at Lee for a second then went back to his paperback.

"That's how it's gonna be?" Lee walked away muttering, "Only customer and he wants to read."

As the clock slowly spun around, Vint read a few chapters, every once in a while, raising his bottle and waving it at Lee. Barely noticing customers coming in and taking stools at the bar, he read on. His concentration was finally interrupted when he heard someone raise their voice.

"Ya mama's boy." A tall man with bony knuckles and protruding ears tapped the back of the head of a short, skinny guy sitting at the bar drinking root beer. "A mama's boy in school, a mama's boy now."

"Elroy, will you please just let me watch Arthur Godfrey?" the smaller man huffed. "Julius La Rosa's gonna sing next."

"Mama, mama," Elroy mocked the smaller man. "Hey, Dickie. Stand up. Let's see if ya got any taller since the fifth grade." Elroy kept tapping Dickie on the back of his red crewcut. "Come on, boy. Git up."

Vint looked at Lee, who seemed to be enjoying the ribbing Dickie was taking.

"I'll buy you another beer if you just leave me alone," Dickie said in a whiny, nasally voice.

"You sayin' I'm poor." Elroy slapped the back of Dickie's head a little harder. "I need yer charity? Huh?"

"No, no. I'm not saying that."

"Yer mama still give you an allowance? Huh, mama's boy?"

"I'm going." Dickie stood and slid his change from the bar into his open hand.

Elroy slapped the bottom of Dickie's hand, sending his change flying every which way.

Lee and Elroy both laughed.

"Sit down!" Elroy shoved Dickie back down onto his stool.

"Please ... just let me go."

"Ya gonna cry now, mama's boy? Huh, ya gonna cry? Boo hoo."

"Know what your problem is, stretch?" Vint called out without looking up from his book. "You have no imagination."

Elroy looked at Lee, then at Vint. "You talkin' to me, slick?"

Vint looked up from the page he was reading and over at Elroy. "Can't you think of something else to insult that little guy with besides mama's boy?"

"Hey, go back to readin' yer book ... mister ... book readin' guy."

"Well now, that was clever." Vint shook his head and went back to his paperback.

Elroy stood up. "How'd ya like it if I came down there, ripped yer head off and shit down yer neck?"

"See, now that's better." Vint turned the page. "More original."

"I think ya better shut yer mouth."

"I think it's a little too late for that." Vint put his book in his back pocket. "Red, get your scrawny ass out of here."

Dickie stood up and Elroy shoved him back onto his stool. "You ain't goin' nowhere until I say so."

"Why don't you get off his back?" Vint stared Elroy down.

Elroy pointed a long knobby finger at Vint. "This is none of yer business."

"No." Vint slowly got to his feet. "It's not."

Lee butted in, "Hey, you better sit your ass back down or get the hell outa here right now."

"I can't do that." Vint downed the last of his beer. "One thing I can't take. That's a big guy picking on a smaller guy. My experience, guys who do are cowards." Vint slammed his empty beer bottle on the bar. "Let him go!"

"Make me." Elroy grabbed Dickie's arm.

Vint picked up his bottle and flung it at Elroy, bouncing it off his forehead. Elroy yelled out and let go of Dickie. Vint rushed the big guy and tackled him, sending him onto his back. He pounded Elroy's face until he felt a hard blow across his upper shoulders. Everything went black for a moment and he rolled off Elroy. Grabbing the back of his neck in pain, he saw Lee stretched over the bar with a baseball bat in his hand.

Elroy got to his feet and kicked Vint several times. Still stunned by the blow, Vint scooted away from him on his back and under a table. Vint kicked back at his lanky attacker, then shoved a chair into the man's upper shin.

"Owww," Elroy screamed, as Dickie ran out the door.

Jumping to his feet, out of Lee's reach, Vint put his boot between Elroy's legs as hard as he could, sending him to his knees. He punched Elroy flush on the nose, knocking him back against the bar.

With Elroy incapacitated, Vint grabbed a chair and flung it at Lee. The bartender ducked behind the bar and the chair broke a few bottles of booze.

"Come out here!" Vint pulled his straight razor. "I'll cut your fucking head off!"

"Here, take it!" Lee's hand reached up from behind the bar holding an expensive bottle of bourbon. "Take it and go!"

Vint left his change on the bar, grabbed the bottle and walked out. He looked up and down the street, then hurried to his car and drove to the outskirts of town. Finding a spot off the road behind a grove of black walnut trees, he pulled over and parked. He looked at his skinned knuckles and rubbed the back of his neck. Examining the fancy label, he uncorked the whiskey and took a sip.

Chapter 14

As the sky drew dark, Vint parked his sedan off the road about a quarter-mile from Adelle's, knowing she wouldn't want his car to be seen near her house. He walked the rest of the way and knocked. When there wasn't an answer, he tried the door. It was unlocked so he walked in cautiously.

"Adelle!" he called out and looked around. A moment later, she descended the stairway, wrapped in a robe that was damp from her freshly showered body. He could tell by the way it clung to her that she wasn't wearing anything underneath. Her large breasts moved side to side as she sashayed down the stairs, her hard nipples poking against the thin silk.

"I want you to move some furniture." She stopped on the bottom stair and casually waved her arm around the spacious living quarters. "I'm tired of it this way."

"You're kidding? You got me over here to move furniture?" He glanced at her spike-heeled slippers. "Don't suppose you'll be helping."

"Don't be droll." She walked closer, turned her back and looked around the room, giving Vint a good look at her tight, round bottom. "It bores me."

After he shoved furniture around, back and forth, for a half-hour, Adelle announced, "Oh, just put it back the way it was."

"You like watching me sweat?"

"When you're through you can take a shower."

* * *

120

Having sex with Adelle reminded Vint of some of the pros he had been with, experienced in performance and little emotion.

He climaxed, then rolled off her. "You had enough or should I keep going?"

"That was for you, not me. Do what you want. I already know you're not much for small talk."

While Vint was getting dressed, Adelle asked, "How did you scrape your knuckles and get that bruise on your back?"

"Got in a fight over at the bar yesterday."

"That's your idea of laying low? What the hell did I tell you?"

"You don't *tell* me. You *ask* me." Vint pulled his t-shirt on. "I couldn't help it. Just one of those things." He squinted at her sideways. "See you around then. Thanks for the horizontal dance."

"Wait." Adelle stood and wrapped a sheet around her, tucking it in half-way down her breasts. She handed him his jacket. "Take everything you need out of your pockets."

"Why?"

"I can't stand looking at that rag." She walked across the upstairs landing, into the other bedroom, then returned. She threw a brown leather bomber at him. "This was my husband's flight jacket when he was in the Air Corps."

Vint slipped it on. "WWII." He walked in front of a full-length mirror. "Fits good."

"He was broad across the shoulders like you. Hold on." She went into her late husband's bedroom again and returned a few minutes later. She handed him a short stack of shirts, t-shirts, boxers and socks, along with a small suitcase. "What are you, about a thirty waist?"

"Yeah." He put a thumb in the waist of his jeans.

"My husband was a thirty-eight in later years. You'd never be able to wear any of his pants." She waved her

121

hand, dismissing him. "You can go now. Let yourself out and make sure the door's locked."

* * *

Vint walked into the nearly empty diner and took his usual seat near the far end of the row of stools.

Lark followed him along behind the counter. "Where'd you get the new clothes? That shirt and jacket look familiar."

"Adelle."

"Her again?" She put her hands on her hips. "What's going on with you two?"

"Nothing." His brow furrowed. "I moved some furniture for her and she gave me some of Mr. Hurst's things."

"Is that all?" Lark looked around, then leaned in closer. "Or is there something else I should know about?"

"We've been discussing a business opportunity. I really don't want to say more than that right now." Vint put his left hand over his right to hide his knuckles. "It's a very sensitive matter."

"What kind of business?" Her face tightened into a scowl. "Monkey business?"

"Get off my back, kid." He stood up. "Or I'll eat at Sally's from now on."

"No. Don't go." She reached over and grabbed his wrist. "I'm sorry. Guess I'm kinda jealous."

"Don't get yourself worked up." He sat back down and she released her grip.

"Adelle's tall, beautiful." She rolled her eyes. "The way she walks and talks. She's so refined. And that body. Wow." Lark motioned an hourglass with her hands. "Don't tell me you haven't noticed."

Vint shrugged slightly.

"I'm not stupid." She pouted. "You're already screwing her, aren't you?"

"Look, you and I aren't married. What I do in my private time is my business."

"How do you think that makes me feel?" Her lower lip quivered.

"There's a lot more to this than you think. I can't get into it all. It's a confidential matter. Not everything's about sex."

Lark's eyes got watery.

"Look, baby. I don't want to hurt you. If this is getting to be more than you can handle, maybe we should stop seeing each other altogether."

"Are you in love with her?"

"What?" Vint's eyebrows shot up. "Of course not."

"Then I still have a chance."

"What is it with you? You could have any man in town. These local yokels don't come in here just for the coffee, you know. They come in to talk to you, to look at you, just to be near you."

"I don't want anyone else. I love you." She grabbed his hand and held on tight. "You know that."

"You make me feel dirty inside. Like I stole some kid's candy or something." Vint pulled his hand away from her firm grip. "I'll talk to you later."

He stood up and walked out the door. Sally's restaurant was just five doors away, so he went in and sat at a table. He ordered a steak and baked potato, washing it down with a beer.

As soon as Vint finished, he glanced up to see fortyish-looking Sally walk up to him.

"It's closing time." She put a hand on her slightly plump hip and winked at him. "I was wonderin' when you were gonna come in and pay us a visit. Heard ya been eatin' at the diner a lot. Sweet on that little blonde number?"

Vint stood and nodded. "Good night, Sally."

"Not much for talkin', are ya, handsome?" Sally's heavy makeup looked stale after a long day and night. Her gray roots were a stark contrast to her jet-black dyed hair.

"That's OK. I don't care if you don't say a word. You can come over and warm up my sheets anytime."

"Thanks." He thought for a moment. The allure of taking a shower and sleeping in a bed was tempting. He looked Sally up and down. "Maybe some other time."

Vint walked out and started back to his sedan that was still in front of Dewey's. Lark was sitting on his front bumper.

"Hi, Vint." She popped up. "Can we talk?"

"Yeah, sure." He unlocked his car and let her in.

She folded her hands in her lap and laced her fingers together. "Where are you going to sleep tonight?"

"Not sure." Vint started his Nash and backed up. "Probably in my car." He smiled. "Just had an inviting offer from Sally."

"Sally? Oh my God. She's twice my age." She scrunched up her face. "You weren't seriously considering it, were you?"

"No." He drove down the street. "But, a nice hot shower, probably breakfast in bed, it's tempting."

"If Grannie died, I could give you those things and a lot more."

"If she died?" He made a left turn and headed toward the river. "She could live another ten years."

"I mean if she suddenly passed away in her sleep."

Vint turned to look at her. "I hope you're not thinking about doing something stupid." He studied her face. "Not for me, kid. Not for me."

"I was just saying. You would always have a place to stay. You could come and go as you please. I wouldn't get on your back. Really." Lark put her hand on his inner thigh. "As long as you came home to me every night."

"You make it sound real nice. But, what I've been trying to tell you all along is, I'm not worth it. I'm used to just looking out for myself. You understand what I'm saying? I'll just end up hurting you."

"And I don't care if you have some kind of business or whatever with Adelle. I'll share you if I have to. I need you."

"I don't think you're listening to me. Find some nice young man to fall in love with. I'm no good for you."

"You can change. I know you could. My love can change you." She caressed his thigh. "I know there's good in you. The way you stuck up for me against the Skinners. Protected me in that bar. And I heard what you did for little Dickie."

"Yeah. I'm a real prize." Vint looked at his knuckles. "I accidently killed one guy and beat up some others." He parked next to a bunch of brambles near the river. "Quit dreaming. I'm not the hero you make me out to be."

"It doesn't matter what you say. I know you did those things because there's goodness in you. I could find it and bring it out." She undid his jeans and pulled down his zipper. "I can bring it out." She removed a condom from her purse and rolled it down on him. She got out and walked to the side of the car with the sound of the river rushing past. Bending over, she rested an arm on the warm hood. With one foot on the running board, Lark hiked up her skirt and called to Vint, "I want to be everything for you. Everything you need."

* * *

Back in the car, sweating and catching his breath, Vint lit a cigarette. "You're too good to me."

"I told you I could make you happy. I'd do anything for you. I'd kill for you if I had to."

"Don't go talking crazy. I don't want to hear any more about killing."

"Just don't ever leave me and I won't do anything crazy."

He started his car. "I better get you home before Grannie calls the marshal."

"I'll kill her if she does."

"What the hell did I just get through telling you?"

"It's just a figure of speech." She giggled. "I probably won't kill anyone tonight."

"I just don't know about you sometime. You talk a little crazy."

"I'm just crazy about you." She rested her head against the upper seat and gazed at him.

"Well, not too many things scare me … but you worry me a little."

"So, I'm starting to get to you, huh?"

Vint scrutinized Lark.

She ran her hand up his leg. "Want me to take care of you again?" she asked with a smile.

"No, I'm cashed. Next time."

"So, there will be a next time? For sure?"

He looked her in the eye. "Yes."

"You promise?"

"I promise."

"Good." Lark sighed.

"Still, I want to remind you. If I had to leave town suddenly, I might not be able to contact you for a while."

"Leave town?" She raised her voice. "How long?"

"I don't know. It's hard to say right now."

"I don't like it when you talk like that. It makes me feel … like I could scream."

Vint let out a deep breath. "Oh, God."

They drove in silence the next few minutes. He shut the headlights off and killed the engine, coasting to a stop in front of her house.

She nestled her head on his shoulder. "Wish I could be with you all night, sleep next to you and feel you, hear you breathe."

"Well, this town is so small they don't even have a motel." He looked at the front window of Lark's house. "We better say good night."

"Good night," Lark said in a low, breathy voice. She put her hand between his legs and gave him a soft squeeze. "Think about me."

126

"Got a feeling I will."

"Mmm." Lark giggled. "I feel it too." She got out, walked to her front door and disappeared for the night.

Vint started his engine and pulled away. Lark's light perfume still lingered in the air as he went over the things she said that night. He turned on the radio and put his window down. Lighting a cigarette, he wondered if he should leave town and come back when it was time to rob the Krauses and burn down Hurst Lumber. He decided he better be on hand until he heard more from Edric.

"Damn it." He pitched his smoke out the window. It didn't taste right. Nothing felt right. He didn't feel comfortable in his own skin. Even the night air seemed foreign to him. Reaching under his seat, he located his bottle of bourbon. It was going to be one of those kinds of nights.

Chapter 15

Walking out of the general store, tapping a pack of Old Golds into his palm, Vint saw a familiar face riding by among crates of apples on the back of a flatbed truck.

"Hey, Mercurio! Hey!" The man jumped off the truck about fifty feet away, his front pockets bulging with apples.

Vint stood frozen on the side of the road watching the lanky man hike up a pair of baggy pants as he took comically long strides.

"Mercurio!" The man's straight brown hair flopped up and down off his forehead with each step.

Giving the long-necked guy a stern look, Vint put a finger to his lips. He glanced around as the man got closer, then quietly said, "Keep it down, Cornie."

"Hey, hey, Mercurio." The man stuck a dirty hand out.

Vint grabbed him by the collar of his prison-issue, blue chambray shirt. "Shut up, you moron. No one here knows me by that name."

"Oh … sorry there." Cornie looked at Vint's thick muscled arm clutching his shirt. "OK if I call ya Vint?"

"Yeah." He shoved Cornie back a step. "What the hell are you doing riding through this town of all places?"

"Remember me tellin' ya I grew up over in Van Buren? I'm hitchin' my way back there."

"What makes you think I paid any attention to anything that came out of your disgusting mouth?"

"What's a matter? Ain't ya glad to see an old prison buddy?" His Adam's apple bobbed as he spoke. "Sure good to see you."

"OK, this little reunion's over." Vint pointed in the direction Cornie was travelling. "Hit the road."

"Can I have one of them smokes?"

"I'll give you the pack if you keep moving."

"A whole pack?" Cornie's smile dropped. "I just got here, pal. Why ya tryin' to get rid of me already?"

"Let's just say it would be in your best interest to get lost." Vint held the pack out. "Here."

"Sounds like ya want this town all to yourself." Cornie gazed longingly at the Old Golds. "What's so special 'bout it here?"

"Nothing."

"Ya must have somethin' cookin'. Otherwise ya wouldn't be wantin' me to go all a sudden like."

"You miserable, conniving stringbean." Vint tapped his fist on Cornie's chest. "If you don't keep moving, I'll wring your scrawny neck."

"Let's keep it friendly." Cornie looked around, then pulled a long switchblade from his back pocket. He flicked it open and started cleaning dirt from under a thumbnail. "I'm sure your tryin' to keep a low profile. Now how 'bout one of them butts?"

Vint undid the pack, tapped one out and handed it to him. "What do you want?"

"In." Cornie held the knife in his left hand and put the Old Gold between his thin chapped lips. Staring at Vint, he lifted his foot, struck a match on the side of his well-worn shoe and lit the smoke.

"I don't have anything going." Vint glared at him. "Believe me."

"Then what ya stickin' 'round a one-horse town like this for?"

"A girl." Vint looked away and put the cigarette pack in his pocket.

"Oh, get the hell outa here." Cornie's smile stretched across his gaunt face, showing a few missing teeth. "I know damn well ya got a girl in every town ya ever been in."

"This one's special."

Cornie laughed. "They're all special when ya shuts the lights off." His face turning serious, he motioned with his thumb. "Your gonna knock off that joke of a bank, ain't ya?"

Vint waited for an elderly lady to pass by on the sidewalk. "No, really. I'm not. I already cased the joint. The marshal keeps an eye on it. I'm serious."

Looking around, Cornie said, "I don't see no marshal."

"Trust me, the guy's around the corner. This one's not worth the risk."

"I don't believe ya." Cornie talked with the cigarette in the side of his mouth. "Think I'll be hangin' 'round for a while. So, don't try nothin' without me, Mercurio. Or I'll go straight to the marshal."

"You ass-licking pervert, I swear, if you mess me up in any way." Vint pulled his razor and flipped it open. "I'll cut your head off, put it in a hatbox and mail it to your mama."

"OK, big man, ya got a razor." Cornie pointed his knife at Vint as he spoke. "We both got blades. What ya say we keep this civil like?" He folded his switchblade and put it away.

Vint glanced around, then put his razor back in his pocket. "I never did like you. You scum."

"Well, hell, don't be like that. I always liked you, ya handsome devil. And now that we're both out, we're gonna be buddies."

"You and I will never be buddies." Vint spit on the ground between them as he backed away. "Stay far away from me."

"You just wait and see, pal. Ha ha. I'm a gonna keep an eye on ya." Cornie spoke louder as Vint walked away. "Make sure nothin' happens to my new partner."

* * *

Adelle opened her front door after the third knock. "I was wondering when you were coming by."

"I slept in my car again last night." Vint stood on her porch rubbing his stubble. "Mind if I use your shower?"

"Come in." She surveyed the area outside, shut off her porch light, then closed the door. "You know where it is."

Vint climbed the wide stairway with Adelle right behind. When they got to the upper landing, she asked, "Have you eaten yet?"

"No. I was going to go to Dewey's for a late dinner."

"Forget about that greasy spoon tonight. Take a shave. We're going out."

* * *

Vint walked out of the bathroom wrapped in a towel. He found Adelle lounging on her bed, flipping through an issue of *Glamour*. Her purple silk robe was open, revealing a lacy black bra, matching panties, garter belt and stockings with seams up the back.

"Where we going?" he asked, slicking his wet, black hair back.

Glancing at her watch, she answered without looking up, "Out of this crummy little town for a few hours." She closed the magazine, sat up and slipped into her black and white spiked heels.

"Suits me."

She stood and let her robe drop to the floor. Walking to her open closet, she reached in and pulled a red dress from a padded hanger. "Zip me up." She stepped into the shimmering gown and turned her back to him. "I've got something for you to wear too."

Vint patted her ass as she went back to her closet. She turned around with a hanger in each hand. One had a

131

white shirt with a silvery silk necktie hanging over it. The other was draped in a black suit with a white, silk square sticking out of the top pocket. "These should fit you."

"You bought these for me?" he said taking both hangers in one hand.

"I had one of Mr. Hurst's dress suits tailored to fit you." She pulled a drawer open and handed him a pair of new silk boxers and black socks.

"What about shoes? This getup won't look too hot with jackboots." He laid the clothes on her bed, let the towel drop and slipped into the boxers.

"You're about an eleven?"

"Yeah, close enough."

"I'll be right back."

Vint got into the outfit and stood waiting for Adelle.

"Here." She walked back, handed him a pair of black and white oxfords, crocodile belt, gold cuff links and matching tie bar.

After putting everything else on, he walked in front of the full-length mirror and adjusted his tie.

She put on diamond earrings and sprayed some perfume around her neck. "How does it feel?"

Turning around and pulling at his cuffs, he said, "I feel like me again."

* * *

After driving over an hour, listening to jazz on the radio, Vint pulled up in front of a night spot with a neon sign reading *Neptune Club*. The doorman opened the passenger door for Adelle and they both stepped out to the muffled sounds of a swing band playing inside the building. The valet took the keys to Adelle's Cadillac from Vint and they walked in as the attendant held the door open.

"Hello. I'm Frederick." The maître d' bowed slightly. "Welcome to the Neptune."

"Hello Freddie." Vint surveyed the spacious, multilevel room that had a stage trimmed in deep-purple velvet curtains.

"Two, sir?" Frederick asked over the soft music of the band playing *Moonlight Serenade.*

"Yeah. Seat us in a quiet spot." Vint glanced around at the 1940s art deco designs. "We want to talk."

"Of course, sir."

Vint gently held Adelle's arm as the maître d' guided them through a succession of white linen covered round tables occupied with patrons dressed in evening wear.

"How is this, sir?" Frederick motioned with a flourish at a table against the wall on the upper-level next to a potted palm.

"This'll be fine." Vint slipped him a couple dollars, then pulled Adelle's chair out for her.

"Sir. I have to ask."

Vint sat and looked up at the maître d' dressed in a black tuxedo. "What is it, Freddie?"

"You wouldn't happen to be ..."

"No. I wouldn't."

"You look so much like him," he gushed.

"I'm taller and better looking."

"Oh, sir." Frederick chuckled and put his hand on Vint's arm. "You're so amusing. Shall I send over a bottle of champagne?"

Vint looked at Frederick's hand on his suitcoat, then peered up at him. "Skip the bubbly. I'm having a dry martini, three olives." He looked to Adelle.

"I'll have the same." She removed a platinum cigarette case from her purse, opened it and took out a short, slim cigar.

"Good choice." Frederick spun on his heel, then walked away with his head back and a bounce in his step, swinging his arms.

Vint patted his pockets out of habit. "Sorry. I don't have a lighter and I left my matches in my pants."

She handed him a silver lighter bedecked with a small emerald on each side. "Keep it. It was my husband's."

"Thanks." Vint lit her cigarillo, examined the lighter, then slipped it in his pocket. "I've seen a lot of things but I never saw a dame smoke a cigar before."

"Bet I do a lot of things you never saw." Adelle slowly let the smoke out of her mouth then breathed it up into her nostrils.

A cigarette girl with a tray strapped around her neck approached the table. "Cigarettes, sir?" She smiled at Adelle and winked.

"Old Gold. The lady will take care of it."

Adelle shot Vint a look, then opened her purse. "Here Susie, keep the change." She handed her a dollar.

"Why, thank you, Adelle." Susie's face flushed. "You look stunning tonight. Haven't seen you in a while. I missed you."

"I'll talk to you later." Adelle waved her away.

"Looks like you have an admirer." Vint watched Susie's hips sway back and forth in her short, satin skirt and white, ruffled panties.

"Nothing more than a schoolgirl crush." Adelle remained typically stoic, her expression rarely changing. "She'll get over it."

He peeled the cellophane wrapping from the top of his cigarette pack and took one out. "More to you than meets the eye." He took out the lighter, admired it some more and lit his smoke.

"There's a lot about me you don't know."

A cocktail waitress set their drinks down, pivoted and wiggled away in her sexy, nautical-styled outfit.

Vint took a big sip of his gin. "I had someone else say that to me just a few days ago." He pulled an olive from a miniature plastic sword with his teeth. "The same way."

"I can only guess." She blew smoke at him, then took a sip. "Let's cut the chatter. I want to go over our plans."

A waiter appeared with two menus. "Will you be dining with us this evening?"

Adelle spoke up, "I'll have a Caesar salad and a T-bone steak, bloody rare." She looked at Vint and raised one eyebrow.

Vint glanced up at the waiter. "Same, except skip the rabbit food and bring me a baked potato." He raised his half-empty glass. "Couple more of these."

As soon as the waiter walked away, she said, "I want to know just how you intend to pull this off." She tapped a finger on the table. "Right down to the letter."

"Nothing doing." He tilted his glass and took another mouthful. "I like you OK. But I don't trust you. Don't take it personally though. I don't trust anyone."

"I want to remind you who's in charge here." She took her spear of olives, dropped them on her bread plate and drained her glass.

"You'll find out when we pull this off. Not a second sooner."

"And you don't get paid until that night. Got it?"

"I expected nothing more. Just make sure you have the cash, lady. I don't think I have to tell you, I don't take checks."

"How am I supposed to judge if your plan is sound if you don't fill me in?"

"Look, damn it!" He slapped his palm on the table.

The waitress came by and looked at Vint wide-eyed. She set two more martinis in front of them, then quickly walked away.

He stubbed his cigarette out in the ashtray. "I know what I'm doing. Things are going to run smooth as long as you don't jinx them. This is a simple operation. I'm going to take care of things and you're going to pay me. End of discussion."

"I sometimes wonder if I picked the right guy." She took a drag, then blew the smoke out forcefully.

"And why *did* you pick me? Because I supposedly killed a guy in a diner? That means I'm a desperate character, an ex-con that'll do just about any crazy thing?"

"Yeah. Something like that." Adelle's laugh was almost imperceptible. "It's not like you guys are in the yellow pages."

"So, I came along and you sized me up."

"Well, you're supposed to be this daring bank robber, aren't you? I figured anyone who has the nerve and brains for a bank heist could help me."

"And you threw in the sex to help seal the deal ... a little icing on the cake."

"Don't play dumb. You knew the score."

"Yes, I did, and took full advantage of the situation."

"All right. Our cards are on the table. You complaining?"

"Of course not." Vint sat forward and smiled. "Come on. Let's enjoy ourselves. This is a swanky joint. The drinks are good and the band's even better. I haven't been out like this in a long time."

"You look good. I have to admit it. If I didn't know you were a jailbird, I wouldn't have guessed."

He stood and extended his hand. "Let's dance. I need to do something to take my mind off my growling stomach."

She rolled her eyes. "How romantic."

"Come on, toots. Want me to tell you you're beautiful first?"

"It wouldn't hurt."

"You got movie star looks and you know it. You don't need me to blow smoke up your ass."

Adelle shook her head and smiled slightly. She slowly stood and took his hand. As the band played *Tangerine*, he guided her down one level of tables, then another.

They glided around the dance floor in close embrace while she hummed along with the melody. She spoke low into his ear, "You're really a good dancer."

"A guy learns things if he wants to move in certain circles. Trust me, I can be charming if I want to be."

"And you just don't want to be?"

"It's not like I'm trying to get you in the sack. I've already been there."

"Yeah." She sighed. "You've already been there."

He held her tighter and moved her around in a couple quick circles.

She pulled her head back, face to face with him. "Is that what I think it is?"

"It's not a roll of quarters, lady."

"Good, God. Is there ever a time you don't want it?"

"You smell great." He kissed her neck and pushed into her harder.

"People are watching us."

"There's seven or eight other couples on the floor. Loosen up."

The song stopped and everyone clapped.

"Let's go back to the table." She said under her breath. "Our food will be out soon."

"OK. Just walk directly ahead of me."

"Oh, brother."

When they got to their table, Adelle nestled into her velvet padded chair and said, "Well, that was embarrassing." Vint sat down after her, lit another Old Gold and finished his second drink.

Their steaks arrived soon after sitting down and they ate in silence. After the plates were cleared away, Susie came back to their table. She handed Adelle a small folded piece of paper, then pushed her hips and tray toward Vint, "Cigar?"

"Sure." He looked at her selection. "I'll take the Upmann."

"Would you like me to cut that, sir?"

"Yeah. And put it on the bill." He nodded toward Adelle.

Susie cut the tip, put it in his mouth and moved in close to light it. "I hope you two come back soon." She gazed into Vint's eyes, then glanced sideways at Adelle. "I'd be happy to be at your service." Looking back over her shoulder, she slinked away.

"Cute kid." Watching Susie's shapely derriere, Vint drew on the rich cigar and slowly let the smoke out. "Don't you think?"

"Yes. Cute. She knows her way around."

"Yeah. I bet." With the cigar in the side of his mouth, he asked, "Why is it a beautiful broad like you lives in that great house all by yourself? Why aren't you seeing anyone?"

"You've been around that stinking, backwater burg for what, two weeks now? You see any eligible prospects for me there?"

Vint laughed. "No one in your league, sister."

"See why I have to get out of there? I belong in a place like Manhattan, Beverly Hills, Paris. Anywhere but that anthill of a town."

"Besides me, how long has it been?"

"After my husband, there was one other person. But that ended."

"Who was he? Anybody I'd know?"

"Please. Let's go. I'm tired and I have to be at that God-awful, smelly lumberyard in the morning."

* * *

When they pulled up to the main entrance to Adelle's home, Vint turned to her and asked, "Want some company?"

"No. Please just go."

He turned off the car and handed her the keys. "What about my things?"

"Hold on." She opened the passenger-side door, illuminating them from the interior light. "I'll bring them down."

Vint got out, pushed the lock button down and waited. Adelle came down a few minutes later carrying his old clothes, leather bomber and boots. She handed them to him and said, "I think it would be better if we didn't see each other for a while."

"Sure." He threw his garments over his shoulder and held the boots. "Why?"

"I have my reasons." She turned from him and looked over at the river. "Besides, with you pulling this thing off, it would be best if no one saw us together outside of work."

"Makes sense."

"Come see me at the plant first thing Monday. I'll square things with Gerald. It'll look better with you working, help keep Amos off your back."

"I hate that place." He grimaced. "All that pounding, buzz saws going off every few minutes. Breathing in all that sawdust."

"Now you know how I feel." She turned back to him. "Come home with my hair smelling like lumber. Place gives me a headache."

"I'm going to miss coming by."

"This whole thing with you, me, that blonde over at Dewey's. It's a little too ..."

"What?"

"Forget it. You better get going." Adelle's mannequin-like face showed no emotion. "You can keep the suit and shoes. Black is your color." She raised one eyebrow. "If the fire doesn't go well, we can bury you in it." She turned, walked back into the house and locked the door.

Chapter 16

Edric removed a gold watch from his vest pocket and popped it open. "You're almost ten minutes late. We can't have this on the big night."

"This isn't the big night." Walking into Edric's aged furnished apartment, Vint looked at him sideways. "Quit bellyaching."

"I see you brought me something?" Edric's eyebrows shot up.

Vint pulled a brown bottle from a slim paper bag.

Edric frowned. "A quart of *beer*?"

"Get a couple glasses," Vint said, strolling into the kitchen across the worn linoleum.

"I'm not in the habit of *swilling suds*," Edric said, following him.

"Just get one then." Vint removed his opener from his jacket pocket and popped the top off the chilled Heidelberg bottle.

"Oh, I suppose it's better than nothing." Edric went to the cupboard, removed two drinking glasses, inspected them, then set them on the kitchen table.

Vint poured them both a glass, forming a frothy head on each. "This isn't a social call. Let's get to it, Eddie."

"Please. Don't ever call me that. The name is Edric."

"All right, don't get touchy." Vint took a seat at the kitchen table. "I'm just pissing in your tea a little."

"Oh, please." Edric picked up his glass, looked at it, and made a sour face. "Not even in jest."

"I picked up a set of wheels."

"Good. That's good." Edric raised his eyebrows. "It fits into my end plan," he said, then took a sip.

Vint rolled his hand impatiently for Edric to move things along.

Edric sat and cleared his throat. "I've found the perfect alibi in one Miss Cumpton, treasurer of this township. My first evening appointment with her is early next week. I've agreed to take a look at the town's financial statements. Told her I wouldn't charge anything unless I could save them funds."

"So, we're doing this next week?"

"No. Not on the initial meeting, that will be brief. We'll move ahead on the follow-up appointment." Edric looked at him solemnly. "You're going to need an alibi too."

"I'll take care of it." Vint tapped his finger on the table. "Let's go over the exact plans. That's what I'm good at. Having a precise plan and carrying it out to the letter."

"A detail man. Good." Edric leaned toward him, making hand gestures as he spoke. "Just before my second appointment with the treasurer, I'm going to stop by the Krauses to drop off some paperwork to be signed. I'll ask to use their lavatory before I leave, at which time I'll unlock that bathroom window. I used their facilities on a previous occasion where I unlocked the window and slid it up with very little effort. It's highly unlikely they'll go in there to check the lock afterwards, they use the upstairs loo. And even if they do happen to glance in there, the shower curtain hides the lock."

"Sounds good so far." Vint sipped his cold beer, scrutinizing the Englishman.

Edric opened his briefcase and produced a drawing. "Here's the layout of the first floor." He spread it out on the table. "Study this. After you do, I'm burning it."

"Yeah. Got it." Vint pointed at the map. "The X in the closet marks the spot where the money's at?"

"Of course." Edric's sarcasm was obvious. "That's what an X usually indicates in a situation like this."

"Hey, Eddie, don't get cocky with me, deal or no deal."

"But I'm supposed to continually take *your* lip?"

"All right." Vint waved a hand. "Let's not lose our heads over nothing."

"That's all I'm trying to say." Edric raised his glass, paused, then took a sip. "I think we're both under a bit of a strain."

"Speak for yourself. I'm cool as a cucumber."

Edric rubbed his forehead and took a moment. "On the floor of that unlocked closet you'll find a heavy-cloth satchel with fancy embroidery. It's very old, so handle it carefully. It contains six-hundred-thousand dollars."

Vint whistled. "Even split. Right?" He finished his beer and poured himself another glass.

"Even-Steven. No reason for anyone to get greedy. There's plenty for both of us."

"Why would that much cash be sitting in an unlocked closet?" Vint brought his glass up, then paused. "It doesn't make sense. Seems to me, in a small town like this where everyone knows everybody else's business, someone would have already come by and taken it off their hands."

"Who knows?" Edric shrugged. "Maybe they had it in a different spot and moved it recently. I just know that I've seen it with my own eyes. The money will appear odd at first glance because it's old, from the mid-1800s."

"But it's good?"

"Legal tender is legal tender. Might be worth more because of its rarity." Edric smiled wide, revealing a gold rimmed bicuspid.

"I can't keep waiting around this town indefinitely. You sure it won't be much longer after that first meeting?"

"Certainly." Edric took a sip of beer, then ran a finger under his neatly trimmed moustache. "Come see me next Tuesday, around the same time."

"This thing has got me on edge. We're running the risk of them moving the money."

"I'm sorry but this is the way it has to be," Edric said, raising his chin. "I can't tell you more than that."

"All right. I'll see you next week. Just make sure there's no delays." Vint finished his glass and stood. "It has to coincide with other plans I have."

Vint left and walked down the street to the diner. He went in, put a nickel in the jukebox, pressed a random button, then sat at his usual stool.

Lark had a bounce in her step as she approached him with a coffee pot in her hand. "Hi, dreamy. I look any different today?"

He looked her up and down. "Look the same to me. You do something different with your hair?"

"Nope. That's not it." She poured him a steaming cup of coffee, then walked away.

Studying Lark, he picked up his cup, blew on it, then set it back down. "Dizzy doll," he said, shaking his head.

She came back a few minutes later. "Figure it out yet?"

"You got me." He brought his hands up. "Don't have a clue. You going to ask me what I want to eat?"

"No." She shrugged. "Did you get me anything?"

"What the hell are you talking about? Look, toots. I'm hungry. What's today's special?"

"You been drinking again?"

"What of it?" He brought his head forward. "Who are you, my parole officer?"

She put her hands on her hips and swayed side to side. "You think I should get some nylons and high heels now?"

"What is it with you?" Vint stood up. "I'm going down to Sally's."

"Oh, don't be a grouch. Not today of all days." She pulled her order pad and pencil from the pocket of her white apron. "C'mon, sit down. Stuffed peppers with mash potatoes. It's pretty good too."

"OK, that's more like it. Put in an order." He wagged a finger at her. "You know, sometimes you don't make much sense."

She gave him a sour look, spun and plodded away. He lit a cigarette, took a sip of coffee and thought about his conversation with Edric. When he was deep in thought, Lark spoke and brought him back.

"Here." She slid a plate in front of him.

He stubbed out his smoke, then ate in silence while Lark took care of other customers. He noticed her giving him side glances while he devoured his meal.

When he was through, he pushed his plate away. She came back and said, "How was it?"

"Not bad. That Shadrack knows his stuff. So, you going to tell me what the mystery is?"

"For a guy who goes around acting so smart, you can be a little thick at times."

Vint put his fingertips to his forehead and remembered something Grannie told him. "Happy birthday, kid."

"I'm twenty years old now. Thank you, but I'm not a kid anymore."

"No." He looked her up and down. "You're not at that."

"You should have known." She pouted. "Could have got me something."

"Birthdays don't mean much to me. Don't even know my own."

"Well, they mean something to me. Today's important. I'm not a teenager anymore." Her voice turned sweet. "Gonna do something special for me?"

"What do you have in mind?"

"Dewey's letting me off early." She looked up at the clock next to the service window, then took off her apron.

"Want me to take you out for a drink?"

"No. Absolutely not." She waved her hands out. "I'm not going to any more bars with you. Someone's liable to get killed. And I don't want it to be you."

"What then?"

"How about we start with a movie? But let's not go back to Booneville. Someone might recognize you."

"A movie." Vint felt his pack of Old Gold for fullness, then slipped it in his pocket. "OK, sure."

Lark rested her chin in her hands with her elbows on the counter. "I never been to one of those drive-ins."

"Check the paper. See what's around."

* * *

Sitting in Vint's car with the windows half-down and the smell of popcorn in the air, Lark nestled her head on his shoulder and asked, "Did you like the first one?"

"You kidding? Giant spiders, dwarfs, a master race of superwomen." Vint shook his head. "I never saw such crap. What was it called?"

"*Mesa of Lost Women*. Maybe the next one's better, it's called *Robot Monster*."

"Good God."

"Do you like this?" Lark asked softly while stroking him up and down.

He looked around at the other cars parked near them. "Yes. But you're driving me crazy. Maybe we should leave."

"I think it's time we talk marriage."

"*Marriage*? Where'd you get a crazy idea like that?" Vint flinched. "Ow. Hey, don't squeeze so tight."

"I'm twenty now and I'm not getting any younger. It's time to start having babies."

"You really think you're … equipped … to raise kids?"

Lark glanced down at her body. "I got all the right equipment."

"That's not …" Vint studied Lark's serious expression. "Maybe it's not quite time for you to be thinking about marriage and babies." He grimaced. "Damn. I told you, not so hard."

"I'm proposing to you. Do you want me to get on my knees? I'll get on my knees for you."

"No. You don't have to do that." He noticed her tightly clenched jaw. "This is kind of sudden. Why don't you let me …"

"If you bend one of these things real hard do they break?"

"Yes, they break. And it's not a pretty sight from what I heard. Come on. Loosen up a little."

"Is that a yes?" She asked, smiling.

"No. It's not a yes. Doesn't someone usually have a chance to think it over? I mean, isn't it customary?"

"What's there to think about? I love you. You love me."

"Well, I never … I mean. Look, sweetie. Um … Ow."

Lark lowered her face nearer his lap. "One of the cheerleaders at school told me about this trick. She used to do it to keep her boyfriend happy and to keep from getting pregnant."

"Oh boy."

She leaned closer and took him in her mouth. Vint grabbed her ponytail, pulled her head up and said, "Whoa. I usually go for this, but, hey, you're not going to bite me, are you?"

"*Bite you*?" She looked him in the eye. "Of course not. Why would I bite you?"

"Well …"

"You're not going to say something to upset me, are you?"

"No. I don't think I'll be doing that." He looked at the huge movie screen. "Hey, look, a robot monster."

"That's just a kid in a space helmet." She sighed and went back to stroking him.

"Oh, yeah." He let out a deep breath. "Whew. Slow down, honey."

"You know, if we were both working, we could fix Grannie's place up real nice."

"You, me and Grannie? You really think that would work?"

"She's not going to be around forever." She rested her head on his chest.

"If we got married she might cut you out of her will."

"Don't be silly. Grannie loves me." Lark stopped stroking and just squeezed. "Well, have you thought about it yet?"

"What's this now?" He watched the screen. "Giant lizards fighting each other? And dinosaurs?"

She lightly smacked his erection. "Are you avoiding my question?"

"When I said I needed time to think, I didn't mean a few minutes. Enough marriage talk for now. All right? Did I tell you happy birthday?"

"Yes. You told me at Dewey's." She looked down at him. "Why don't you put that thing away for now?"

He lowered his jeans and stuffed himself back in.

She flopped back in her seat.

"Now that's a robot monster." He pointed with his chin. "Or … a guy in a gorilla costume with a deep-sea helmet."

"Why don't we get out of here?"

"Sounds good to me." Vint lowered his window, removed the speaker, then set it in its cradle on the pole. He started his car and said, "What happened to Clark Gable, Gary Cooper, Rita Hayworth? I don't understand why anyone would bother to make garbage like this." He backed up and pulled away as the sound of the movie echoed in the vast parking area. "Want to park by the river?"

Chapter 17

Vint pitched his cigarette and walked into the diner during the after-dinner lull. He saw the wild look in Lark's eyes and knew immediately that something was wrong.

With a tremble in her voice, Lark called out, "Dewey, I need to take a break." She took off her apron and threw it on the cooler. Hurrying out from behind the counter, she grabbed Vint's hand and led him outside.

"What is it?"

"Let's talk in your car." She squeezed his fingers tightly. "Please."

"Sure, kid. Sure." He opened the passenger-side door, let her in, then walked around and got behind the wheel.

"Oh, Vint ... something terrible happened." She put her face in her hands. "Grannie died in her sleep last night."

"She *died*? Just like that?"

"Yes." She peered at him. "Isn't it sad? Drive somewhere dark."

"You got it." He started his sedan, backed up, then drove down Main Street.

"I couldn't wait to tell you." She fidgeted and squirmed in her seat.

"Yeah." He watched her from the corner of his eye. "Something like that. Can come as a shock."

"I've been out of my head all day. Can't eat, can't think straight. I got to make funeral arrangements ..."

Vint turned down a dark side road and pulled over. "I'm sorry." He turned in his seat to face her. "Was it natural causes?"

"Sure. What do you think?"

He stared at Lark. "You didn't do anything? I mean ..."

"Of course not. How could you ask me such a thing?"

"You were just saying the other night."

"It was her time to go. Now you can stay over again. We won't even have to worry about making noise."

"She seemed full of life when she was whacking me with that cane."

"Grannie was old, Vint." Her hands flew up. "Old people die all the time and nobody gets suspicious."

"You sure you didn't do anything to help her along?"

"Oh, come on now. She lived a good long life. All she ever wanted was to be with Gramps again."

He brought his fingertips to his forehead. "Please tell me you didn't do something stupid."

"I didn't do anything stupid. Vint, we can be together now. It'll be even better than before."

"You're a nervous wreck but you don't seem very broken up."

"I cried about it all day." She frowned. "Grannie's in a better place now."

"You scare me, kid. Sure you won't put a pillow over my head one night when you're mad?"

Lark suddenly giggled. "Well, just behave yourself and nothing will happen to you." She ran a finger along his chin and smiled.

"What makes you think I'll move back in with you?"

"Don't say that!" She clenched her fists. "Not now!"

Vint's eyes flashed at her.

Her demeanor changed again in an instant. "Mmm. Just think about it, sugar." Her voice turned soft and sweet. "No more sleeping in your car. You can do anything you want to me." She caressed her breasts, gazing into his eyes. "Any time you like."

He backed away from her. "I think maybe you really *are* crazy."

"Crazy about you, lover." She hiked her uniform skirt and spread her legs. "Think about it."

"How the hell do I keep ..."

Lark rolled onto her stomach, then pulled her skirt up higher and yanked her panties down. "Do it, Vint. Please. Stop my mind from racing."

A knock on the passenger window made Vint jump. "What the fuck?"

She tugged her underwear back up, pulled her skirt down and shuffled into her seat.

"Hey, what y'all up to in there?" Cornie appeared out of nowhere, peering inside with his hands on the window.

Vint hopped out of his Nash and yelled over the top. "You cocksucker! What do you think you're doing?"

"Vint, ole buddy," Cornie spoke loudly. "I'm just checkin' up on ya. Makin' sure my partner's all right."

"I ought to kill you." Vint dashed around the front of the sedan and up to Cornie. "Don't ever come sneaking up on me." He grabbed the lanky man by the collar and shoved him against the car.

"Sneakin'? Who's sneakin'? I'm lookin' out for ya. Better'n an insurance policy."

Vint banged him off the passenger door a couple times, making Lark cower. "You and me don't have any kind of future together. Got that? You better blow this town before I make sure you got worms crawling around on you."

"Hey!" Cornie shoved back. "Remember, Mercurio. I don't wanna have to go to the marshal 'bout you."

"If you're six-feet under, you won't be talking to anyone but the devil, you sick bastard."

Cornie pulled away from Vint's grip. "You and me both know it'd be better for ya to cut me in than to kill me.

I know how much ya hate prison … a guy like you who hates takin' orders. Ya wouldn't wanna take a chance of goin' there till you die."

"Get out of here!" Vint balled up his fists. "Now!"

"OK, pard. I can see ya got your hands full." Cornie leered at Lark through the window. "Ya ole pussy hound," he said, laughing and backing away. "I know ya smell money and I want some of it. See ya soon, Mercurio."

Vint got back in the car and slammed a fist down on his steering wheel. "Lousy goddam mother fucking son-of-a-bitch. I could kill that prick."

"Calm down." Lark rubbed his arm.

"Damn it," he said, through clenched teeth.

"Anyone who's a threat to you is a threat to me." She caressed his cheek. "Want me to make him go away?"

"What the hell are you talking about? How can you make him leave?"

"I didn't say leave. I said go away. Like disappear."

"What are you driving at?" He squinted at Lark.

"I don't like seeing you upset. It makes me upset. A little rat poison in his soup …"

"Whoa." He put his hands out. "Don't talk like that. Don't even think about it."

"Vint. Do you want me to make him go away?"

"You are. You really are crazy."

"Stop saying that! I'm not crazy!" Her voice softened. "I just get things done that need getting done."

Vint stared at her wide-eyed. "I better get you back before Dewey fires you." He started his car and backed up.

"Oh, who's talking crazy now? That place would fold without me. Besides, Dewey worships me."

He put it in forward and sped up. "Still, I better get you back."

Grabbing his arm, Lark pleaded, "Don't leave me alone tonight. I couldn't take it. Not after …" She choked on her words. "Drive me home after work."

Looking straight ahead, not saying a word, he kept driving.

"Please, Vint!" She cried out, "Please!"

Breathing heavily, he answered, "All right. I'll be by Dewey's at closing time."

Lark turned the radio on and sang along, "*How much is that doggie in the window?*"

Chapter 18

"Who the …?" Vint woke up from a deep sleep to hard knocking on the front door. He got out of Lark's bed, picked his jeans up off the floor and pulled them on. The pounding got louder and Vint called, "All right! Damn it. I'm coming." He opened the door dressed only in his pants.

"Surprise, surprise." Gilstrap looked down at Vint. "Playing house *already*?"

Vint finger-combed his hair off his forehead. "What do you want?"

"The truth." The marshal put his fists on his hips. "Where's Lark?"

"Sounds like she's in the bath. What's this about?"

"I want y'all at the station in an hour. If you're not there, I'm swearing out warrants for your arrests."

"Arrests? What for?"

"Murder." Gilstrap turned and walked toward his squad car in the driveway.

Vint knocked lightly on the bathroom door, then walked in.

Lark beamed at him as she sat in the tub lathering her hair, but her smile dropped when she saw his expression. "What's going on?"

"The marshal was just here. He wants us both in his office in an hour."

"Oh, no. Is it about Grannie?"

"Sure sounds like it." He rubbed a palm across his thick black stubble. "You have a lawyer?"

"No. And I don't need one." She lay back and dunked her hair in the water. "If I brought a lawyer with me, I'd look guilty as sin."

"Maybe we should talk to Edric Randall before we go in. He's not licensed to practice law here but he could advise us."

"I told you no. That numbskull marshal doesn't scare me. I'll answer anything he wants."

Vint lathered his face, then sharpened his razor. "This is serious business. Better know what you're doing."

* * *

Vint held the door open for Lark and they walked into the police station.

"Right over here." Gilstrap motioned toward two chairs across from his desk. Mrs. Sinks sat next to the marshal at a card table with an old Underwood typewriter. Deputy Anfield stood behind her, rocking from heel to toe.

Lark and Vint took their seats, glancing at one another.

Gilstrap removed his hat and set it on the desk. "Lark, I got several calls so far from concerned citizens suspecting foul play in the death of your grandma, Ortense. Mostly from ladies she knew at church. Said she seemed very healthy for a woman in her late seventies and they're shocked that she went that way, so suddenly."

"That what this is about?" She raised her eyebrows. "Gossip?"

"I've always been of the belief that where there's smoke there's fire." The marshal pointed a pen at her. "What time did you last see your grandma alive?"

"Yesterday, about 10:45 am." Lark spoke over the click-clack from Mrs. Sinks' typewriter. "Right before I left to walk to work."

"Didn't you check on her when you got home?"

"No. I'm not in the habit of … I mean …" She crossed her legs and smoothed her plaid skirt. "I wasn't in the habit of checking on Grannie."

Gilstrap leaned forward. "Are you saying she might have been dead when you got home?"

"No. She was alive when I got there."

"Already you're contradicting yourself. You just said the last time you saw her alive was 10:45 in the morning. Now you're saying she was alive when you got home." Gilstrap stood and waved his pen at her. "Which is it?"

"Well, both. I didn't see Grannie alive when I got home but I know she wasn't dead."

Gilstrap threw down his pen, leaned forward on his knuckles and stared at her intently. "How do you know that?"

"I heard her snoring."

"Oh." The marshal sat back down. "Did she sleep with her bedroom door open or closed?"

"Closed." Lark shrugged. "She was a loud snorer."

"What time did you get home Thursday night?"

She put her palms out. "The usual time, about 9:15, 9:20."

"Are you the beneficiary of your grandma's life insurance?"

"Yes." She put a finger alongside her cheek. "I believe I am."

"How much do you stand to gain for her death?" the marshal asked, folding his arms across his chest.

"I don't think that's any of your business."

Gilstrap sat staring into Lark's eyes. "I can find out."

"What about this joker?" Anfield interrupted, motioning toward Vint.

"Shut up, boy. I'm getting to him." Gilstrap turned his attention to Vint. "Smith, where were you when Ortense died?"

"*Me?*" Vint brought a hand to his chest. "I don't know. I mean I don't know when she died, exactly."

"Doc Harris suspects she took her last breath somewhere around midnight. Then she laid there until the next morning when Lark claimed she first became aware that Ortense had passed."

"Midnight Thursday I was sleeping in my car. Parked by the river, down where Pine Street trails off."

"Were you alone?"

"Yes." Vint nodded slowly. "Of course." He pulled out his pack of Old Gold.

"Put those away." The marshal scowled at him. "So, there's no one to collaborate your whereabouts?"

"No. You don't think I ..."

"I think you're not only capable of murder, you had opportunity and motive."

"You're nuts." Vint sat forward. "What motive?"

"With Ortense out of the way, you could have the run of her house. Take it over like it's your own. Have Lark here at your beck and call."

"No one's going to buy that. And I'll tell you right now, you're not pulling another one of those deals on me with that Judge Chester as prosecutor and judge. I checked, that's not legal. A judge can't try a case."

"That time no one was charged with anything. It wasn't even a trial, just a fact gathering session." Gilstrap wagged a finger. "If I bring formal charges against either one of you, you can bet we'll do things by the letter of the law. Right now, I don't have enough evidence on y'all. But I'm not through poking around. Smith, I told you to get out of town. Now you better stick around for a few days."

"You through?" Vint stood up.

The marshal waved a hand. "You're both free to go. For now."

Vint and Lark walked out to his sedan. He let her in, lit a cigarette, then hopped behind the wheel. "I don't have to tell you. This doesn't look good. I'm half tempted to split." He started his car and pulled away.

"You're not going anywhere without me. My story can *change*, you know."

Vint's tone turned harsh. "What do you mean by that?"

"Never you mind." She looked out the passenger window as they drove past Dewey's. "Just don't cross me."

"How much is that policy worth?"

"$5,000." She crossed her leg and swung her foot. "Take me back home."

* * *

Lark leaned over her kitchen table and poured Vint a cup of coffee. "Damn marshal, snooping around. I could kill him."

"That guy's really reaching." Vint rubbed the back of his neck. "Got me worried."

She put the coffee pot back on the stove. "Don't worry. If he makes trouble, I'll fix him."

"First you want to fix Cornie, now him too? Maybe we should wait and see what happens. Not get ahead of ourselves. OK?"

"He has no right to threaten either one of us. Big ape in a uniform."

"I'm thinking the smart thing would be to lay low. Wait it out." He raised his cup. "Say, put a spot of bourbon in here, will you?"

"I'm not going to work today." She retrieved Vint's whiskey bottle from the cabinet under the sink and added a splash to his cup. "I wanna go see Grannie."

"You'll see her at the wake."

"There's not going to be one." She put her hands on her hips. "Are you going to drive me or am I walking?"

"Where is she?"

"The funeral parlor. It's on Elm, just south of Main."

"Give me a few minutes." He took a sip of his spiked coffee. "I'm going to get my suit out of the car trunk."

"*Suit*? Where'd you get a suit?"

"I got it from Adelle." Vint stood up. "Don't make a big deal out of it."

"Why would she give you a suit?" Lark wagged a finger at him and leaned forward. "What did you do to earn that?"

"Part of the same business opportunity I told you about. I'm going to need a nice set of clothes."

"I don't like all this mysterious stuff." She poked his chest. "I wanna know what's going on. Right now."

He pushed her hand away. "Drop it, little lady. I told you before, don't stick your nose in my business."

"All right." She pouted. "All right. But I don't like it."

* * *

Parking in front of Wilkes Funeral Home, Vint peered through the windshield. "This looks like someone's house, not a mortuary."

"It's both," Lark said casually.

To Vint, it seemed all the odd things in this town were somehow deemed normal if spoken about matter-of-factly often enough. He tilted the rearview mirror down, straightened his tie, then got out and opened Lark's door. "Places like this give me the creeps."

The muffled sound of the doorbell carried out to the wraparound front porch as Lark pressed the button. A moment later, Mr. Wilkes, dressed in a charcoal gray suit with a pink carnation pinned to his lapel, swung the door open. "Why, Miss Stookey, so good to see you. Please come in."

Vint followed Lark into the spacious living room. Striped couches and stuffed easy chairs lined the walls. The smell of unseen, decaying flowers permeated the stale air.

"I wish it wasn't under such tragic circumstances." Wilkes bowed his head slightly and extended his hand. "So sorry for your loss."

"It's everybody's loss, Mr. Wilkes." She gave his hand a quick shake, then let go. "She was everyone's friend. I'll miss her terribly."

Vint felt the back of his head where there was still a small lump from Grannie's cane.

"And this is?" Wilkes smiled and extended his hand toward Vint.

"He's …"

Vint interrupted her, "I'm Mr. Smith." He shook Wilkes's hand. "Friend of Miss Stookey."

"Yes." An uneasy look came over Wilkes face. "I've heard of you, sir."

"Mr. Wilkes," Lark spoke up. "I'd like Grannie cremated. How soon can you do it?"

"Cremated? I see. Well, right after the wake."

"What if we don't have a wake?"

"No wake?" Wilkes' baritone voice cracked. "Why not?"

She shrugged. "I just don't want one."

"But all her friends from church, including me, we'd like a chance to say goodbye to our dear friend."

"I'd consider a memorial service once she's been cremated. How soon can you take care of it?"

Wilkes stroked his dark, pointy goatee with his fingertips. "I suppose we could take care of things in a couple days."

"I want it done today. Right now, while I wait."

"This is highly irregular. Maybe I should consult Marshal Gilstrap first. To make sure everything is in order."

Vint interrupted, "Excuse me." He took Lark by the arm and tugged at her. "I need a word with Miss Stookey." The two walked into the next room, out of earshot but in view of Wilkes. "Why you doing this?" He put his hands on her shoulders and looked her in the eye. "What's the big rush?"

"Why do you think?" she said quietly. "That marshal's trying to make trouble for us. He practically accused you of murder. I can't have that."

"He suspects you too."

"That's just screwy. I suppose he thinks we strangled her together."

"Who said anything about *strangling*?" He leaned in closer. "Look, the marshal doesn't have anything substantial on me and I doubt that there's anything he can pin on you."

"He should know that I loved Grannie. She put a roof over my head when I had nowhere else to go."

"You having her cremated like this looks suspicious as hell."

"I don't care how it looks. With Grannie's body burned up there's no evidence."

"Evidence of what?" Vint looked over at Wilkes who watched them with his hands folded in front of him.

"I don't know. I just don't want the marshal railroading either one of us. You heard the way he was talking. He's liable to trump something up against you."

"I don't know about that. I know he's not too wild about me but ..."

"If he locked you up, I'd kill him and Anfield, and break you out of jail." She scowled. "I swear."

"Keep it down." Vint noticed Wilkes studying them intently. "You're getting yourself worked up."

She took a deep breath. "I'm OK."

"Let's get back to Wilkes."

When they walked back to the funeral director, Lark said, "She was my grandmother, not the marshal's. He shouldn't have any say in the matter." She opened her purse and pulled out a stack of money. "I've been saving up for a car. But this is more important."

"I, I just don't know." Wilkes stared at the bills in her hand. "I don't want to get in any trouble. There are certain protocols ..."

"Did Doc Harris give you a death certificate?"

"Yes. But the cause of death hasn't been established yet. There was some talk of an autopsy."

"I don't want anyone cutting up my Grannie like a frog in biology class. Her last hours in this world shouldn't be spent having someone slicing up her naked body and poking at her. Grannie was powerful modest. She'd be humiliated."

"I understand your concerns but ... people will talk."

"Grannie was old. She died." She tapped the cash into her right hand. "How much will it cost to cremate her?"

"$125, plus $20 for a nice brass urn."

"Here's $250. Everything I got. Go start your oven or whatever you do."

"Maybe I should call Doc first, or the marshal." Wilkes stared at the wad of cash.

"You either do this now or I'm taking Grannie out of here. I'll tote her on my back if I have to." Lark shoved the cash back in her purse. "Damn it! I'll take her to Booneville and have her taken care of there!"

Wilkes' voice softened. "Would you like to say goodbye to Grannie one last time?" He held his hand out, palm up.

"Yes." She took the money out again but held onto it. "Where is she?"

The smell of embalming fluid became stronger with every step as Wilkes led the two down to the basement where Grannie lay on a table, covered head to toe by a white sheet.

As the three gathered around the table, Wilkes pulled the cloth down revealing Grannie's discolored, contorted face.

"Poor old Grannie." Lark slapped the stack of bills into Wilkes' hand. "Looks like she's sleeping."

Vint studied Grannie, who looked anything but peaceful to him. "God rest her soul."

Chapter 19

"Bunch of busybodies." Lark scowled as she clung to Vint's arm while scanning the crowd in Wilkes Funeral Home. "Look at them all watching us … whispering."

"What did you expect?" Vint talked out the side of his mouth. "Let's stick around for another hour, then thank everyone for coming."

"I think most of them came for the cake and cookies. That one over there …" She waved a finger. "Grannie thought she was a birdbrain. Don't know what *she's* doing here."

"Well, they came straight from church. Already had their Sunday best on. Yeah, just about everyone in town's here except the Skinners."

"And a certain female." She pinched Vint's arm.

"Stop that." He pulled his arm away. "I don't think we'll be seeing Adelle today. Not the type to rub elbows with common folk. She's pretty uppity for an ex-stripper who married into money."

"Look at them munching away like they're at an all-you-can-eat buffet. They're standing around watching Grannie's urn on that pedestal as if she's going to pop out like a genie."

"Get a load of Wilkes back there in the doorway." Vint smirked and nodded his head back. "Looks like the damn cat that swallowed the canary. That man must *really* love money."

Pimply faced Grover walked in, took off his cowboy hat, saw Vint and went right back out the door.

Ned, the barber, saw what happened and smiled uneasily at Vint, nodding his head.

"Looks like Grannie's memorial service is the social event of the year." Lark ran her hand across Vint's chest. "You look scrumptious in that suit. My, my."

"I never saw *you* so dressed up. Look pretty sexy." He leaned closer and took a whiff. "Smell good too."

"This was my graduation dress. There's not much in the way of fashion in this town. Most of these ladies make their own dresses."

"You must have drove the boys crazy back in high school, probably some of the teachers too."

"Oh, I don't know. I only had eyes for Danny." She sighed. "We were king and queen of the prom."

"Still miss him?"

"Not anymore." She put her arm around Vint and gave him a squeeze. "I appreciate you being here. You didn't have to come with me and put up with this circus. I'll thank you later, handsome."

"You read my mind."

Vint nodded to Pete, who followed his chubby wife around while he ate forkfuls of yellow cake with white coconut frosting. "I worked with him over at Hurst." Vint pointed with his chin. "Even in that cheap suit he's wearing, he looks like he's going to start hauling lumber around any second."

"I liked it better when you were working." She lightly elbowed him. "Got in less trouble."

"Even old Jacob from the hardware is here." Vint motioned with his thumb. "Still wearing that polka-dot bowtie. Got some real characters in this town."

"I heard the only time he takes that pipe out of his mouth is to eat. Probably sleeps with it."

"I can't wait for this to be over." He made a sour face. "Even with all these flowers you can still smell that embalming fluid coming up from the basement."

"See the way those church ladies keep looking over here. Bunch of dried up old biddies. You know that they're talking about me. Saying I killed my own Grannie. I don't know why I should put up with this. Ought to go over there right now and give them a piece of my mind."

"Don't bother. They're not worth it." Vint took Lark's wrist and glanced at her watch. "Less than an hour and this'll be over. We can go back to your place and get out of these clothes."

Dewey walked in and went straight to the two of them. He took Lark's hand and said, "I want you to know I don't believe any of the rumors about you. You couldn't hurt a flea."

"Well, thank you, Dewey. So nice to know you don't think I'm a murderer."

"I told everyone, our Lark, she can't even squash a bug, let alone kill her own grandmother."

"Euw." Lark shivered. "I hate bugs."

"Think I'll go over and try one of those lemon squares."

"You do that, Dewey." She shook her head as he made a beeline to the sweet table.

Vint's face tightened as he looked out. "Notice how that ass-kissing foreman, Gerald, stays on the other side of the room with that wife of his? She reminds me of Olive Oyl." His voice turned gruff. "Prick won't even look in my direction. I ought to drag him outside and smack him around a while."

She lightly slapped his arm. "Don't start anything."

Edric slowly opened the front door of the funeral home and glanced around. He spotted Vint, then approached him and Lark, extending his hand. "Miss Stookey, so sorry for your loss."

She shook his hand. "The mysterious Edric Randall. Did you know Grannie?"

"Why, no. Never had the pleasure." Edric cleared his throat. "Vint, my dear boy. May I please have a moment of your time? I'd like to speak to you about an urgent matter."

"Sure, counselor."

"Outside?" Edric raised his eyebrows, spun on his heel and headed for the door.

"Be right back." Vint went to pat Lark's rear but stopped himself.

He followed Edric out onto the elongated wooden porch into the early afternoon sun. He pulled out his pack of Old Gold and put one in his mouth. "What's so important? I don't think we should be seen hobnobbing too much." He took out the silver lighter Adelle had given him and lit his smoke. "Considering what we have planned."

"To use an American colloquialism, I'm a little short, Vint."

"Look about six-foot to me." Vint blew smoke in his direction.

"Oh. You jest." Edric flashed an insincere smile. "I find myself low on funds at the moment and was wondering if you could advance me a few quid?"

"Talk English."

"I thought that's what I was doing."

"I mean American English like a normal guy." Vint flicked his ash onto the porch.

"Vint, could you please lend me three dollars? Is that better?"

"A little thirsty, are we?"

"Considering the high-stakes proposition I'm dumping in your lap, one would think you'd be more than happy to share whatever you have with me."

Vint put the Old Gold between his full lips and removed his wallet from his inside suitcoat pocket. He pulled out two dollars and held them out.

Edric took the money and looked Vint in the eye. "You ought to be a bit more courteous to those that have the power to change your life, for better or worse."

"I'm just having a little fun with you, Limey. Don't get your knickers in a twist."

"Exactly what I'm talking about." Edric turned and sternly peered back at Vint as he went down the porch steps.

"Have a great afternoon guzzling gin." Vint took a deep drag, then pitched his cigarette onto the neatly mowed front lawn. He walked back in blowing smoke out the side of his mouth.

As he headed toward Lark, Adelle's secretary, Margaret, locked her arm through his and strolled along. "Honey chile, you clean up nice. Look like a movie star. Mmm, I could eat you up."

Vint stopped and pulled his arm from hers. "Where's your husband today?"

"Oh. That lazy bastard. On Sunday, all he wants to do is read the paper, listen to the radio and drink his homemade hooch. Won't even shave. Calls it his day of rest. I don't know why. That's what he does every day."

"You need a hobby, lady."

"I could make you my hobby."

He looked over at Lark who watched the two of them steely-eyed. "I already got one."

"When're you coming back to work? Place isn't the same without you."

"Looks like I'll be reporting back tomorrow morning. Not that I want to."

"Well, see you then, big boy. Maybe we could take a break together sometime and get to know each other better."

"Yeah, maybe. I got to get back to Lark." He bowed his head slightly. "If you'll excuse me."

"What did Margie want?" Lark put her hands on her hips as Vint approached. "As if I didn't know."

Changing the subject, he said, "See who's sitting in the corner over there? The Harrells. Haven't seen those two since they identified me in jail. Notice how they avoid eye contact with me?"

"You're not going to win any popularity contests in *this* town."

"Well, well. Lee, our friendly neighborhood bartender's here too. Prick." Vint spoke with a tight jaw. "And check out little Dickie over there with his mother, eating fig newtons like they're some kind of delicacy. I got one piece of advice for that squirt, stay out of the tavern."

"I could say the same to a certain someone. I don't know what it is about you, trouble seems to follow you wherever you go."

"At least that Dumbo-eared barfly, Elroy, had the good sense not to show up here." Vint nudged her. "That Anfield doesn't quit giving me dirty looks, I'm going over there and push his face in."

"Please don't start any trouble. Have a little respect for Grannie."

"Never saw him out of uniform before. Figured he slept in the thing." Vint smirked. "Who's that runt he's with. She's got a face like a Pekingese."

"Some girl from over in Gray Rock he's dating. Seems nice."

"Yeah, if you like midgets. Looks like she's part leprechaun. Could you imagine if they had kids?"

Lark giggled. "Stop it, Vint. This is supposed to be a solemn occasion. If these people see me laughing they'll think I really did murder Grannie."

"Yeah, well, I'm still not convinced you didn't give her a little boost toward Heaven somehow."

"How could you think such a thing about me?" She scowled at him. "Even for a moment?"

"Trust me, it's not that hard."

She shook a fist at him. "I ought to kill you for just thinking such a thing."

"OK. Truce." He put his hands out in front of him. "Let's just say, I think any one of us could kill under the right circumstances."

"Yeah? Well, let's just say, I think you have a way of getting under people's skin. And someone's liable to find the right circumstances with you someday."

Vint huffed and folded his arms in front of him. "Why is that Anfield such a prick all the time?" He grimaced. "Little bastard."

"He always had a thing for me." She ran her fingers along the mohair material of his suit sleeve. "Jealous, I guess."

"I thought something was up. The way he's always eyeballing you. Ever go out with him?"

"I let him take me to the show one time. He kept trying to hold my hand." She frowned. "I don't like him like that."

His shoulders tensed. "I'd like to beat the living piss out of him sometime."

Lark turned from Vint and looked at the front door. "Oh, how nice. Shadrack's here."

His mood softening again, Vint said, "His wife's really nice looking, you know, I mean for him. Whoa, look at all those kids. Four, five … six of them including the baby girl tucked in his arm."

Shadrack lumbered up, his upper body swaying side to side. "Hello, Lark. You know my wife, Jewel." He put a huge hand on his spouse's shoulder.

"How do you do?" Jewel folded her hands in front of her and bowed her head. "So sorry about your Grannie."

"Thank you." Lark caressed the cheek of the little girl cradled in Shadrack's left arm. "Well look at this pretty little lady."

"Looks like her mama," Shadrack said, smiling at his wife. "Thank the Lord."

Noticing the children eyeballing the bakery goods, Lark said to Jewel, "Why don't you take the kids over to the sweet table? There's plenty there. We'll talk more later."

Vint watched the kids grabbing cookies from paper plates. "Six kids. Looks like they're all about a year apart. Now I know what he does when he's not cooking. Guy's a regular pistol."

Lark put her hand over her mouth to hide her smile. "Stop it." She forced back a laugh. "Please."

"Guess Sally had to close up for a while. No one's in her restaurant, including her."

"I see the way she keeps giving you the eye. Sure you never did anything with her?"

"Come on. Give me more credit than that. I'm not that hard up." He rubbed his smoothly shaved chin. "Maybe if she had a lot of dough."

Vint saw Cornie slink in from the rear entrance of the room, still dressed in his prison blues. He went straight to the snack table, loaded up his pockets and carried out a slice of cake in each hand.

"Oh, great," Vint said through clenched teeth, "Gilstrap."

Dressed in his marshal's uniform, Gilstrap went straight to Vint and Lark. "Think you outsmarted me, young lady? This is far from over. I'm just getting started with you."

Vint interceded, "Hey, go sell your wolf tickets somewhere else."

"I'm not through with you either, boy. So, don't push your luck." He turned back to Lark. "I could arrest you for obstruction of justice, destroying evidence."

"Well go ahead, arrest me," she said, raising her voice. "You don't scare me, ya big palooka."

Everyone in the room stopped talking and watched the three.

Lark clenched her fists at her sides. "How dare you come into Grannie's memorial service and threaten me."

Gilstrap looked around. "Calm down."

"I won't calm down. Try and make me. I can turn people against you in the next election if I want."

Vint took her arm but she shook him off.

"If I was you, I'd find another place to eat." She glared at Gilstrap. "You come into the diner again you might not like what you get."

"What's that supposed to mean?"

"Just watch yourself, buddy, that's all." She waved her finger around with a wild look in her eyes. "You and all these other people with your gossip and rumors. Get out! All of you! Leave me and Grannie be!"

The marshal leaned forward and pointed. "I think you better get hold of yourself."

"Or what?" She put her fists on her hips.

"I'll arrest you for threatening an officer of the law."

"Oh, really." Lark stomped over to the pedestal in the center of the room and grabbed Grannie's urn. "Think I'm guilty of something? You want evidence? Here you go." She removed the lid to the brass urn and dropped the lid on the floor. She heaved the urn toward Gilstrap, causing ashes to fly in his face.

The marshal gasped, causing him to breath in ashes. He coughed uncontrollably and rubbed at his face wildly. "Agh, agh!" he yelled between coughs.

"Well? What're y'all waiting for?" Lark walked among the crowd holding the urn. "Get out!" She started shaking Grannie's ashes onto people as they backed away. They dropped their snacks and ran toward the door.

"This isn't over." Gilstrap wheezed and brushed himself off as he stumbled backwards.

Vint looked around the empty room that was littered with ashes, partially eaten pastries and other goodies. Scattered on the floral designs of the carpet were tipped over paper cups, spilled coffee and lemonade. He nodded to Lark and said, "You know how to throw a party, kid."

Lark stood silent, breathing heavily while clutching the urn. She stared off as tears began filling her eyes.

Mr. Wilkes gingerly approached them from the corner of the room. "I think this will conclude today's services. Wouldn't you agree?"

* * *

Later that night, Vint shoved open the front door of Cooper's tavern. All eight customers, plus the bartender, Lee, turned to look at him. He went straight to the bar and slapped two dollars down.

Lee, chewing on the end of a stick match, went right up to Vint. "Turn around and git. Don't want your business."

"Come on, big guy." Vint stuck his hand out. "Let bygones be bygones."

"Last time you were in here," Lee looked at Vint's hand and spit the match out, "you busted four bottles of booze."

"Plus the one you handed over to get rid of me. That was pretty good stuff." Vint laughed, then put a couple more dollars on the bar. "How about we split the difference," he raised his voice, "and I buy a round for the house."

"Hell yeah," patrons called out in approval, "I'll take another, Lee."

"You crazy son-of-a-bitch." Lee shook his head, then went up and down the bar setting up drinks. He came back to Vint and asked, "What're you having?"

"Highball."

Lee set his drink in front of him. "No fighting tonight. All right?"

"I'm not looking for trouble." Vint took a sip. "But if it finds me …"

Lee grabbed some of Vint's cash from the bar and walked away muttering.

* * *

"Lee." Vint looked up from his paperback after four drinks and called out, "Give me one more." He noticed that the highballs Lee was serving him were very strong.

"Here ya go, buster." The bartender set another bourbon and ginger ale on ice in front of Vint.

Looking at the rich brown color in his glass, Vint remarked, "I like the way you're pouring."

Lee smirked, took some of Vint's change and went back to talking to other customers.

Vint took a sip and found it even more potent than the last one. He swirled his glass and took another mouthful, trying to shake the feeling that things seemed off. Two beefy guys that he never saw before came in about an hour after him. They were playing pool and shooting him dirty looks.

Twangy guitars and nasally voices emanated from the jukebox as Vint stubbed out his cigarette and took another gulp of booze. Glancing up at the clock on the wall over the bar, he figured that Lee kept the time about ten minutes fast to help get the last few drunks out a little early at closing time. The real time was a little after 10:00 pm. Lark would still be up.

The two pool players dropped their cue sticks on the green felt of the table, then walked past Vint on their way out through the haze of cigarette and cigar smoke that hung suspended in the air. They mumbled something while watching him out of the corner of their eyes.

He was tired, just wanted to go back to Lark's and sleep. Downing his cocktail and getting to his feet, he put his book away feeling a little unsteady. Walking out the door and into the dark, Vint heard something odd. It sounded like muffled voices. He stood on the street and looked around listening but didn't notice anything out of place. As he walked toward his Nash, he heard a rustling sound but couldn't tell where it was coming from. He followed the dull glint of the moon reflecting on top of his sedan, wondering if Lark had set something out for him to eat.

When he got a few feet from the car, he saw something fly over his head. He ducked, thinking it was probably a bat, but whatever it was, it hit the ground with a dull thud about six feet behind him. Taking a couple steps closer, he saw that it was a dead crow.

A sudden burst of commotion alarmed him, but before he could tell what was going on, everything went black. Feeling scratchy wool on his face, he realized a blanket had been thrown over his head. He felt a sharp pain on his shin, a quick blow to the back of his head, then was shoved to the ground by a number of hands.

He gasped when something hard hit him across the back. Fending off repeated blows, he heard a familiar sounding voice say, "Bust his teeth out." Another man called, "Yeah, mess up his face."

Bringing his arms up, Vint felt hard objects hitting his forearms and elbows. He shot to his feet and tried pushing the blanket off but stumbled back against his car. He stood, taking a pounding, leaning against the sedan, then fell to the ground when something hit him hard on top of his head. The only thing he could see were boots and shoes kicking at him and he managed to roll under the car. Kicking back, he pushed himself further under, lifted the blanket off his face and pulled out his razor.

Only able to see out of one eye because of the blood running down his face, Vint saw the legs of the men running away, then disappearing around the corner of the drug store.

Vint crawled out from under his car with pain radiating from his head, arms, back and legs. He got to his knees and squinted at his car, blinking away blood. Pulling a handkerchief from his back pocket, he wiped his eyes. He reached for the door handle and pulled himself to his feet but his bloody hand slipped off the handle and he went down again. Fighting hard against passing out, he pushed himself to his knees again with the help of the running board. He wiped the blood from his eyes again, then tied the handkerchief around his forehead like a bandana to keep the blood from streaming down. Looking back at the bar, he saw that the outside lights were still on but no one was in sight. Grabbing the handle again, he pulled himself up and opened the door. He got behind the wheel, turned on his dome light, and looked in the rearview mirror. His face was a mess.

Starting the car, Vint felt woozy. He was tempted to lie down and sleep but fought the urge. Putting his sedan in reverse, he backed into the street, then put it in first gear.

"Come on," he slurred, "it's only a few blocks." He drove along the street weaving, trying to keep his eyes open. His head dropped, then he quickly lifted it, steering away from a ditch. He turned onto Lark's street and told himself, "Keep going, a little bit more."

Parking crooked in Lark's driveway, Vint got out and put one foot in front of the other, over and over as his eyes rolled back. He stumbled up the steps and opened the front door. "Honey, I'm home."

Lark jumped up from the couch and screamed as Vint fell over.

He opened his eyes a couple minutes later with Lark shaking him and slapping his bloody face.

"I thought you were dead," she cried.

"Ice," he mumbled.

"What?"

"Ice. Bring some ice."

She ran into the kitchen and returned with a bowl of ice cubes, a dishcloth and a dishtowel. "I should call the doctor."

"No." He scooted a few feet and sat up with his back to the couch. "Bring me a mirror."

She placed the dishtowel on the couch behind him, then brought back a hand mirror and kneeled next to him. "You're not going to like it."

Vint held the mirror to his face. It was covered in blood. His once white bandana now totally red. "Where am I bleeding from?"

Lark inspected him closely. "You have a gash on top of your head. I'm getting the doctor. You need stitches."

"No. No doctors. No cops." He turned his face side to side looking in the mirror. "Ice the cut. You're going to sew me up."

"I can't do that."

"You can sew, can't you?"

"Yeah." Her lower lip quivered. "But not skin."

"Fill that cloth with ice and hand it to me."

"Please, let me get Doc Harris."

"No. Damn it." Vint took the compress and put it on his wound. He flinched and said, "We're keeping this to ourselves. I'm not going to let this get around, not giving anyone the satisfaction."

"Oh, Vint." Tears streamed down her cheeks.

"Go get a damn needle, some black thread and scissors. Let's get this over with. It's not going to be any more pleasant for me than it is you."

Vint sat on the floor holding the ice to the gash until Lark returned with a needle and thread. He held the mirror over his head inspecting his wound. "How big is it?"

"About an inch."

"That's not so bad." He put the ice-filled cloth back on his head. "Only about five stitches. I'd do it myself but I can't see what I'm doing up there and I'm in a lot of pain."

"I think I'm gonna be sick."

"Come on. Hang in there with me. Get my bourbon and a small bowl."

When she returned, Vint took the bottle from her hand and took a swig. He poured a little in the bowl and said, "Dip the needle in there, then pour some on my cut." He handed the bottle back.

She threaded the needle, then set it in the whiskey. "Put your head back. I don't want to get any in your eyes."

Vint's body stiffened and his fists tightened as she poured. Through clenched teeth, he said, "OK, let's get this over with."

Lark took the needle from the bowl and straightened up on her knees. "Are you sure?"

"Push the hair away from the cut. You don't want to get any in there. Then squeeze the skin together."

"It's still bleeding."

"I know." He took another belt of booze. "Put the first stitch in."

As she pushed the needle into his scalp, he groaned, "Good girl. Keep going."

"Oh, my God. I don't feel good."

"How do you think I feel?" He held the mirror up. "Tie it off and get on to the next one. This'll be over soon. Then I can get cleaned up."

After she finished the last stitch, Vint said, "Give me a hand." He winced in pain as she helped him to his feet. "Let's inspect the damage," he added, stumbling toward the bathroom.

"Here, let me help you." Lark put the plug in the tub and began filling it with warm water. She helped him out of his clothes and when he was undressed, she said, "Dear, Lord. You got marks and cuts all over."

Vint sat in the tub and let her scrub the blood from his head and face. After she washed his hair and rinsed him a few times, she said, "Your face doesn't look as bad as I thought. Just a mark under your left eye. When I saw you covered in blood …"

He held his forearms up. They were decorated with small lacerations and lumps. "This is how my face would've looked if I didn't cover up."

"I don't see any broken bones or anything." She lathered his hairy chest. "You wanna talk about it?"

"Some of the local boys, maybe a couple out-of-towners, threw me a blanket party."

"Do you know who they were?"

"No. But I have a few ideas." Vint's face tightened. "Go get me that bottle, sweetie."

Chapter 20

Vint opened his eyes late in the morning to find Lark dressed and kneeling next to the bed, watching him. He winced, propping himself on one elbow. "God, it hurts."

"What hurts?" She caressed his cheek.

"Everything. Bring me something for the pain."

Lark returned with a glass of water and three aspirin.

"I'm going to rest up today." He sucked in air through clenched teeth as he sat up. "But tomorrow I'm showing my face up and down Main."

"Aren't you afraid something'll happen again?" She sat next to him on the bed.

"Nothing's going to happen to me." He popped the pills in his mouth and washed them down with cool well water.

"Why do you want to do that?" She put her hand on his shoulder. "You should just stay in for a few days."

He handed the glass back. "I'm going to the bar, Sally's, Dewey's ... I don't care how much pain I'm in, I'm going to walk around, smile and act like nothing happened."

"Well, if you go around smiling, people will suspect something's off right away."

"Real funny, blondie." Vint looked at her sideways. "You know what I mean. I have to show whoever did this to me that I'm invincible. I have to give that appearance. It'll make anyone think twice about messing with me again."

"You have that much pride?"

"It's not just pride. It's for my safety. Why do you think I had you use black thread?"

Lark inspected her handiwork. "So it blends in with your hair?"

"Exactly." He nodded. "Light me a cigarette, doll."

* * *

"That was Grannie's recipe." Lark took the soup bowl from Vint as he lay in bed. "How was it?"

"Great. Thanks."

She set the bowl on the floor. "I'm not through taking care of you yet." Pulling his cover and sheet down, she gave him a sly smile.

"Whoa." He held onto his boxers as she began tugging on them. "Hey. I'm too sore to even move."

"You're not gonna have to." She yanked his boxers down to his knees.

"Look. Maybe in a day or two."

She began stroking him. "You sure about that?" she asked, as he became hard.

"Uh, yeah. I mean no. I mean ..."

Lark stood and removed all her clothes, then pulled her hair loose from its ponytail. She kneeled on the bed, straddling him, then lowered herself onto him, guiding him in with her hand. She gently rocked back and forth while moving up and down. She gazed into his eyes. "Want me to stop?"

"No. No." His chest heaved. "Keep going."

"I know how to take care of my man." She laced her fingers behind her head and sped up her movement.

Vint caressed her breasts while she shoved herself against him harder and harder. She leaned down so she was cheek to cheek with him, thrusting until they both climaxed simultaneously.

"You OK?" she asked breathing heavily next to his ear.

"Happy as a beaver with a log."

Chapter 21

After staying in bed most of the day and night Monday, Vint got up late morning Tuesday, shaved, took a bath, and got dressed. He brought a wet rag with him out to his sedan and wiped his dried blood off the seat and steering wheel.

In sunny, mid-eighties weather, he drove to Main Street, and parked in front of Dewey's, where Lark had already been waiting on customers for a couple hours. He walked down to the drug store, went in and nodded to the pharmacist. Heading back to the soda cooler with his body and head aching, he pulled out a bottle of Orchard peach soda. He bent down with a wince and popped off the cap with the built-in opener, trying hard to conceal his pain.

"Anything else for you today?" The pharmacist peered at Vint over half-glasses perched on a long nose decorated with a few short dark hairs.

Vint placed a nickel on the counter. "That'll be all."

Stepping out onto the sidewalk into the light breeze, he headed east up one side of Main then back again on the other side as a few cars passed. After pausing to look at the newspaper in the window of the barbershop, he kept moving. Vint gulped some of his drink, crossed the street and walked into Cooper's tavern.

Lee's eyes flashed at the sight of Vint strolling in as though nothing had happened to him.

Vint put the half-finished bottle of soda on the bar. "Give me a real drink, Lee." He plopped a quarter down. "Shot of bourbon."

Filling a shot glass to the brim, Lee looked at Vint cagily, then slid it toward him. "How ya doin' today?"

"Fine." Vint picked up the shot, careful not to spill any, and downed it. "You?"

"I'm great. You git home all right the other night?"

"Yeah." Vint set the glass down on the bar harder than necessary. "Why wouldn't I?"

"Oh, nothing." Lee glanced around the room. "You had five highballs. Just checkin'."

Vint stared at Lee until he returned his gaze. "Because you're so concerned about me?"

"Well, I like to make sure my customers ..."

Vint shoved the shot glass toward him. "Hit me again." He flipped one more quarter on the bar.

Lee poured him another ounce of whiskey. "A little early in the day for you, ain't it?"

"I'm on vacation." Vint threw his aching head back and swallowed the booze in one gulp. He looked Lee in the eye for a moment, then tossed a dollar on the bar. "Give me a pint of that Gordon's gin."

Lee slipped a bottle into a small paper bag, set it on the bar in front of Vint and took the dollar.

"See you around." Vint grabbed the bottle, walked out and went down a few doors to Sally's. He opened the door and nodded to her. "What's your dinner special today?"

"Hey, handsome. I was wonderin' when I'd see you again." Sally glanced up at her Dr. Pepper wall clock. "I'm servin' up chicken fried steak in a few hours."

"Maybe I'll see you then."

"Please do," she called as he closed the door.

"Son-of-a-fuck," he muttered in pain under his breath as he slowly paced down to Dewey's and tossed the bottle of gin through the open window of his Nash.

Vint pushed the diner door open, then strolled back to where he usually sat. Lark set a plate of black-eyed peas and collard greens with biscuits and gravy in front of a customer. She turned from the table and watched him struggle to look at ease.

Dewey put down the glass he was drying as he stood behind the counter. He walked down to Vint and pushed his white sailor cap back. "Heard some talk in here earlier that there might've been some trouble in town Sunday night."

"Who'd you hear that from?"

"Deputy Anfield."

"Anfield," Vint said through clenched teeth. "Doesn't surprise me."

"You OK?"

"Sure. Any reason why I shouldn't be?"

"No ... no." Dewey backed up a step. "How'd you get that mouse under your eye?"

Lark put her order pad in her apron pocket as she walked up to Vint.

Vint pointed toward his eye. "That's nothing." He turned and smiled at Lark. "A little love-tap from Lark. She's got a great right-cross."

"Oh, don't be silly. That was an accident. I opened the door into him." She touched his face. "How does it feel?"

"Don't feel a thing. Why don't you bring me a glass of beer, a raw egg and some hot sauce."

Dewey scrunched up his face, shook his head, and went back to drying glasses.

Lark went behind the counter, grabbed a can of Pearl Lager from the cooler, a beer glass, and said, "Shadrack, hand me an egg."

Shadrack's face appeared in the service window. "Hardboiled?"

She stuck her hand out. "Raw." She took the egg and brought all four items to Vint. "Here you go, killer," she said, opening the can.

Vint cracked the shell, plopped the egg into his glass, added a few shakes of hot sauce, then poured beer in over it. He drank it all down and wiped his mouth with a paper napkin.

"You in a big hurry to be somewhere?" Lark put a hand on her hip. "I could've had Shadrack cook it first."

"I went through Gramps' closet. Spotted an old fedora, coat and pants I'd like to borrow."

"You don't have to borrow them." She turned his cup upright and poured him some coffee. "You can have them if you want."

"Good." He glanced around and spoke in low tones. "Keep your ears open. There's bound to be some talk about what happened in front of the bar. Whoever knows too much was probably involved."

"What're you gonna do when you find out who did it?"

Vint made a fist. "I'm going to catch them, one by one."

"Do you know how many there were?"

"Five or six." He winced in pain as he brought his boot up to the rung of his stool. "Five ... pretty sure. Almost positive one of them was Anfield. Recognized his voice."

"He's the law, better not mess with him."

"That badge isn't going to help him."

"Please don't." She put her hand on his.

"I'll need a good alibi. And an old blanket."

* * *

Vint drove to Hurst Lumber, got out of his car and tried not to hobble as he made his way into the outer office.

"Well, look what the pussy dragged in." Margaret beamed at Vint. "This place's been a bore without you."

"She in there?" He nodded toward Adelle's private office.

"Where else? Knock first." Margaret lowered her voice. "She's not in a good mood."

"Is she ever?" Vint rapped on the door and over the sporadic racket heard Adelle call out, "Come in."

He closed the door behind him and walked up to her desk. "How've you been?"

"Never mind how I've been." She looked at her watch. "It's two in the afternoon, and you were supposed to report here yesterday morning."

"Couldn't make it. Got jumped by a bunch of guys Sunday night." He eased down onto the chair across from her desk. "I'm sore as a whore with the fleet in."

"So that's how you got the mark under your eye? When you walked in I thought maybe you got caught screwing someone's wife."

"That's a line I don't cross. I don't mess with married women."

"*You* have scruples?" She smirked slightly.

"There's plenty things I won't do."

Adelle sat studying him for a moment. "You know, you're not that hard to figure, Mr. Tough Guy. You'll have sex with a woman but you won't make love to her. You'll screw her but won't kiss her."

"I don't need your amateur psychoanalysis, lady."

"You're a rolling stone," she continued in a cool, matter-of-fact manner. "Can't get too close to anyone. You treat women like doormats so they won't love you or get too close. Love makes you uncomfortable because you don't know how to love. Never had it in your formative years when a kid really needs it."

"OK, enough." He put his hand up. "Shut up about it. You don't know me."

"I don't, huh?" Adelle sat back and crossed her legs. "You're just like my father, God rest his soul. The only way he knew how to love me was the wrong way. He related to me the only way he knew how to relate to a female."

"Do I need to hear all this?"

"I think you need to hear it from someone." She gestured. "Look at you, your body tightens up just at the talk of intimacy."

Vint waved his hand and looked away.

"You're mad at the world because no one loved you, no one held you and comforted you as a child. You go around fighting all the time because you're trying to get back at everyone who didn't give a damn."

"I'm going." He stood up. "We'll talk later when you get off your soapbox."

"Come on. Sit down. That's all I have to say on the subject."

"No. I'm going." He grabbed his lower back. "Give me a few days before I come back to work. Can you handle Gilstrap?"

"I'll see what I can do. I really do need all the hands I can get right now. So, heal fast."

* * *

Vint drove from Hurst Lumber straight to the bakery and parked out front. He got out of his old Nash and stiffly climbed the outdoor wooden steps.

Edric opened his door after the second knock. "I wasn't expecting you so early." He stepped aside as Vint entered. "You don't look so good, old chap."

Vint pulled the pint of gin from the slim paper bag and held it toward Edric. "Because you've been such a good boy."

"Thank you." Edric took the bottle and scrutinized the label. "But do you have to be so flip?"

"As a matter of fact, I do." Vint took a seat at the kitchen table. "It's in my contract. Read the small print."

"I should know better than to say anything." Edric went to the cupboard and produced two glasses. "I prefer my gin chilled but, oh well, what the hell." He couldn't contain a smile as he poured them both a generous amount of spirits.

"OK, Eddie, fill me in."

Edric huffed, rolled his eyes, then sat down. "One week from tomorrow, Wednesday. Let's plan on you being at the Krauses', 9:00 pm, precisely."

"Sounds good." Vint took a sip of gin, then looked at his glass. "You wouldn't happen to have some ice and a couple olives?"

"Afraid not." Edric gulped some liquor. "Do you have your alibi in place?"

"Yeah. I think I got it covered." Vint noticed the handle of a pistol protruding slightly from inside the Englishman's suitcoat.

"Don't think." Edric tapped an index finger to his temple, then pointed at Vint. "Know."

Vint set his glass down. "I'm having second thoughts about this whole thing."

"Losing your nerve, old boy?"

"No. I'm not losing my nerve." Vint looked at him harshly. "Things just don't add up. That much loot just sitting there waiting for me to come by and pick it up." He waved a finger. "Another thing. How am I supposed to spend this old money? It's bound to be reported missing."

"The wise thing would be to take it out of the country and exchange it. That's what I plan to do. Why, you could go to Mexico and live like a king on that kind of wealth. Either that or exchange it a little at a time in small state banks around the country. Your choice."

"I'll give it some thought." Vint rubbed his chin. "Mexico. That's an idea."

"We'll see each other one last time. To split the money. I'll meet you outside of town. As soon as you have the cash, drive west on Main, past Hurst Boulevard approximately five miles. You'll see an old brick silo set back on the left-hand side. There's a dirt road there. Turn left. Follow it back roughly a half-mile. To your right, you'll find the foundation of an old house."

"Yeah." Vint picked his glass up again. "Got it."

"I'll arrive approximately twenty minutes after you. My old DeSoto isn't much to look at, but it's dependable." Edric finished his glass. "You'll give me my share and we'll part company. I'm going to bury my end and head back to town. I don't plan to touch the money for at least one month. Only after I settle all my affairs here and answer all the questions I'm sure the marshal will throw at me. What about you?"

"Not sure." Vint hesitated, then said, "I got something else I'm supposed to wrap up before I leave town. But, if this thing goes as planned, I might just take off without a word."

Edric looked at Vint solemnly. "One more thing. You're going to need a gun."

"A gun?" Vint's inquired with tight a jaw.

"Yes, dear boy. One of those things with bullets, that goes bang bang."

"You told me this was a simple in-and-out job. Nobody gets hurt."

"It is," Edric said, his voice softening. "I promise. I'm only offering you a gun because I don't want an unforeseen incident to cause you any harm. I've grown fond of your peculiar ways and manners. I think about some of the things you say with a chuckle."

"Yeah. I'm a barrel of laughs." Vint's eyes narrowed. "Does Mr. Krause have a gun?"

"A shotgun," Edric answered matter-of-factly.

"When were you going to mention that tiny bit of information?"

"I didn't want to alarm you."

"Alarm me?" Vint raised his voice. "You trying to get me killed?"

"Of course not. If you get shot, I don't get my end of the money." Edric went into the other room and returned with his green alligator briefcase. He set the case on the table, opened it and pushed it toward Vint. "Here. Try this snubnose out."

Vint reached in, took out the small caliber revolver and handled it a bit.

"How does it feel?" Edric's eyes lit up.

"Not bad."

"Perhaps you'd like something more accurate, distance-wise." Edric pulled a .32 Colt revolver from his inside suitcoat pocket and handed it over. "Try this one."

Vint tried it out for feel and sighted down the long barrel. "Yeah. That's more like it."

"Thought so. It's really more your style."

Opening the cylinder and spinning it, Vint said, "Good. It's loaded."

"Put that thing in your trunk as soon as you get to your car. You don't want to take a chance of getting caught with a gun on you in this town. The marshal's a stickler for carrying weapons outside the home. One can transport an unloaded rifle in a case for hunting purposes only."

"Heard all about it." Vint set the pistol down.

"I'd suggest you have it with you when you go to the Krauses'. Just in case."

Vint nodded.

"We've been talking around a certain aspect of this deal." Edric poured himself some more gin. "I was hoping you'd be the one to bring it up."

"The double-cross? You think I might just head out of town the other direction and keep it all? I'd be lying if I said it didn't cross my mind. I may be a thief but I'm no swindler. I'm a bank robber. Except for an occasional pie from a windowsill, a chicken from a coop, a shirt off a clothesline as a kid, I've never robbed anyone of their personal possessions, nothing substantial. The Krauses' will be my first."

"Well, I feel a bit better." Edric downed his glass.

"I'm ambitious but I'm not greedy." Vint pointed at him. "Three-hundred Gs is plenty to get me on my way. I never cheated a friend or partner. That stuff always has a way of coming back and biting you on the ass." He put his hand out. "You have my word. I'll be there with your share."

"All right, Vint." He smiled and shook Vint's hand. "I believe you. Yes. Feel much better."

"Now that brings us to the part where you're supposed to convince me that *you're* not going to pull a fast one on *me*."

"How so?" Edric shrugged.

"You know how so. Like a loaded pistol waiting for me when I pull up, or turn my back."

"I wouldn't dream of it, my good man. I abhor violence." Edric put both hands out. "I'm a barrister, not a gunslinger. Please believe me. I would never cross you."

"Guess that'll have to do. We're just going to have to trust each other." Vint raised his glass in salute, then drank what was left. "What're you going to do with your split?"

"Going back to the motherland. I'll have enough to get myself out of the legal mess I left behind and actually practice law again in a civilized land."

"Level with me." Vint poured himself some more spirits. "What's your story?"

"Ahh. I was at the top of my game." Edric looked up at the ceiling. "A respected attorney in the London courts. I don't want to go into it all, but I found myself in a sticky wicket. Seems I was damned if I did, damned if I didn't."

"Bent the rules a little?"

"Yes. I broke my vows and ... what ended up happening was beyond my imagination. A total mess."

Vint waved his glass in Edric's direction. "So, you made a quick getaway."

"With this suit on my back and the money in my pocket. I hopped a freighter and arrived in New York a couple weeks later. Made a few bob here and there giving legal advice. I'm not licensed to practice law in this country and received a stern warning from the authorities. So, I moved around the country, finding it safer to hang a shingle in little nowhere towns like this where they don't ask as many questions."

"So, your dream is to go back and clear your name."

"I had a home, family, friends. Everything I love is in Great Britain." He raised his glass high and proclaimed, "God save the Queen."

"Hell with that. Here's to the US of A. Greatest country in the world. Land of opportunity." Vint downed his glass.

"What about you?" Edric raised an eyebrow. "What're you going to do with your share?"

"I kind of wanted to open an upscale saloon, live in a suite above it. Maybe out in California somewhere. But that much money, three hundred Gs, has me rethinking my plan. I don't know. A racetrack sounds nice. Always liked the ponies." Vint looked at his empty glass, slid it closer to Edric and pointed at it. "Maybe even a whorehouse, with only the finest prostitutes one could imagine. Have to give it some thought."

"To dream. Ahh, to dream." Edric poured some more into his glass, then Vint's. "We are such stuff … as dreams are made on …"

"That sounded kind of poetic. You a poet, Eddie?"

"Oh, for God's sake, quit referring to me with that pedestrian epithet. That was Shakespeare, my dear boy. The Great Bard."

"Well, I wrote a poem, just now, for this special occasion."

"You surprise me, Vint. Please go on."

"Roses are red. Violets are blue. You double-cross me and I'll split your fucking head open."

"Indeed. You're a natural born poet." Edric drained his glass. "A Pulitzer Prize winning ode, no doubt."

"I don't need any prizes, just a lot of dough."

Edric stood and stumbled slightly. "I'm going to take a nap. Do what you wish." He undid his tie, pulled it off and hung it over his chair. "Finish the bottle if you'd like. Just lock the door as you leave."

As Edric walked into the living room area and untucked his shirt, Vint picked up the bottle. There was less than an ounce left, so he drained it, then let the drops fall on his tongue. He stood, stuck the revolver in the waist of his pants and pulled his jacket over it. After turning the door lock, he stepped out into the late afternoon sun. Vint closed the door behind him, then slowly descended the stairs, keeping an eye out for the marshal.

Chapter 22

Vint glanced around the nearly empty diner after finishing his late morning breakfast. "Pretty slow in here since you showered ashes on everyone." He lit an Old Gold. "Guess you could say they all took a little piece of Grannie with them."

"Oh, they'll come around again." Lark freshened up Vint's coffee. "Only other place in town to eat is Sally's. You can only take so much of that heavy food over there."

"It's been three days. You know Gilstrap's going to be in here sooner or later. Or he'll show up at your house. You're going to have to answer for what you did."

"I know. So far, no news is good news."

"What the hell possessed you anyway?" He motioned toward her with his cigarette.

"I don't know. I don't know." Lark brought her hands to her face. "I don't want to talk about it." She raised her voice. "Don't want to think about it."

"All right." His voice softened. "Settle down."

"I don't know what to do. My mind keeps going around in circles." She rubbed her temples with her fingertips. "I feel like my brain is caught in a twister."

"You got to get a hold of yourself. Try thinking about something pleasant. Like being on a picnic or something."

She stood with her eyes closed, breathing deeply.

Vint reached out, took her hand and patted it. "Calm down."

After a minute, her breathing slowed and she opened her eyes. "What's that concoction I see you brushing your teeth with?"

"Peroxide and baking soda." He laughed a little. "Keeps your teeth white."

"I was wondering. With all those cigarettes and all that coffee."

"Got to say, never met anyone like you." He looked at her quizzically. "And I've met a lot of people."

"What're you saying? Is that good or bad?"

"Just different, that's all," he said, with the cigarette in the corner of his mouth.

Lark paced back and forth behind the counter. "I can't stand hanging around here with no customers. When I'm not keeping busy, my mind starts going ... where I can't stop it."

"Oh, boy." He looked out the wide front window of Dewey's. "Speak of the devil. Look who's pulling up."

"Oh, God. Oh, God." She wrung her hands.

"Try not to get upset."

"Am I going to jail?" She grabbed her apron in her fists.

"Wish I could say." He stubbed out his cigarette. "Really don't know."

They both turned and watched Gilstrap open the front door and walk in. He approached them, looked at Vint and motioned with his thumb. "Take a hike. I want a word with Lark."

She grabbed Vint's hand. "No. He's not going anywhere. Anything you have to say, you can say in front of Vint."

"She's having a rough time. I'd like to stick around."

"OK, but stay out of it." The marshal wagged a finger at him, then turned to her. "Lark, I'd be perfectly within my rights to arrest you right now." He put his left hand on his handcuffs. "You assaulted an officer of the law in front of witnesses."

"I'm sorry. I really am."

"I can't let people in this town thinking they can go around breaking the law, disrespecting me and go unpunished. It leads to big problems."

Lark looked down at the floor. "I understand."

"You realize how hard it is to get someone's ashes out of your clothes? Huh? I was blowing Grannie out of my nose for two days." Gilstrap yanked his hat off and slapped it against his leg. "Never in my life have I seen such contemptuous hardihood against authority."

She held her wrists out in front of her.

Gilstrap stood looking down on her. "Oh, put your hands down. I'm not going to arrest you. I should but I'm not."

"I don't know what came over me," she pleaded. "When I think about it, it seems like someone else did it. I apologize."

"That's good enough for me. I came here to tell you I have no evidence against you in the death of your grandmother. So, I'm dropping my murder investigation."

"Thank you." Her shoulders dropped and she let out a deep breath. "What about Vint?"

"I don't have anything on you either, Smith."

"She apologized to you." Vint nodded toward Lark. "Don't you think you owe her one for getting her so upset? I mean, it was Grannie's memorial and all."

"All right. I can live with that. Sorry." The marshal hooked his thumbs in his holster belt. "Now, you promise to drop any smear campaign against me in the next election?"

"Oh, I didn't mean any of that." She tilted her head to the side. "I was just upset, that's all."

"Everything's settled then." Gilstrap took a seat at the counter. "Why don't you tell Shadrack to rustle me up some steak and eggs?"

Vint stood up. "I'm going to get going."

The marshal pulled out his night stick. "As long as you're here, there's something I want to talk to you about." He held the stick out, blocking Vint's path. "Heard you got in a scrape outside the bar Sunday night. Know who jumped you?"

"Yes and no."

"What's that supposed to mean?"

"I mean, I don't think you should have to look too far, that's all."

Gilstrap tapped his stick on Vint's chest. "That's all you got to say?"

"That's it."

"Now that the murder investigation's over, the only reason I'm letting you hang around this town is to pitch in at the lumber yard."

"I'll be there to help get the big load out. I'm just taking a couple days off. I'm pretty sore from getting jumped."

"I'd suggest you stay out of Lee's place. You're not too popular with most people around here. The men folk anyway." Gilstrap put his stick away. "You have no business being in this county after a week from Friday. So after that, you just git. Or I'll make sure you wish you did."

Vint looked at Lark's worried expression. "I'll talk to you later," he said to her. "Try to take it easy. I'll see you back at the house." He turned and walked out of Dewey's.

* * *

"Lark," Vint called out, standing in front of the open medicine cabinet in her bathroom.

She walked in from the living room. "You realize that's the first time you called me by my name?"

"Really?" He looked at her, holding a small bottle. "How old is this?"

"Gramps' morphine?" She raised her eyebrows. "About six months. He was taking it at the end."

"Hmm." He removed the cap and took a whiff.

"That's potent stuff," she warned.

"I'm still pretty sore." He took a sip and made a face. "God, that's bitter. Why don't you make me a cup of coffee?"

"I wish you'd forget about this crazy plan and stay home. I don't know why you just can't let things be."

Vint followed her to the kitchen. "Take a beating and forget about it? No, little lady, I'm not built like that. No one pulls that kind of bullshit on me and just walks away."

She lightly touched the side of the coffeepot, then poured him a cup of warm coffee. "Anfield's a deputy marshal. He's armed."

"I know he's a deputy, damn it." He gave her a sour look. "Remember, you and me were working on this jigsaw puzzle all night, listening to the radio." He sat at the kitchen table in Gramps' old bib-overalls, lacing the deceased man's work boots. "I never left the house."

"Please don't go through with this." Lark paced the cracked linoleum flooring.

Vint stood, pulled Gramps' tweed cap on, then put a handkerchief in his pocket. "That runt has it coming."

"He may be short but he's not little. I saw him fight. He's tough."

"Quit worrying. I know what I'm doing." He gulped some coffee, then set the cup on the table next to the pile of puzzle pieces depicting a windmill setting.

"Promise you'll come right back here?"

"Of course." Vint pointed a thumb at his chest. "They'll probably suspect me right off. I'm going to get back as soon as possible."

"Please be careful. I don't know what I'd do if anything happened to you. I'd go crazy."

"Get going on the puzzle. Don't empty the ashtray. Leave my butts right there."

"You know your way?" Lark grabbed one of his overall straps.

"Yeah. 18 Bluebird, three blocks over." He turned his head side to side and shrugged. "Hey, that stuff's pretty good. I'm feeling better already."

She threw her arms around him. "Please don't go."

"OK, kid. Let go. I got to get out of here." Vint put on Gramps' faded denim coat and pulled on his own work gloves. Grabbing the old blanket that Lark set out for him, he went out the back door just as the clock struck 10:00, and walked close to the house. When he got to the street, he looked around, then crossed. Making his way to Anfield's by way of backyards, hopping fences, and avoiding barking dogs, Vint went around to the back of the deputy's one-story house and climbed onto the roof using a garbage can and windowsill to boost himself.

Vint walked on the roof to the front of the house, then sat in the dark over the front door, shielded by branches of an old willow tree. Waiting and holding the blanket, he craved a cigarette but knew the aroma would give him away.

He sat, thinking over his plan, watching the road. When it was close to 11:00 pm, he saw the deputy drive up in his patrol car. Vint took out his handkerchief and tied it over the lower half of his face. The deputy pulled into the driveway, got out of his car, and walked up to the front door whistling *Honeymoon on a Rocket Ship*.

Just as Anfield reached for the lock with his key, Vint jumped on him with the blanket out in front of him. His knees landed on the stocky man's chest, driving him to the ground. Anfield cried out in pain and surprise. Vint immediately reached under the blanket, pulled the deputy's pistol from its holster and flung it across the yard. The deputy yelled and struggled but Vint kept the man pinned down with his knees on his shoulders and pummeled his face. Anfield drew a knee up hard and caught him between the legs. Vint rolled off and groaned loudly. The deputy sat up and began taking the blanket off him. Vint kicked Anfield in the face with both feet, sending him onto his back. He stood and jumped on the deputy's stomach, knocking the wind from him. After kicking him in the ribs a few times, Vint took off running.

Hurrying back to Lark's in terrible discomfort, Vint was careful not to be spotted. When he flew in through the backdoor, she jumped to her feet. "Are you all right?"

Vint pulled the hankie down from his face. "I got kneed in the nuts," he said, breathing heavily. He took off the cap, gloves and coat. "Hurts like hell but I'll be OK."

"So, this is it then? You're through with this whole thing?"

He sat, untied the boots and pulled them off. "Yeah, with Anfield. If I find out who the others were …"

"You're lucky you didn't get a bullet in that stubborn head. Please drop this thing."

"Here." He jumped up, undid the metal buttons of the overalls and let them drop to the floor. He stood in his jeans and t-shirt and handed all of Gramps things to Lark. "Hurry up and put this stuff away."

She took the old clothes and hustled into Grannie's bedroom with them.

Lighting a cigarette, he sat and picked up a piece of the puzzle, trying to figure out where it went, but it was all just a blur to him.

"Sure you weren't recognized?" she asked as she reentered the kitchen.

"Positive." Vint pushed a chair out for her with his stocking foot. "Sit down and relax."

"You better comb your hair and dry your face." She sat and picked up a puzzle piece.

He slicked his damp hair back, then untied the handkerchief from around his neck and patted his forehead with it.

Lark flinched when she heard a loud knock on the front door.

"That was quick. Go ahead and answer it. Act surprised as you normally would having someone pound on your door this late."

After opening the front door a crack and peering outside, she swung it open and exclaimed, "Marshal, what are you doing here?"

With his back to the front door, Vint heard Gilstrap ask, "Can we come in?"

"Well, sure. What's this about?" Her voice got louder. "Deputy! What happened to you?"

Vint turned in his seat to see Gilstrap in his uniform with his shirttail hanging out. Anfield stood next to him, his face a bloody mess of lumps.

"There he is!" Anfield pointed at Vint. "Arrest him!"

Strolling into the living room, Vint asked, "What's this all about?" He looked at the deputy and smiled. "You fall down some stairs?"

"Cuff him." Anfield shook his fist. "He's the one did this to me."

"What are you talking about?" Vint replied calmly, "I didn't do anything to anybody."

"Where were you just a little while ago?" Gilstrap asked Vint.

"I've been in all night, with Lark, working on a jigsaw puzzle."

"That true?" Gilstrap stared at Lark with his beady, deep set eyes.

"Vint's been with me all night, for the last few hours. Working on a puzzle, like he said."

"They're both lyin'." The deputy squinted at Vint with one eye, the other swollen shut. "I kneed him in the balls. Go ahead and check."

"Go ahead and check?" The marshal looked down at Anfield. "You mean, look at this man's testicles?"

"Yeah. Make him pull his pants down."

"Not in front of me, you're not," Lark objected.

Vint smirked. "Normally, someone has to buy me dinner first or at least ask real nice before I take my drawers down."

"You done lose your mind, Deputy?" Gilstrap shook his head. "I'm not examining this man's *cojones*."

"If it'll help clear things up, I'll take my pants down. But I got to warn you, you'll be embarrassed by comparison."

"That won't be necessary." The marshal gestured. "Let me see your knuckles."

Vint held his hands out.

Gilstrap looked them over. "Where'd you get that cut?"

"That?" Vint pointed to it. "Got that Sunday night defending myself against five guys who threw a blanket over my head on Main and worked me over."

The marshal put his fists on his hips. "So, you were out tonight evening up the score?"

Vint stood silent, glaring at the bloody deputy.

"Were you part of that ruckus, Anfield?" Gilstrap wagged a finger at his deputy. "I will not tolerate a bunch of men taking the law into their own hands and ganging up on someone. I'm the law in this town and I'll dish out justice as I see fit." The marshal pushed his hat back. "I want you two to shake hands and be done with this."

"This man jumped me and you want me to shake his hand?" the deputy complained loudly. "I'll kill him before I do."

"You'll shake and you'll do it right now," Gilstrap commanded. "Either that or take off your badge. A lot of men in this town would line up for your job. I said shake!"

Vint smiled smugly and extended his hand.

Anfield hesitated, then briefly shook Vint's hand.

"I'm telling you both, this monkey business is over with, as of right now. I find out either one of you breaks the truce, you'll both be run out of town."

Walking out behind the marshal, Anfield turned and ran his finger across his neck while giving Vint a menacing look.

Vint slammed the door, nearly hitting the deputy's face.

"The marshal knows I lied to him." Lark wrung her hands and fretted.

"You're worried about *that*? After threatening him in front of witnesses and heaving Grannie's ashes in his face? Of course he knows you lied, he knows why and he doesn't care. Forget about it." Vint flopped back on the couch. "Damn, I'm sore. I could use a drink."

Chapter 23

"How you coming along with that book?" Lark topped off Vint's cup with steaming coffee.

"About three-fourths of the way through." Vint closed his paperback. "You were right. Didn't take long for your fan club to come back."

"These old boys?" Lark smiled and glanced up and down the counter. "They're nice guys. Not much else to do around town."

"Don't kid yourself." He grimaced. "You could spit in their coffee and they'd ask for seconds."

"Oh, boy. You're in one of *those* moods."

"I can't take another night of sitting in this diner." Vint peered side to side as he spoke. "Watching you run around, serving pie to a lot of googly-eyed creeps, dreaming they were with you." He stood and stuck his book in his back pocket.

"You jealous?" Lark replied with a big smile.

"I don't get jealous. I get bored."

"Where are you going?" She pouted. "Adelle's?"

"No. I'm not going to Adelle's." Vint waved his hand away. "Think I'll stop in the bar."

"Sure that's a good idea? What if the Skinners are around?"

"I'm not afraid of those Li'l Abner characters."

"Please don't." She set the coffeepot on the counter. "Last time you were there you got in that fight out front."

"Maybe that's just what I need right now, a good tune-up." Vint shoved the front door open and was met with a cool blast of early evening wind. Watching the toes of his boots kicking forward with each step, he made his way down to the tavern. He opened the door, glanced around, then walked up to the bar and sat on one of the worn, leather-covered stools.

Lee went up to Vint and leaned both hands on the bar. "Here again, huh?"

Vint squinted at him. "You got a problem with that?"

"No." Lee straightened up.

"Good." Pointing at a bottle of bourbon, Vint said, "Four Roses. Straight up."

Vint took his time with his drinks, listening to mournful country music about midnight trains and purple skies coming from the jukebox. He was sipping his third whiskey and watching a couple guys play pool when the front door flew open. Merk Skinner stepped in along with a balding man who resembled him, only bigger and wider. They both glared at Vint.

"I don't want no trouble in here," Lee called out.

The song on the jukebox ended and the room went silent as the two men walked up to Vint. The bigger man yelled at Lee, "Shut up, boy! Or I'll come 'round that bar, bend ya over and ream your ass like one of my hogs."

The two pool players set their sticks down and backed away from the billiards table.

"Just the mudsill we were lookin' for." Merk came up on Vint's left and slapped him on the back.

"*This* is him? Doesn't look like much to me." The other man came up on Vint's right. "I'm Polk Skinner, buzzard bait." He leaned in close to Vint, smelling of moonshine and bad breath. "I'm gonna kill ya for what ya did to Lester."

"Meet my big brother." Merk laughed. "They let him out a few days early for bad behavior."

Vint took a sip of his bourbon, looking straight ahead, ignoring the two.

Merk stood close, giving off a stench of body odor and pigs. "Heard ya was in here buyin' drinks."

Looking around to see who had left the bar since he arrived, Vint answered back, "Heard wrong, tubby."

As the brothers stood crowding Vint, Polk pulled a bowie knife from a sheath on his belt. "Go for that razor I heard about and I'll slice ya up."

Calmly holding his glass, Vint replied, "I don't need a razor to take you two gorillas."

Merk looked at Polk. "Ya believe the balls on this nob?"

Polk brought the knife close to Vint's neck. "I'm gonna cut your fool head off, ya Yankee pile of crap."

Watching their reflections in the mirror behind the bar, Vint replied. "You're not stupid enough to kill me here in front of witnesses."

"How do you know?" Polk sneered, slowly bringing the knife away from Vint's neck.

Still holding his glass, Vint finally turned to Polk. "You mean, how do I know how stupid you are?"

Merk grabbed the collar of Vint's jacket, "Don't get smart, slick."

"Too late for that." In an instant, Vint threw whiskey into Polk's eyes and smashed the glass on Merk's nose. He jumped back out of his seat, grabbed the cue ball and a pool stick from the billiard table.

The brothers yelled out in pain and turned to Vint in shock. Polk wiped his eyes with his sleeve. Merk had blood dripping from a gash on the bridge of his nose.

"Drop that Arkansas toothpick," Vint commanded Polk.

"*Drop* it? I'm gonna split ya open, balls to belly."

Vint threw the cue ball, hitting Polk between the eyes. He fell backward against the bar still holding the knife. "Mother fucker!" he yelled. "Kill 'im, Merk!"

Merk produced his own knife and stepped toward Vint.

Waving the pool stick in front of him, Vint told the younger brother, "Come on. I'll crack this over your head and jab your eyes out."

Polk blinked and stumbled a couple steps toward Vint.

Lee fired a shotgun toward the ceiling. "Outside! All y'all!" With bits of plaster raining down, he pumped the action. "Or I'll scatter all three of you with buckshot." He yelled at Vint, "Drop that stick. I got a right to defend my bar and the marshal's gonna be on my side if I shoot y'all."

Vint tossed the stick onto the pool table and pulled his razor. He turned and backed out the front door with the open blade out in front of him.

A knot formed between Polk's eyes, and blood dripped from the tip of Merk's nose as they stumbled outside after Vint.

Once all three were in the street with their weapons drawn, Vint heard a familiar voice.

"Two against one, huh." As the night air filled with drizzling rain, Cornie walked up next to Vint with his knife out.

"Who the fuck is this, now?" Merk scowled at Cornie.

"Stay out of this, beanpole." Polk pointed his long knife at Cornie. "We's two cats ya don't wanna mess with."

"I can't let ya kill my pard, here." Cornie circled his blade in the cool evening air. "He's too valuable to me."

"Stupid bastard," Vint said to Cornie out of the side of his mouth. "You don't know what you got yourself into."

The brothers stepped closer to Vint and Cornie. "We'll kill both y'all right here in the street and claim self-defense."

As Vint and Cornie waved their blades in front of them, the marshal's patrol car flew up to the four. The vehicle screeched to a halt. Gilstrap and Anfield jumped out with their revolvers drawn.

"Drop the weapons!" the marshal commanded. "Now!"

The metal blades dropped with clangs on the concrete street. "Hands over your heads and step back," Gilstrap barked.

Anfield grabbed his ribs and stiffly bent over to pick up the weapons. "Havin' a little Thursday night hootenanny, are ya?"

"You Skinners can start walking to the jail." Gilstrap pointed down the street with his thumb. He turned to Vint and Cornie. "Both of you in the back of the squad."

With Gilstrap behind the wheel, the car followed the brothers as they lumbered down the middle of the street, illuminated in the headlights along with drops of rain. "Who are you and what are you doing in my town?" The marshal inspected Cornie through the rearview mirror.

"Name's Cornelius Jenkins. I was just passin' through when I seen this gentleman bein' threatened by those big galoots. I was comin' to his rescue."

"I seen this guy slinkin' around here the past few days." Anfield, with two black-eyes, nodded his head toward Cornie. "Man his description been reported rummagin' around in garbage cans like a raccoon."

"I'd say you look more like a raccoon than me, bub." Cornie smiled.

"Shut up!" the deputy sputtered. "And don't say nothin' unless you're asked a question."

"You know this man, Smith?" Gilstrap asked.

"Can't say that I do," Vint replied, looking out the side window.

Gilstrap frowned at Vint through the rearview mirror. "Can't say, huh?"

Once all four were inside the marshal's office, the Skinners were put in one jail cell and Cornie was placed in the one next to them.

"Here." Anfield came back to the cells after a couple minutes and tossed a bandage at Merk, then handed an old rag filled with ice to Polk.

"Sit down, Smith." Gilstrap gestured to a chair in front of his desk. As they both took a seat, the marshal shook his head in disapproval. "You're still not working."

"Like I told you …" Vint turned and glared at Anfield, who stood behind him, slapping his night stick into his palm. "I needed a few days to heal up from that beating I took."

"So, you're too sore to work but well enough to scrap with the Skinners and my deputy? I'm telling you, I don't want no more bloodshed in my town. I'm ordering you to steer clear of any trouble for the next week. Then leave town for good. If you don't, I guarantee you'll regret it."

"I have no reason to stick around after that."

"See that you don't," Gilstrap growled. "I'll tell you what we do with outsiders around here who cause trouble. We drive 'em out to the woods, handcuff 'em to a tree, and beat 'em with our billy clubs."

Anfield chuckled. "Never had one of 'em come back and bother us again."

"I've been Mr. Nice Guy so far but don't push your luck." The marshal slapped a palm on the desk. "Go on, *vamoose*. I swear, if it wasn't for Adelle Hurst …"

Vint stood. "Can I have my razor back. I like a close shave."

"Here." Gilstrap tossed the folded razor onto the desk in front of Vint. "Close shave." He shook his head. "Git out before I change my mind."

* * *

The Skinner brothers sat on the one bed in their cell and talked to Cornie through the bars. "You don't know what ya let yourself in for," Polk said quietly. "We're gonna have some fun with ya when we git outa here."

"Know what we like to do with dirty tramps like you?" Merk jumped in. "We like to give y'all a special welcome to town."

"See, we're gonna take ya back to our place and throw ya in the barn." Polk took over again. "Then we're gonna beat hell outa ya for a couple hours. Then after you're all soft and mushy, we're gonna chain ya to a barn pole and yank all your teeth out with pliers."

Cornie curled up on the bed in his cold cell, staring at the bars in front of him.

"Know why we do that?" Merk asked. "Cause when we make ya suck our cocks ya can't bite us."

Polk laughed. "Then after your through blowin' us, we're gonna fuck ya up your pooper real good and hard."

"Yeah." Merk stood and grabbed the bars separating the cells. "Then the real fun starts."

"That's when we live up to our name," Polk said with glee. "First we slice your skin all round your neck. Then we cut ya down the middle."

Merk stared at Cornie through the bars. "After that, we carve ya 'round the waist and wrists."

"Ya know what comes next, don't ya?" Polk's voice took on a maniacal tone. "We pull your hide off like a shirt and try it on over our bare skin while ya watch. And if ya pass out, we keep ya up with smellin' salts."

"When we're all through slicin' ya up, we feed ya to our pigs." Polk stood next to Merk, reached through the bars and pointed at Cornie. "They eat up everything, even the bones."

"Hey, look at me when I'm talkin' to ya." Merk spit at Cornie. "Not so brave without your buddy, are ya?"

"Look at 'im shakin'," Polk growled. "He's a chickenshit without that knife."

The Skinners kept it up for a few hours while Cornie lay on his bed in a fetal position, trembling.

Chapter 24

Cornie finally got to sleep around 7:00 am and had a nightmare about the Skinner brothers devouring him alive. An hour later he heard Anfield yelling, "Up and at 'em, Jenkins."

Seeing his cell door open, he sat up and put his stocking feet on the floor. When Anfield unlocked the Skinners' cell, Cornie jumped up and slammed his door shut again, shaking.

"What do you think you're doin', Jenkins? Time for you to skedaddle. We're not a hotel. You're not gettin' breakfast here."

"Hey there, slim." Polk laughed. "You can come over to our place for breakfast."

"Please," Cornie pleaded. "I'll stay around and wash the floors, windows. Anything you want. Please."

"What'd y'all say to this man?" the deputy asked the brothers as he wagged a thumb toward Cornie. "He's about to have a nervous breakdown."

"We was just tellin' him bedtime stories." Merk smiled, revealing greenish-colored teeth.

"Yeah. Scary ones I bet." Anfield turned to Cornie. "Alright, you can sweep up and mop the floors. Then we'll feed ya."

The Skinners stood in front of Cornie's cell, glaring at him.

"Go on, you two," Anfield commanded the brothers. "Scram."

* * *

As Vint pulled up in front of Dewey's that afternoon, he was surprised to see Lark standing next to the driver's side of Adelle's Cadillac. Lark glanced sideways at Vint, then patted Adelle's hand that rested on the open window. Adelle didn't turn to look at Vint. She started her car and pulled away as he got out and approached Lark.

"What was that all about?" He watched the Caddy head west on Main. "You discussing me?"

Without looking at him, she replied, "Not everything's about you, Vint."

"Just seems odd." He turned his head and squinted at Lark. "You and her."

She crossed her arms under her breasts and tapped a foot on the cracked concrete street. "Nothing odd about a little girl talk."

"I want to know what was said." He pointed a finger at her.

"Sometimes ladies have things between them that don't concern men." She shrugged slightly and stuck her lower lip out.

"Seems unlikely that my name didn't come up."

"What you have going on isn't enough, buddy?" There was a flash of coldness in her eyes. "You need to be in the middle of our conversation too?"

"Just how well do you know Adelle?"

"Please, just drop it. I've got customers." She pivoted and spoke over her shoulder as she walked away. "I'm going back in."

Vint stood glaring at her.

Holding the door open, she asked, "You coming in?"

"No." He stood breathing heavily. "Maybe I'll be back later."

* * *

As Lark walked up to Vint's sedan after her evening shift at Dewey's, he pushed the passenger door open with his boot. She settled in and said, "Thanks for picking me up. I get scared I'm never gonna see you again."

"Let's go for a ride." Vint put the Nash in gear. "The thought of sitting around your house again makes me buggy. Feel the walls closing in on me."

"Wish you could just settle down like most folks."

"I can't stand being in one place too long." He motioned forward with his finger. "Got to keep moving."

"What makes you like that?"

Vint drove west on Main and didn't answer.

"Where do you go when you're not around?" Lark pouted. "Got another girl?"

"No." He turned to her and frowned. "Sometimes I just like to be by myself. Can you understand that?" He watched the road disappear under the car in the beam of the headlights. "I park by the river. Like to watch it. Just keeps flowing, day and night."

Lark moved closer and ran her fingers through his hair. "Most people want a home they can go to, family, loved ones. Not you. You're like a hummingbird. Can't light down anywhere unless you sleep. Gotta keep flapping those wings or you'll die."

"God, you're gabby." He pulled his head away from her hand.

Her demeanor suddenly changed. "I want to know what you and Adelle have going. You say it's business. What sort?"

"She didn't tell you when you were talking with her?"

"Don't be funny. That was just small talk." She huffed. "Look, I got a right to know what's going on."

"Drop it." He turned off Main. "Doesn't have anything to do with you."

"OK. You have your secrets, and I'll have mine." Lark folded her arms in an exaggerated manner and slumped in her seat. She sat like that for several moments then reached to turn the radio on.

"That's a nice bracelet." He took her wrist and examined the jewelry. "Never saw you wear it before."

"I only put it on once in a while."

"Looks like solid eighteen-carat. Must have cost a lot."

Lark pulled her hand away. "It was a present."

"Not from that boy you were going with?"

"No. Someone else." She took it off and put it in her purse. "Please tell me what's going on. Why is everything about you such a mystery?"

"I'm sorry, but there's things you're better off not knowing."

"You can tell me anything. Really. You can trust me."

"I trust nobody but me." He pulled up to a spot under a winged elm that overlooked the river. "I'm the only person I've ever been able to rely on."

"I feel sorry for you. You've been kicked around so much, you don't even know when there's something good right in front of you."

Vint turned and rolled down his window, listening to the rush of the wide river.

"You gonna go the rest of your life like that ... turning away?"

Pulling out a cigarette and lighting it, Vint sat silent for a couple minutes, staring off. "I don't know what the hell I keep doing wrong." He pulled his paperback from his pocket and tossed it on the floor of the Nash. "My life keeps turning out like one of these dime-store novels."

"I can make it better." Lark unbuttoned her white uniform and took it off. She pushed off her saddle shoes, then climbed over the front seat in her bra, panties and bobby sox. Lying on the back seat, she said, "Throw that butt out and come back here. I'll show you something I read about in one of those dime-store novels."

* * *

Cornie hid out in alleys, searching for fresh scraps of food in garbage cans, waiting for dark. After several hours of laying low, he walked west along the dirt road leading out of town. Hearing a vehicle approach, he turned to face the headlights with his thumb out. Realizing it was the Skinners in a pickup truck, he quickly put his hand down.

The brakes screeched and the truck skidded to a halt. Through the open passenger window, Polk yelled, "Lookie, lookie, a little nookie."

With the sound of crickets chirping from every direction, both Skinners jumped out and surrounded Cornie.

"Ain't this somethin'?" Polk chuckled. "We was just talkin' 'bout ya."

"And here ya are," Merk added. "Good thing we come along. Hop in. *We'll* give you a ride."

"I'll w-walk. If it's all the same to you." Cornie tried backing away but Polk stepped behind him.

"It ain't all the same to us." Polk smacked Cornie on the side of the head, then shoved him from behind. "Get in, stringbean."

Cornie pulled his knife and lashed out at the two, missing them as they jumped back out of the way.

Merk laughed and said, "Our girlfriend wants to play."

Polk went to the bed of the pickup and came up with a chain. Merk jumped back as his brother swung the heavy chain in a circle over his head. Cornie backed away brandishing his blade as Polk kept stepping closer. Lunging forward, Polk hit Cornie's hand with the chain, knocking the knife away.

Cornie took off running but Polk went after him and swung the chain toward his ankles. The chain tripped Cornie and he hit the ground with a thud.

Grabbing Cornie by the back of his collar, Polk yanked the tall, lean man to his feet and shoved him into the front seat while Merk got behind the wheel. Polk squeezed in next to Cornie, then grabbed a bottle of moonshine from under the seat and uncorked it. He took a swig, howled, then passed it to his brother as they bounced along the bumpy road. Merk took a sip, then handed it to

Cornie. "You're gonna be needin' this," Merk said with a giggle.

Cornie took a sip and gagged. "Please let me go. I'll do anything ya want. Anything."

"We know you will." Polk laughed and pulled the bottle from Cornie's shaking hand.

As they drove into the night, the brothers talked and laughed about a wild dog they caught and chained up, then skinned alive.

Cornie quietly said the Lord's Prayer over and over as they turned off the road and continued on along a tire-path with branches slapping the windshield.

When they came to a stop in a small clearing, Cornie pleaded, "No, don't stop. Please, keep drivin'."

"Shut up, sissy boy." Polk got out first and grabbed Cornie by the ear. "Git out," he growled, as he yanked Cornie out onto the grass. The slim man's wobbly legs buckled and he went to his knees.

Merk joined his brother. "What ya wanna do to 'im first?"

"Oh, let's just have a little fun with 'im for starters."

Cornie put his hands up. "Please, please. I'm beggin' you."

Polk punched Cornie in the face, knocking him on his back.

"Not too hard." Merk pulled Cornie up but he went right back down sobbing. "You knock 'im out and he won't feel a damn thing."

"Som-bitch can't even stand." Polk motioned with his hand. "Here. Grab his wrists. I'll get his ankles."

The brothers carried Cornie next to a tree and swung him back and forth. "On three," Polk ordered. "One ... two ... three!" They let go and sailed Cornie's body against the wide cottonwood tree.

"Ugh," Cornie emitted, as air was forced from his lungs when his chest hit the rough bark. He fell to the ground and tried to crawl away. "Please. Please don't kill me."

"Hear those ribs crackin'?" Merk howled and laughed.

"Again." Polk grabbed his ankles.

After several more throws against the tree. Polk said, "This is getting borin'. Besides, it's too much work."

"Yeah." Breathing heavily, Merk bent over and looked at Cornie's contorted face. "Think he's still alive?"

Polk stomped his boot onto Cornie's throat making a crunching sound. "Not for long. Let's have some real fun with 'im."

Chapter 25

"Shadrack. Wake up." Jewel shook her sleeping husband as they lay in bed. "What was that?"

Shadrack shifted and mumbled.

"Get up!" She sat up and shook him harder. "Something's wrong."

"Damn, woman. What're you wakin' me up for." He rolled over to face her. "I worked all day and night. I'm workin' again today like I do every day."

"I heard something."

"You always hear somethin'. We're out in the country, you fool woman."

"This is different. It's not a skunk or a raccoon. I heard voices."

"You were dreamin'. Go back to sleep."

"There." Her eyes opened wide. "I heard it again."

Shadrack shot up in bed. "Oh, Lord." He got up and hastily put his pants on.

He raced into the main room and looked out the one window in the house. A wooden cross was in flames about twenty-feet from their front door. A group of eight men stood behind the cross, their white hoods and robes aglow from the firelight. There were two vehicles. One of them was Merk Skinner's pickup truck.

Grabbing his rifle, Shadrack watched with a horrified look on his sweating face as the cross burned.

Two of his six children wandered into the room. The younger boy rubbed his eyes, the other boy yawned. "What's goin' on, Daddy?"

"Get your sisters up, tell 'em to get dressed. Right now!"

Jewel ran into the room holding their baby tightly. "What're we gonna do?" With the little girl clinging to her nightshirt, she screamed, "What're we gonna do?"

Hooting and hollering broke out in the night. Clutching his rifle, Shadrack watched the men in robes run within ten feet of his wooden shack, then throw lit torches. He broke the window with the barrel of the rifle and fired, hitting one of the men in his chest. The man fell onto his torch and his robe went up in flames as he lay writhing and screaming. Another man ran to help him but Shadrack shot at him, winging his arm.

The wounded man quickly retreated back by the others as they ran behind their vehicles. The men lit more torches, then ran in opposite directions in a wide circle around the house. They threw the torches hitting all four walls and the roof. Within seconds the place was up in flames.

As the children screamed and raced around, Shadrack went to the back door. The fire was too intense to get near it. The whole front of the house was ablaze. Smoke filled the air as they all coughed and choked.

"Gimme the baby!" Shadrack yelled over the roar of the flames. "And follow me!"

He covered the little girl in a blanket and ran toward the wall with the least amount of flames. Right before he got to the wall, he turned his broad shoulder toward it, put his head down over his baby girl and crashed through the old wooden slats. He ran as fast as he could toward the dense woods behind their house. When he got about ten feet away from the shack, a rifle shot echoed in the night. He felt a sharp pain in his thick leg. In agony, he kept running, then felt another bullet enter his muscular arm.

While shots rang out, the children shrieked and backed away as the hole in the wall exploded in a fiery ring.

Jewel tried in vain to pull her children from the deadly inferno as they were all quickly engulfed in flames.

Fighting through the pain, Shadrack held his baby girl tightly as she wailed in the night air that was thick with white smoke. He was no more than fifteen feet from the dense trees when a bullet hit him in the back of the head. He went down on his knees, then fell over on his side, cradling the baby. The last sounds he heard were the screams of his wife and children as the flaming roof collapsed on them.

Chapter 26

As the black preacher led a handful of mourners in hymn at the cemetery, a few sang along, most cried. A middle-aged lady in a black dress rocked Jewel and Shadrack's baby girl, the only survivor.

"The Skinners must have been part of this," Vint said under his breath, loud enough for only Lark to hear as she clung to him in tears. "Lousy scum."

"It won't be the same at the diner," Lark whimpered. "Just won't be Dewey's without Shadrack."

"His family died because he helped me. I know it." He stood with his fists clenched, breathing in the smell of damp black earth. "I don't care what happens to me, I'll get those redneck bastards for this."

"You can't put it all on yourself." She rubbed his arm. "Shadrack stood up to the Skinners to protect me. He couldn't stand anyone giving me a hard time."

"He didn't deserve any of this." Vint stared at the seven cheaply-made caskets lined up next to their respective holes. "His family certainly didn't deserve it." Vint's words caught in his throat. "When I think of what it must have been like ... trapped in that house, burning alive, screaming."

"Please stop. I can't ..." Lark's legs gave out and she collapsed.

Vint went down on one knee and patted her face as the mourners stopped singing and watch them.

She opened her eyes. "What happened?"

"You fainted." He helped her sit up. "Did you sleep last night?"

"Barely."

"When's the last time you ate."

"I don't know … can't remember."

"Come on." He pulled her to her feet and led her away. "I'm taking you for some breakfast."

* * *

Vint parked in front of Sally's Restaurant, kicked his car door open and got out. He pulled off his tie, threw it in the backseat, then went around and opened Lark's door.

Lark gazed up at Vint with puffy, reddened eyes. Taking his extended hand, she stood and said, "Oh, a gentleman."

"I can be."

"You look peachy in that black suit but you could've shaved." A look of shock came over her face. "Oh, no."

Vint turned to the sound of honking horns and looked up the street. "What the hell?"

A line of vehicles, three pickup trucks and two cars were driving in their direction. A passenger in the lead truck waved a confederate flag. The men in the small parade drove by, yelling and shouting.

After they passed and continued up the street, his voice shook as he said, "They can't be."

"Yes, they can."

"Please tell me they're not going to drive past while Shadrack and his family are being put in the ground."

"Let's go in." She tugged on his arm. "Don't get involved. There's too many of them."

"Isn't there anything anyone can do?"

"By the time we call the marshal, it'll be all over and they'll be gone again. Please, Vint."

"Why is it that Gilstrap never seems to be around when you need him? Where the hell does that guy get to anyway?"

"He likes to fish," she said, pulling him into Sally's.

"I don't think I could live around here." He pulled out a chair for Lark at a small table. "Thought I was a son-of-a-bitch. These people add insult to injury." He plopped into a chair next to her.

"There's a few bad apples like the Skinners and their buddies, but this is a really good town. None of the ones who drove past are from here. I recognized a couple of them, they're from the next town over."

"When I think about those poor people at the cemetery. How horrible they already feel. And then to have to put up with that crap. Makes my blood boil."

A young waitress, with too much eyebrow pencil and a wavy, Italian-style haircut, walked up with a bounce in her step and a big smile on her face. "How y'all doin' today?"

Vint just stared at her.

"We just came from a funeral," Lark said softly. "Lost a good friend."

"Oh, my. I'm so sorry. I'm new 'round here but I heard about that awful fire." The waitress held out two menus. "Can I git ya anything?"

Lark answered, "Bring us a couple coffees." As the waitress walked away, Lark patted Vint's arm. "We'll get through this together."

Vint glared steely-eyed at the wall. "I feel like getting drunk." He balled his hand into a fist. "But I have to be ready. There's something important I have to do."

* * *

Vint pulled into Lark's driveway. "Can you walk to the diner after you get ready?" he asked her. "I need to take care of something."

"It's just up the road a piece." Lark shrugged. "Walked it plenty of times before you come along."

"Good," he said, getting out of the car. "I need to borrow a shovel and flashlight."

"What do you need those for?" She stood and looked at him quizzically. "I don't like the sound of this."

221

"There's times in your life when you're just better off not having your curiosity satisfied. Trust me on this."

Vint grabbed what he needed, then drove out of town and parked down by the river. After a few hours of digging, he threw the shovel back in his trunk, then slammed it shut. He accomplished everything he set out to do, including scattering dry leaves over the mound of fresh dirt.

Heading back to town and parking as close to Dewey's as he could, he glanced back and forth at all the cars lining the street, then went into the diner.

Lark saw Vint enter and went straight to him. "What've you been up to?" She looked him up and down. "Why don't you go back and get cleaned up?"

"Place is pretty busy."

"Should have been here an hour ago, the place was packed."

"I don't like crowds," Vint said, surveying the place. "Still, it was nice of Dewey to do all this."

"Him and his wife and couple others are doing all the cooking. Everything's on the house tonight. In honor of Shadrack and his family." Lark motioned toward the middle of the long counter. "Did you see that big jar? People have been leaving donations for the baby girl."

* * *

A few hours later, after most of the customers had left, Vint sat at the counter reading his book. The front door slammed, grabbing his attention. Merk Skinner walked straight to him with a scowl on his brutish face.

Vint's head swung around when he heard a voice behind him say, "This is the night ya die, Yankee puke." He realized Polk must have snuck in the backdoor while Merk entered the front.

Lark had a terrified look on her face. "Should I try to find the marshal?"

Vint motioned her away. He reached into his pocket, put his hand around his straight razor, and looked Polk in the eye. "So, this is it then."

"Too many people 'round." Polk grinned, showing bits of corn between his teeth. "But we'll be outside waitin' for ya."

Listening to the low mumblings of the small crowd at the counter and tables, Vint pushed his half-empty beer away and peered out the front window. The Skinner brothers were sitting on the front bumper of Merk's pickup truck, watching Vint and passing a bottle of hooch back and forth.

"Damn it," Vint said under his breath. "One more week was all I needed, one more fucking week." He knew someone was going to die tonight and hoped it wouldn't be him.

Vint sat thinking, then waved Lark over. "Give me a bottle of Grapette." He took the top off a salt shaker and emptied the contents into his left-side coat pocket. Reaching over, he grabbed another salt shaker and did the same.

She pulled a cold bottle of soda from the cooler, popped the cap off and set it in front of him. "What are you gonna do?"

"Don't worry. I got a plan." Vint gulped some sweet soda.

Polk grabbed the clear bottle of corn liquor from his brother. He took one last swig, stood up, then threw the empty bottle behind the front seat of the pickup. The two stepped behind the truck and began urinating in the street.

Knowing it was time to make his move, Vint jumped up, ran to front door, then took a step out while holding onto the door handle.

"Get that blue belly carpetbagger!" Polk yelled out, as the two scrambled to pull their zippers up.

Vint ran back in and headed for the backdoor. When the Skinners ran around the outside of the diner toward the rear entrance, he knew they had fallen for his ruse. He flew out the front, hopped in his sedan and pulled away. Polk and Merk saw what he had done and went after him in their pickup. Vint slowed down a little to make sure he didn't lose them as he headed out of town.

Checking his rearview mirror, he could see Polk behind the wheel of Merk's pickup. Keeping an eye on their headlights in the dusk, he sped along the dirt road. When he reached his destination, he skidded to a stop, hopped out and yanked a canvas glove over his right hand.

The Skinners pulled up behind him and jumped out. "Run outa gas?" Merk howled and laughed.

"This is it, boy," Polk growled. "This is the night ya die. How's that feel?"

Vint ran next to an ancient maple tree, stepping on the thick roots. Standing in a clearing, he pulled his razor. With his heart pounding, he answered in a sweet voice, "Come and get me boys."

Merk looked at Polk and pulled a long switchblade. "This cooter's crazier than a stomped pissant."

"Admit it." Polk flicked open his bowie knife. "Ya killed Lester didn't ya?"

"Not on purpose. But yeah, I killed him. He was coming at me with a broken bottle. It was him or me. And I'm not sorry it wasn't me who died."

"Well, we took care of your beanpole buddy." Polk's full face contorted into an evil grin. "Took *real* good care of him. Wouldn't have recognized the scumbag after we got through pullin' 'im apart with pliers."

"Enough talk," Merk said to Polk, staring at Vint. "Let's finish 'im."

"Don't rush me," Polk commanded. "I like lookin' into a man's eyes when he knows I'm gonna cut him up, when he knows I'm the last eyes he'll look into before I chop his head off."

"That's right, Polk. Look into my eyes. Do I look afraid to you?" Vint smiled. "Let's do this."

"OK, you got it, buster." Polk glared at Vint. "Let's bum-rush 'im." He yelled, "Go!"

With his legs set apart, Vint hunched forward, his gloved hand extended, gripping his razor. He tried his best to not let fear overtake him as they charged. Merk was a couple steps ahead of Polk as they ran at him.

"Aghhh." Merk yelled as the ground beneath him gave away and he fell into a six-foot-deep hole. "Ugh," was the last sound to come from Merk.

Polk stopped just short of falling in after his younger brother. He looked down to see Merk impaled on sharpened branches that Vint had half-buried at the bottom of a hole with a collapsible, sod-covered top. The poles came through the front of the man's body and out his back.

"Ya done killed two of my brothers!" Polk screamed. He walked around the hole. "Nobody in the world's as good with a knife as me. I'm sendin' ya to Hell."

Slowly stepping closer to Vint, Polk waved his long blade in a circle.

When Polk was about five feet away, Vint put his left hand in his jacket pocket and said, "All right, I know when I'm fucked. I thought you'd both fall in the hole. Before I die, there's one thing I got to confess."

"Go ahead, make your peace and do it quick."

"I just want to say ..." Vint pulled his hand from his pocket and threw a handful of salt into Polk's eyes. As Polk shut his eyes and yelled out in pain, Vint reached out and slashed the big man's throat. He jumped back a couple feet and stated calmly, "It isn't always the meanest, the biggest, the strongest guy that wins a fight. Sometimes, it's the smartest."

Polk tried to speak but only gurgling sounds came from his throat that oozed blood. He stumbled toward Vint brandishing his knife. He lunged at Vint, but he jumped back. Polk went down on one knee, swinging the blade back and forth in front of him.

As his eyes started closing, Polk waved his weapon for a couple minutes. Bleeding profusely, his arm slowly dropped and Vint pushed him onto his back with a shove of his boot. He removed Merk's truck key from Polk's pocket and put it in his own. He took the knife from Polk's hand, threw in into the hole, then rolled the big man in on top of his brother. Inspecting his glove, he saw that it was splattered with blood. Pulling it off, he tossed it into the hole too. He shoved the blade of his straight razor into the ground several times, cleaning the blood from it.

Vint took the shovel out of the car trunk and filled the hole back in. When he was through, he patted the mound down, then covered it with dried leaves. He drove Merk's pickup to a steep embankment closer to the river and left it in neutral. He got behind the vehicle and pushed it until it went down the slope on its own, picking up speed as it descended. The truck crashed into the rapidly flowing river and slowly disappeared from sight.

Walking back to his car, he surveyed the area, then pushed his boot back and forth over any footprints and tire tracks, working his way backward to his driver's side door.

Wanting to be seen in public as soon as possible, he drove back to the diner. There were fewer customers than before but a half-dozen remained. Everyone turned to look at him as he walked in and took a seat at the counter. Vint acted nonchalant as he ordered a beer from Lark.

Lark's eyes were wide as she asked quietly, "What happened?"

"Not much. I ditched those knuckleheads." He spoke loud enough for those sitting close to hear. "Probably still riding around looking for me."

"Do you think they'll come back here?" She uncapped a bottle of beer and set it in front of him.

"Not likely." Vint smiled and took a sip. "Probably too embarrassed after the way I made fools of them."

"You better watch it. Those guys are meaner than a skilletfull of rattlesnakes."

"Don't underestimate me. I can take care of myself."

"You going to be around when I get off?" She leaned her elbows onto the counter.

"I could be."

"Well, stick around." She winked at him. "I'll make it worth your while."

* * *

Vint sat in his sedan smoking while waiting for Lark. She exited the diner with a smile and walked up to the passenger door. He opened the door from the inside and pushed it open.

She hopped in and said with a sigh, "I'm so glad you waited, honey." She turned her head, rested it on the upper seat and gazed at him.

"Yeah, sure." Vint started his car and backed out.

"Come on, let's go park down by the river." She reached over and rubbed his stubbly cheek.

"You're going to wear me out, kid."

Lark just giggled.

"You're a beautiful young lady. I really like you and don't want to hurt you. You make me feel guilty for getting involved with you at all."

She slid next to him, put her head on his shoulder and ran her hand lightly on his thigh. "Don't talk like that. It scares me."

"I don't know what to do with you," he said as he drove in the direction of her house. "Remember I talked about leaving town suddenly? Well, that time is near."

She straightened up and slapped his leg. "Don't say that. You're not going to leave me."

"Oh, boy. What did I get myself into?" After pulling into Lark's driveway, he turned, lightly grabbed her chin and looked into her eyes. "Don't go falling in love with a guy like me."

"I already love you." She shoved his hand away. "You know I do. I don't just go around having sex with guys. This is special to me." She cried into her hands.

"You realize how exceptional you are? So pretty, talented. Don't waste yourself on me." He stroked her hair. "I don't like staying in one place too long. About time for me to move on."

"I could make you happy." She looked at him with quivering lips and tears running down her face. "I know I could."

He turned from her and looked at her house. "If I was the type to get married and settle down, I'd want you. Really."

"Give us a chance. Please."

"It's not going to work out." His voice turned harsh. "Get that out of your head."

Lark cried harder, then jumped out of the car and ran into the house.

Vint's shoulders dropped and his head fell back against the seat. He felt exhausted, physically and mentally. Starting his car, he looked to see if she was in the window but she wasn't there. He pulled away and drove to a remote spot where he could sleep and not think about everything.

Chapter 27

Vint sat facing the entrance in Sally's Restaurant, finishing a bowl of Brunswick stew. As he pushed his empty lunch bowl away, Lark walked in wearing high-heels, a tight-fitting dress, red lipstick, heavy makeup, and her hair up.

She strolled up to his table with a wiggle. "Hi, Vint. I missed you so last night. I kept waking up and looking over but you weren't there. It made me so sad."

Letting out a big breath, he said, "You look so different."

"It's time I did some growing up." She pulled out a chair and sat next to him. "There's something important I have to talk to you about. Can you come over tonight about 8:00? I'm not going into work."

"Yeah, sure." He rested a boot on another chair and pulled out a cigarette.

"Thank you. Thank you," Lark repeated, as she stared at him with her mouth open and touched his arm. She stood and fingered Grannie's pearls that hung around her neck. "I'll see you tonight then. Just come right in."

* * *

The windshield wipers slapped back and forth as Vint watched the road in the beam of his headlights. He pulled into Lark's driveway, then stepped out into the light rain and cool night air. Putting his collar up, he strode to the porch and hopped up onto it. Walking into the darkened house, he saw a flickering light from Lark's bedroom. He entered her room that was aglow from a handful of candles.

Lark lay in bed under a white sheet that covered her body from her breasts down. "Welcome home."

"What's with the candles?" He motioned outside the room with his thumb. "Want me to check your fuse box?"

"Are you serious? I'm trying to set a romantic mood."

"Oh." He looked her up and down. "I thought there was something you wanted to talk about."

"I swear you don't have a romantic bone in your body." She threw the sheet off her, revealing her nude body.

"Never saw the point of it." Vint took off his jacket, dropped it on the floor, then pulled his t-shirt over his head.

"I haven't been able to think about anything but you all day." She ran her fingertips down her belly. "Come lay down with me."

He undid his jeans and tugged them down along with his boxers. Sitting on her bed, he pulled off his pants and boots. Without any foreplay, he lay on top of Lark and entered her.

After a few minutes, Lark said softly, "Kiss me, Vint. You never kiss me. When two people love each other …" She brought her lips to his but he pulled away. "Love me, Vint," she whispered, "please love me."

He continued on silently, and when he finished, he climbed off her and sat on the edge of the bed. "You're not going to like this." Vint looked down and grabbed his forehead. "We can't see each other again."

"You're not serious." She sat up quickly. "You can't be. You're gonna screw me, then leave me?"

"I'm sorry it has to be like this," Vint said, staring at the floor. "I wish things were simpler."

"Did I do something wrong?" She leaned forward and put her hand on his shoulder. "I'm sorry."

"You didn't do anything wrong." He massaged his forehead. "There's some heavy stuff coming down in the next few days. I can't have you involved."

"I don't care what it is. You can't leave me."

"I'm telling you it's dangerous." He stood and pulled up his boxers. "I shouldn't even be telling you this much."

"If it's dangerous, we can see it through together."

"No, I told you!" He tugged up his jeans and zipped the fly. "You don't understand."

"Then make me understand."

"Only reason I'm leveling with you is because I like you. Like you better than most." He put on his t-shirt. "More than just about anyone I've known."

"This can't be. This can't be," Lark repeated, as her eyes glazed over. "I can't be left alone again. I can't. I'll …"

"Seems like no matter what I say, you don't get it." He sat and pulled his boots on, then grabbed his jacket. "I don't know what else to tell you. I'm sorry. I have to get out of here." He walked out of the bedroom and into the living room.

"Wait! Wait! Where are you going!" she screamed and came after him. "Adelle's?"

"No." He put his hand out, stopping her. "I'll sleep in my car again. I can't ever come back here."

"I'm sorry I yelled at you. I didn't mean to act so crazy. I can be better. As long as you don't leave me, I can be better."

"Please stop pleading. It only makes it harder. I warned you over and over that I might have to leave town." He turned and went out the front door.

She ran after him into the cold rain, totally nude.

"Get back in there. What're you, nuts?" Vint grabbed her by the hair and smacked her across the face. "Snap out of it. Someone might see you."

"I don't care!" Lark cried out. "If you leave I don't care what happens to me! I'll do something crazy. Vint. I'll do something." She fell to her knees onto the wet grass, sobbing. "Please, Vint. Please, don't go."

Getting into his car, listening to Lark beg and wail, Vint felt something inside of him. He didn't know what it was. It was foreign to him. He felt worse than he had ever felt.

Driving away, he tried to swallow his emotions, as he had since he was a boy, but this time it was different. It was someone else he felt bad for, not himself.

Continuing on and turning onto Main, Vint knew he had blown his chance for Lark to lie for him and say she was with him when the Krause robbery was to take place two nights later. He just couldn't do that to her. Couldn't use her and take the chance of her getting into trouble for him. He would just have to figure something else out.

After driving around aimlessly for a while, Vint headed to Adelle's and pulled his car off the road in a dark area. Looking around to make sure he wasn't spotted, he walked to her front door and rang the bell a couple times.

A few moments later, the door swung open. "Good, God. What're you doing here?" Adelle stood holding her silk robe closed with one hand.

"I need to talk to you about something."

"Well, hurry up and get in here." She grabbed his jacket and tugged at him. "I was getting ready for bed." She tied the sash of the robe around her waist. "Come on upstairs."

Vint could tell by the way the thin silk clung to her body that she had nothing beneath the robe.

She led him to her bedroom, then lay on top of her bedspread. "What's so damn important?"

"I need an alibi for Wednesday night." He stood next to the bed looking down on her.

"You're serious?" She brought a knee up, separating the robe from her navel down. "You really came here to talk?"

"Yes. Think you could help me out?"

"What's this all about?" She moved her knee back and forth.

"I can't say." He gazed at her nude lower half. "Just need someone to vouch for my whereabouts two nights from now."

"You know we can't take the chance of anyone tying us together. Last thing we needs is something interfering with our plans."

He looked away from her body briefly, then returned his gaze. "Know of anyone who could keep me in the clear, for a price?"

"Leave me out of this." Adelle brought her other knee up and ran her hands down her bare thighs. "Aren't you going to get undressed?"

"No. Look, I didn't come here for that." Vint paced the floor. "I just had to do something that was extremely hard. Not in the mood."

"That's a first." She brought her legs back down and pulled her robe closed. "You OK?"

He stopped pacing and looked her in the eye. "I'm not myself." He rubbed his aching forehead. "Seems like years since I felt anything … real. Now all of a sudden … I don't know why I'm telling you this. I should go."

"You don't look good. Sit down for a while." Adelle got out of bed. "I'll get you a drink."

Vint sat on her bed with his back to the headboard, rubbing his temples.

Adelle returned a few minutes later with two snifters of brandy. She handed him one, then sat down next to him.

He took a gulp, then turned his head and scrutinized her. "I saw you talking with Lark outside Dewey's a few days ago."

"I'm quite aware of that," she snapped back, looking straight ahead.

"What the hell would you have to discuss with her?"

"Oh, nothing much." Adelle peered into her glass. "She was out front taking a break. Saw me passing by and waved."

"So, you just pulled over?"

"What does it matter to you?" She slowly sipped some brandy.

"It matters. What did you two say about me?"

"Say about *you*?" She smirked. "Your name never came up."

"Quit being so cagy. I want to know what's going on. How well do you know her?"

"You're getting paranoid."

"Don't give me that shit." Vint raised his voice. "And look at me when I'm talking to you."

Adelle turned to him with a mockingly understanding expression. "Lark and I talked about something very private between the two of us. It's none of your business. So, quit asking."

"I'm not stupid. I can tell when something's up. I can feel it."

"I don't know what you're talking about, mister."

Picking up a solid gold bracelet from her night table, he said, "These must be popular. Someone we both know has one exactly like it."

She snatched it from his hand, rolled over, and put it in the other nightstand drawer. "I hope you don't have sticky fingers."

"Are you serious? I rob banks, not people. If I *was* going to rob you, I wouldn't start with a damn bracelet." He sipped more brandy.

"You're telling me you've never robbed anybody?"

"That's so hard for you to believe? After I ran away from the orphanage, I did what I had to, just to eat and get by, but it was just petty stuff. Never took anything of any real value from anyone. There's a difference, banks are insured. But lately, I don't know, maybe I'm getting greedy."

"I'm the wrong one to be telling any of this to. I'm not your bartender and I'm not your shrink. And frankly, I really don't care."

"Forget it. I've been in one spot too long." Vint downed the rest of his drink and stood. "It's making me a little nuts." He walked out of Adelle's bedroom and continued on into the night to his car.

Chapter 28

"Oh, God," Lark moaned, "that was so good."

"Better than any man could." Adelle moved up so she was face to face with Lark as they lay nude in Adelle's bed. Caressing Lark's face, she purred, "I know how to take care of you, honey. I love you. No one else knows how to keep you grounded like me."

"I can't be left alone. The thought of it makes me ..."

"I know, I know. As long as we're together, you'll never set foot in that hospital again."

"I hated that place. Oh, God, I hated it. All those shock treatments." Lark breathed heavier staring at the ceiling. "There were two guys that worked there. They'd come into my room at night. Stuff a rag in my mouth. Strip me down and force me into a straight-jacket. Then ... it was awful. They didn't do it the regular way. Said if I got pregnant everyone would know what they done."

Adelle rose up on one elbow. "I'll never let anyone hurt you."

"They threatened to cut my face up if I told. Said they'd swear I did it to myself." Lark shot up. "I'll get both of 'em one of these days." Lark's bare chest heaved as she stared with a wild look in her eyes. "I'll fix 'em so they can never do it to anyone again!"

"Calm down, Lark." Adelle caressed her shoulder. "Forget about the past. Our future is so bright."

"I told Vint he was the only guy I was ever with besides Danny. Those guys at the hospital don't count. Do they? They forced me."

"That'll never happen to you again. I promise," she said softly, kissing Lark's cheek. "Not as long as you're with me."

"I feel safe with you." Lark turned to look at her. "You know how to smooth me out."

"It'll be just you and me again, sweetheart. Just like it was. Before you got involved with that black-hearted womanizer. I'll be free from the lumber plant soon. We can go wherever you want. You name it."

"I've grown to like this little town, but I heard Paris is beautiful in the spring. And I wondered what it would be like to get all dressed up and play roulette in Monte Carlo."

"You got an expensive imagination, little lady." Adelle threw her head back and laughed. "I love it. I can just picture all those rich guys drooling over you in your expensive gowns. But, it'll be me pleasuring you when we go back to our suite."

"You make it all sound so good." Lark looked down at her folded hands. "But I love Vint."

"Oh, forget about that bank-robbing Romeo. He didn't hesitate to come to my bed and leave you alone. Did he?"

"No."

"You can never trust a guy like that." Adelle pointed a finger. "Did he ever once say, I love you?"

"No."

"The sooner you get him out of your system, the better off you'll be. Trust me. I've been around the block a few more times than you." Adelle moved closer to Lark and kissed her softly on the lips. "I love you."

"Last couple days ... I feel ... strange." Lark took her head in her hands. "Like I don't know who I am sometimes. Things are getting to be a blur."

"I'll make everything better." Adelle gently pulled Lark back down, nuzzled her neck, then kissed her over and over, as she moved down her body.

* * *

237

"Piece of shit." Vint tried over and over to start his sedan. Hopping out, he slammed the door, then kicked it, leaving a dent. He walked a few blocks over to the diner a little before 9:00 pm but all the lights were out. Peering in the front window, he could see that everyone had left.

He lit a cigarette and sat on Dewey's windowsill for a few minutes, then decided to walk to Adelle's. When he got to the edge of town, he was surprised to see Lark walking his way with her head down, her hands deep in the pockets of her checked wool coat.

"Lark," he called out in the waning moonlight.

She kept shuffling in his direction. When they came face to face, she looked at him with a blank stare.

"What're you up to?" Vint was shocked at the change in her demeanor. Even her face looked different. "I've been worried about you. You all right?"

"It's you. Vinton Mercurio. That guy from the diner."

"Of course it's me. What's going on?"

"Nothing. I don't know what you're talking about, mister." She continued walking.

Vint went after her. "Hey, what's … you sure you're OK?"

She ventured on as though in a trance.

"Where you coming from?"

"Why are you asking me all these questions?" She replied calmly, looking straight ahead. "Dewey closed early tonight so I went for a walk."

"There's nothing back that way except Adelle Hurst's place." He motioned behind them.

"Good a direction as any for a walk."

He stood in her way, causing her to stop. "Just because I'm leaving town doesn't mean I don't care what happens to you."

Lark stepped around him and kept going.

"I don't think it's safe for a lady to be walking alone at night."

"I'm fine." She pulled a revolver from her coat pocket. "Don't worry."

He stared at the gun wide-eyed. "Where the hell did you get that?"

"It was my Gramps'."

Vint kept pace with her. "You never told me you had a gun."

"I don't remember you asking me."

"Whoa." He grabbed her arm. "What's going on with you?"

Lark spun and pointed the revolver at his stomach. "You should never grab a person with a loaded gun." She slowly let her arm drop to her side. "Anyone ever teach you that?"

He stood staring at her. "You know Gilstrap has strict rules about carrying guns in town."

"The marshal's an idiot." Her eyes remained cold. "A gun's a good thing to have in these parts. Every now and then we get a razorback boar wander into town. They can be very dangerous. When you see one, you're better off shooting it right away, before it gets a chance to hurt you. You got that?"

"Yeah. I think I catch your drift." He watched her turn and move along. Catching up to her again, he asked, "Would you like me to walk you home?"

"I'm a big girl now. I'll be twenty any day."

"What are you talking about? You're already ..." Vint hesitated, then asked, "Why don't you let me hold that pistol?"

"No." Lark shot him a stern look. "Don't you think you caused enough trouble in this town already?" Looking away, she said, "I can make it the rest of the way by myself. Just go back to what you were doing before you saw me."

He took a few steps, then stopped and watched her walk away.

Chapter 29

Vint slept in his Nash right where it died, on a woodsy side street off Main. After unsuccessfully trying to start it a few more times, he worried about how he was going to make it outside of town to meet Edric and split the robbery money. It would be a long walk with a lot of cash and he'd be late.

Avoiding Dewey's, he washed up and had breakfast at Sally's Restaurant. When he was through eating, he went to the General Store and spent the last of his money purchasing a pack of cigarettes, two quarts of beer, a loaf of bread, and some baloney.

Going back to his sedan, he tried to get it going again. On the third attempt, it kicked over and started. He drove down to the river with his paper bag of items, Lark's flashlight, and the revolver Edric gave him in the trunk. The day, afternoon, and part of the evening were spent parked by the flowing current, smoking, drinking, and reading a little here and there.

Falling asleep behind the wheel with his book in hand, Vint opened his eyes, feeling a chill in the air and realized it was getting close to the time he had to go to the Krauses'. He tried starting his car but the battery was dead. Getting out of the car and looking around, he opened the trunk and retrieved the fedora, short trenchcoat and pants he got from Gramps' closet a week earlier. He changed clothes and put the pistol in the pocket of the coat. Under a hazy, half moon, he took off on foot, avoided streets and sidewalks whenever possible, staying mostly in the shadows.

When he arrived at the house on the edge of the woods, he crept through the grass to the bathroom window. Noting that all the lights in the house were out, he pushed up on the vintage privacy-glass window. It slid up without a problem but he got a bad feeling. Why hadn't he thought of it before? What good would Edric's alibi be if it wasn't for the whole night? Once the Krauses were in bed asleep, they would have no idea what time the money was taken. For that matter, would they check the next morning before going to work to see if the cash was still in the closet? Providing it was even there to begin with. All he had was Edric's word on everything.

After coming this far and putting so much hope into the deal, he had to see if the money was there. If it wasn't in the closet, he'd get out as quickly as possible.

Vint grabbed hold of the sill and pulled himself up. As quietly as he could, he climbed through the window and into the bathroom. Pulling the flashlight from his jacket pocket, he flicked it on and kept the dim beam aimed at the floor as he stepped lightly on the creaking floorboards. Making his way down the hall and to the closet; he opened the door and searched with the narrow shaft of light.

And then he saw it. The large satchel with a design of grapes and leaves embroidered on the age-darkened cloth. He opened it and shined the light into the bag. It was filled with paper-banded stacks of cash. His heart beat faster as he picked up the bag. "This is it," he whispered. "What I've been waiting my whole life for."

He turned to leave the same way he came in but heard a noise from outside. A beam of light flashed across the room from the large picture window at the front of the house. He hit the floor and lay on his stomach as the light from a flashlight scattered its rays. Vint flinched when he heard a heavy knock on the front door and pulled out the revolver. Springing up, he ran toward the rear entrance, pushed the kitchen door open and scrambled to the back door. When he got halfway across the dark room, he fell to the floor on his stomach with a gasp as the bag and pistol flew away from him. He tried to push himself up from the tiles but something syrupy on the floor made him slip onto his face. As the pounding on the door got louder, he rolled to his side to try and see what he tripped over.

In the dim moonlight coming through the window, Mr. Kraus lay stretched out on his back in a pool of blood. Focusing his eyes, he saw a bullet hole in the dead man's forehead. Next to him lay Mrs. Krause, also shot in the head. On the floor next to her was a small caliber snubnose revolver. Vint got up, covered in their blood and grabbed the bag, but could not locate the pistol that slid away when he fell. He heard the front door open with a crash. Unlocking the back door, he quickly looked around, then ran toward the thicket of trees behind the house.

A gunshot rang out in the night and a voice called out, "Stop or I'll shoot!"

He recognized Marshal Gilstrap's voice. More shots were fired. One of the bullets grazed his arm with a burning sensation. When he got to the trees, bark flew off one of them when a bullet hit it.

Vint ran through the woods without looking back. He ran so long and fast that he felt his heart would burst. When he could no longer continue, he collapsed in a clearing under the moon and stars. Vint studied himself. His hands and clothes were covered in blood. He touched his face. It too was coated in the drying thick fluid. Somehow, he had to clean up. He needed a change of clothes. He needed to get out of town.

Getting to his feet again, he walked and stumbled through the thick forest. Searching his mind for answers, he moved further and further away from town and toward the river.

When he got to the riverbank, he took off the fedora and blood-covered coat, then washed his face and hands in the cold, flowing water. Shivering, he removed his shirt and used it to dry off. Examining the injury from the bullet that grazed him, he saw that it was bleeding, then he tied the shirt around the wound.

He put the coat back on, picked up the bag and sat against a wide tree. None of it made sense to him. Even in the Krauses' darkened kitchen, he could tell the snubnose revolver on the floor looked identical to the one Edric had him handle at his apartment. Thinking back, he never saw Edric touch the snubnose. But his own prints were on it.

"But, I've got all the money," Vint said to the cool night air. He opened the bag and pulled out a few stacks of bills. They looked different, older, larger than the cash he was used to. He examined them in the moonbeams. The bills were legal tender and worth a fortune. At one time.

Pulling out more stacks, he scrutinized them. Tossing them aside, he removed more. Dumping the remaining contents onto his lap, he knew he had been had. The money was worthless. They were Confederate bills. He stuffed all of the money back into the bag and set fire to it.

Edric must have killed the Krauses, Vint realized. But why? One thing was obvious. He was the fall guy.

* * *

Vint followed the river west toward Adelle's house. It was close to 11:00 pm when he arrived at her door. He looked around and knocked loudly. There was no answer so he rang the doorbell and pounded harder. He saw a light go on in her upstairs bedroom. Peering in the window next to the door, he saw Adelle coming down the stairs with a pistol in her hand. She turned the porch light on and peeked out through her curtains.

Throwing the door open, she exclaimed, "What in God's sake are you doing here this time of night?"

"I'm in trouble." He felt faint. "I need your help."

"What's that all over you, mud?"

"Some of it. The rest of it's blood. Look, I can't keep standing out here." He looked up her long driveway. "Kill that light."

"Take off your boots." She flicked off the porchlight. "And don't touch anything."

Vint removed his filthy boots and held them as he walked into her house. "I appreciate this." His body visibly shook. "I'm in a real jam."

She looked around outside, then slammed the door. "Am I going to get in trouble by having you here?"

"Not if you're unaware of what's happened."

"Come on. Let's go upstairs. And quit looking at me. I don't have my makeup on."

When they got to the top of the stairs, he said, "I need a hot bath and a stiff drink." Stepping into the bathroom, he took off all his clothes and left them in a heap on the tiled floor. He untied his bloody shirt from around his wound. It was still bleeding.

Inspecting his arm, Adelle said, "You're going to need a bandage and some clean clothes."

Vint filled her large tub and eased into the hot water.

She came back without her automatic handgun and handed him a rock glass filled halfway with cognac. Standing in front of the bathroom mirror, she began applying makeup. "If we didn't have our little deal in the works, I'd call the police on you. Who'd you kill now?"

"I didn't kill anyone but I look guilty as hell." He took a long sip of spirits, set the glass on the edge of the tub and submerged his head under the water. Coming back up, he pushed his hair back.

"How did you manage that?"

"I'm the fall guy in a double murder. The Krauses, the ones who own the bakery, they were both shot in the head tonight. More than likely with a pistol that has my prints on it. You're looking at the perfect patsy."

"Let's say I'm buying this. Who put you in the box?"

As he lathered his hair with Adelle's shampoo, the suds turned red with the Krauses' blood. "A sleazy Englishman by the name Edric Randall."

"The attorney?" She glanced at Vint. "I know him."

"How do you know that character?" He stopped scrubbing.

"He came by the plant. We talked business. He was very charming."

Vint dunked his head in the water again. He sat up and glared at her. "Charming? What kind of business would you have with a guy like that?"

"Finances. It has nothing to do with you."

"It does when he's trying to frame me." He gulped some brandy. "I want to know everything he said."

"He came by. Went over my books at no charge and said he could save me a lot in taxes."

"I thought you were smart. He's looking for a way to chisel you." Vint stood and soaped up. "Did my name come up?"

"Your name? No. Of course not."

"Look me in the eye and say that," he demanded.

She turned from the mirror, watched him lather, then moved her eyes up to meet his. "Your name never came up."

Vint pulled the plug, closed the black curtain and turned the shower on. After he rinsed off, he pulled the curtain open. Adelle handed him a thick bath towel. He dried off, avoided the bloody wound, then hung the towel around his neck.

"Stand still." Adelle stood before him holding gauze and tape. "Let me bandage you."

Standing naked, his black body hair glistened with moisture. She finished dressing his wound, then said, "Follow me. I'll find you something to wear. Then you have to get out of here."

Walking after Adelle, he grabbed her arm and spun her around. "I'm not going anywhere. I need a place to hide out until I start that fire. And this is it, sister."

"What happens if the marshal or his goober-eating deputy show up here looking for you?" She yanked her arm from his grip.

"Not likely. Even if Gilstrap recognized me, he'll figure I'm long gone. Probably out combing the countryside right now." He finger-combed his wet hair back out of his eyes. "We've been careful. Who knows about us?"

"Yes. Who *does* know about us? How about that little cheerleader you've been screwing?"

"She won't say anything. The kid's crazy about me."

"Crazy being the operative word." Her eyes worked their way down to his dark-haired chest. "Be careful. When a woman in love turns on you, Hell hath no fury."

"I'm familiar with the phrase."

Adelle gazed at him and noticed he was becoming aroused. "Talking about that slip of a girl getting you hot?" She took his cock in her hand and squeezed. "She a good lay?" She stroked him until he was rock hard. "You like that young blonde trim?"

Vint scooped her into in his arms, carried her to her room and threw her on the bed. He got on top of her and bucked as hard as he could, as if trying to excise all of his demons through his cock.

Chapter 30

After sleeping a few hours, Vint got up and rummaged around in Mr. Hurst's closet and drawers. He found a zipper jacket, military boots, and other clothes that were a reasonable fit, including a pair of the deceased man's army pants from his slimmer days. After retrieving his razor, wallet and other things from the pockets of his bloodied clothes, he carried the soiled items in a ball to the top of the stairway and listened. Carefully descending the stairs in the quiet house, he realized that Adelle must have given her help the day off and she had left early for work.

Vint went to Adelle's three-car garage and located a shovel. Running his hand across the hood of a black, mint-condition Hudson Commodore, he pondered his chances of getting caught if he drove it straight west out of town. After some consideration, he thought it would be best to stay off the roads for now and stick to his plan. Wait until Saturday night, let things die down a little, get the $5,000 from Adelle, and hop a freight train out.

First looking out of all the windows, he hurried out the back door to the wooded area close by, carrying the old clothes and shovel. He quickly dug a hole, threw the incriminating items in and covered it up before running back to the house.

He tried having a little breakfast, but was too nervous to finish. After closing all the drapes on the lower floor, he settled down with his book, trying in vain to read with his mind racing. Turning on the television in hopes of a distraction, he watched the images on the round, black and white screen but couldn't concentrate on what was being said. He clicked the radio on and flipped from station to station searching for news about the Krauses, but heard nothing. Constantly getting up and peering out through the curtains, his mind kept going around, trying to figure out how everything went so bad.

Every time he heard a noise, he jumped. Finally going upstairs, he spent most of the day and afternoon pacing from one bedroom to the next trying to think of some way out of the mess he was in. Becoming exhausted, he eventually slept a couple hours on Adelle's bed.

Vint flinched when he heard the front door open. With his heart pounding, he heard Adelle's voice echo from downstairs, "It's me!"

As he descended the stairs, Adelle was stepping out of her high heels, carrying the newspaper.

"Looks like I'll be cooking tonight," she said to him as he approached. "It's not my strong suit so I don't want to hear any complaints. We'll eat in the study, wait there."

"Let me see that paper." He took the daily newspaper from her hand and headed into the study.

* * *

Vint wiped his mouth with a linen napkin and dropped it on his plate of half-finished ham and potato hash. "There's a story about the Krauses. Closed casket funeral tomorrow." He motioned toward the newspaper on the floor next to him. "Doesn't say much else. Just that they were murdered and a person of interest is wanted for questioning."

"Maybe Amos didn't recognize you in the dark." Adelle stood up, holding her empty plate.

"I don't know. Hard to tell, he only saw me from behind and I was wearing different clothes."

She took Vint's plate from the leather ottoman in front of him. "How was it?"

"Not bad." He grabbed his cigarettes from the end table. "I'm not in a position to complain."

"I'll be right back."

Lighting a cigarette, Vint sat in Mr. Hurst's leather easy chair feeling trapped.

Returning to the study, Adelle took her seat across from him on the sofa. "How could you be so stupid?" she admonished. "I'm having second thoughts about using you for this job. You're not as bright as I thought you were."

"There's a big difference between the Krauses' deal and the one we got planned." He jabbed a finger in the air. "I made the mistake of trusting someone. I'm in control of the arson job. I'll make sure everything goes smooth."

"You sure about that?"

"Positive." He rested his feet on the ottoman. "That Hudson in the garage run?"

"Yes. That was Mr. Hurst's. Why would that concern you?" Her eyes flashed at him. "Don't even think about taking off in it. That's worth a good buck."

"I'm not taking off. There's something I have to do tomorrow and I can't have anyone recognize me."

"Don't be stupider than you already are. Just stay put until Saturday night."

"I have to do this. Look, I'll be careful and take the backroads."

Adelle scrutinized him. "You look like a bum. Next time you shave stand a little closer to the razor."

"I've been so jittery, I'm liable to cut my own throat." Vint shot up in his seat when the doorbell rang.

Slowly getting to her feet, with a worried look she ordered, "Stay here. I'll see who it is."

A moment later, Adelle said louder than necessary, "Amos, what are you doing here?"

"May I come in for a minute?" Gilstrap's husky voice echoed.

"Of course. What's this all about?"

Vint dropped his cigarette in the ashtray and jumped up. Grabbing a letter opener from the desk, he stood with his back to the wall next to the doorway of the study.

"What do you think it's about?" the marshal replied.

"Well, I heard about the Krauses."

"Exactly." Gilstrap walked from the foyer into the great room.

Adelle followed him. "What does that have to do with me?"

"Have you seen anything suspicious?"

"Suspicious?" She put a hand on her hip. "I stayed an extra two hours at the plant supervising the big shipment. Then I came straight home and made myself some dinner. When am I supposed to see something suspicious?"

Gilstrap paced around and glanced into the dining room. "Got the table cleared already, I see."

"I didn't eat in the dining room." Her voice turned harsh. "Would you please stand still while you're talking to me?"

"I'm gonna come right out with it." He removed his hat and held it at his side. "Have you seen Smith?"

"No. Of course not. He never even reported back to work. I should've let him rot in your jail."

"Is that cigarette smoke?" the marshal asked as he kept wandering about the great room, moving closer to the study. "Mind if I look around?"

Brandishing the letter opener, Vint's chest heaved as he breathed through his mouth.

"Yes, I *do* mind." She raised her voice. "Damn it. I have to be up early again tomorrow and stay at work an extra two hours like I did today. I haven't seen anything suspicious and I haven't seen Smith. I'd appreciate it if you left now. I've got to get to bed."

"You know I can get a warrant."

"Don't threaten me, Amos." Adelle poked his chest. "Or I'll finish you in this town."

"When did you get so cold?"

"I was always cold. You were just too mesmerized to notice."

"I wish it could be like it was before." Gilstrap lowered his voice. "When your husband went on his hunting trips."

"Quit dreaming, you fool. I did what I did to control you. You're the one who started talking nonsense about love. Don't forget, I have the photos in a safe place."

"That hunting accident …"

Adelle interrupted him, "You better not say another word."

"Why?" The marshal glanced around.

"Go! Just go!" She paused, then lowered her voice and glared at him. "Before I say something I might regret."

Putting his hat back on, the marshal stared at her for a moment, then headed for the door. He stopped and turned to face her. Raising his finger, he looked as though he was going to say something, but his head dropped and he continued out of the house.

Adelle went back into the study and saw Vint standing next to the doorway, clutching the letter opener with a wild look in his eyes.

"Damn. My heart's pounding," he said in a breathy voice. "I need a drink."

Walking to her liquor cabinet, she produced two glasses, then poured them both a snifter of Grand Marnier. She set a glass on the end table next to her late husband's chair. "Sit down. You're making me nervous." Watching him pace around, she added, "And put down that opener."

Vint tossed the silvery blade onto the desk, went back to the easy chair and flopped into it. "What was all that about photos, and a hunting accident?"

"Nothing that concerns you."

"At this point, anything that has to do with you concerns me."

"Don't go jumping to conclusions," she shot back. "Things aren't always as they appear."

"You don't have to be a genius to connect the dots." He swirled his snifter.

"The only thing that should concern you is burning down the plant and not getting caught. Don't get distracted by things that are none of your business."

Vint took a long sip of the cognac liqueur without taking his eyes off her. "That what you have on the marshal? He bump your hubby off?"

"You're talking crazy. I loved Mr. Hurst."

"Yeah. Sure, you did." He took another sip. "Did Hurst have a first name or did his parents name him Mister?"

"Of course he did. I never addressed him by his given name."

"Daddy issues, huh?" Vint smirked. "Older guy, in charge, powerful. He look anything like your old man?"

Adelle shot to her feet and flung her glass into the fireplace. "Shut up!" she screamed. "I got half a mind to call Amos back here!"

He sat back and crossed one leg over the other. "That's the second time I saw you lose your cool. And twice in one night."

"I'm warning you. You better keep your mouth shut about … everything."

"OK, lady. Sit down and relax. Don't like it when the shoe's on the other foot, do you?"

"What's that supposed to …" A look of revelation came over her face.

"Yeah. That's right. Keep your elegant looking nose out of what makes me tick and I'll do you the same."

"You can sleep in Mr. Hurst's bedroom. And lock the door."

"Or sleep with one eye open?"

"I can't wait for all this to be over. The sooner I never have to look at your face again, the better. You get under my skin more than anyone I've ever met."

Vint threw his head back and laughed. "And here I thought we were going to get married and live happily ever after."

"Don't mock me." She glared at him.

"Come on. Truce." He got up, poured her another glass of spirits, and handed it to her. "What do I care how Hurst bought it. Long as it doesn't happen to me." Vint's head spun toward the doorway when the phone rang in the distance.

"Who's this now?" She got up and walked into the great room.

Standing and walking next to the doorway again, he listened as Adelle answered the phone.

"Hello ... look, this isn't a good time ... no ... I ... no ... I can't talk right now ... yes ... all right. Good night."

When she hung up, Vint sat back down and picked up his glass. "Who was that?" he asked as she reentered the study.

"No one."

"It must have been someone."

"It's none of your business."

"Guess nothing's my business tonight." Vint got up again and poured himself a full snifter. "I'm going to hit the hay." He left the room and climbed the high, broad stairway to the second floor.

Chapter 31

Vint stood in front of the foggy mirror after his shower and lathered his seven-day stubble. Using his straight razor, he shaved everywhere except his upper lip, then carefully carved out a moustache, shaving even lines on the top, bottom and sides.

"What's this?" Adelle walked into the open bathroom doorway on her lunch break and inspected his new look. "You look like that actor. What's his name? From *The Mark of Zorro*."

"Hear anything more about the Krauses?" He turned from the mirror patting his face with a towel and faced her.

"Everything's pretty hush hush. Gilstrap's playing it close to the vest."

"That suit you got me is back in my Nash. They're probably keeping an eye on it. I'm going to borrow some of Hurst's clothes."

"Take what you want. I don't know what to do with any of it. Maybe give it all to Goodwill." Adelle left the room.

Vint slid open the mirror-covered closet door in Mr. Hurst's bedroom and found a shirt, tie, and dark suit he could wear. He put everything on and picked out a belt, needing it to hold the pants up. Inspecting the array of hats on the shelf, he selected a dark-gray, cashmere Borsalino and tried it on. He looked in the mirror and pulled the brim down, half covering his eyes. Thumbing through an assortment of topcoats, he picked out a tan trench coat. He slipped it on, tied the belt around his waist and turned the collar up.

Adelle entered the bedroom and laughed. "Well, look at you. Right out of a detective movie."

He picked up a pair of sunglasses off a dresser and put them on. Turning to face her, he asked, "Think anyone'll recognize me?"

"Doubtful. Not unless they get a good look at your mug."

"I only plan on getting close to one person."

"You're either stupid, crazy or both."

* * *

Vint pulled Hurst's Hudson off the bumpy gravel road that led into the cemetery, then parked and got out. Through dark sunglasses, he saw a group of town regulars gathered together, minus the marshal and deputy. Everyone was dressed in black except for one man. He wore a gray flannel suit.

With the mourners' backs to him, Vint walked across the grass through rows of headstones toward the group. As he approached, the preacher's voice became clearer as he presided over the Krauses' funeral. He stopped about thirty yards away, lit a cigarette and pretended to pray over a grave.

After several minutes, the preacher wrapped things up and Vint walked toward the gatherers. Keeping his head down, he moved closer to the dispersing crowd and watched Edric from under the brim of the fedora. Making sure the Brit's back was to him at all times, he got close enough to hear him talking to an elderly couple.

"A tragedy, simply a tragedy," Edric said with a flourish. "I hope they get the man responsible for this heinous crime. And I think we all know who that is."

"Would you like to ride back with us?" the elderly man asked Edric.

"Why, yes. So kind of you. Did you know that I'm a lawyer? I specialize in finance and estate planning."

"That a fact?" the man asked, putting his hat on. "I was just tellin' Cora that we need to set up a will."

"Why don't you pull your car up?" Edric patted the man's shoulder. "I'll be right along."

As the man took his wife's arm and walked toward their vintage Hupmobile, Edric removed a flask from his inside suitcoat pocket and took a swig. "Country bumpkins. They grow on trees out here."

With everyone except Edric dispersed from the Krauses' gravesite, Vint walked up behind him and pulled his razor from the pocket of the trench coat.

Edric flinched when Vint shoved his unopened razor into the Englishman's back. "Don't move," Vint whispered in his ear. "That's a gun in your spine. Open your mouth and you get it. I got nothing to lose at this point."

"I-I-I." Edric gulped.

"Wave those people on," Vint commanded under his breath. "Tell them you don't need a ride."

"Go on without me," Edric called to the couple. "I've changed my mind. A walk will do me good. We'll talk again soon."

"Good boy." Vint kept the razor in Edric's back and moved next to him. "Just walk slowly. Make any sudden movements and you'll be staying in this graveyard permanently."

"Vint, you got me all wrong." Edric's voice broke. "Things aren't as they appear."

"Don't give me any double talk. I heard what you said back there, about getting the guy who killed the Krauses. You and me both know you shot them and sent me to their house as the patsy."

"No. It wasn't like that. Someone else must have heard about the money and got to it before you. I swear it wasn't me."

"Don't insult my intelligence," Vint said through clenched teeth. "Think I'm stupid? Like the Krauses were?"

"You've got to believe me. Why in the world would I do that? Anyone could see that I was the one who was double-crossed. Either you or someone else made off with the cash. I was the brains behind the operation and came away empty-handed."

"I'll give you this, you sneaky, limey bastard. You talk a good game. Yeah, I got the dough, but it was worthless. Confederate bills, all of it. And I'd bet anything you knew it."

"Confederate? How was I to know?"

"You said you saw the money in the house," Vint replied, leading Edric toward the Hudson.

"Well, yes. That's true. I did see the money. Just a glimpse of it for a brief moment. How was I to know it was worthless? All of your money here looks foreign to me. Especially older bills."

"You're good. I never heard anyone lie as convincingly as you. What was your angle? What did you get out of this?"

"Nothing! Nothing! I promise on the throne."

When they reached the Hudson, Vint stepped behind Edric and put the razor in the left pocket of his trench coat and pointed it at the Englishman. Vint watched the last of the cars pull away. "All right, squire. Turn around with your hands up. We're going to have to do this the hard way."

"You're going to shoot me? Right here?" Edric raised his trembling hands. "What good will that do you?"

With the razor directed at Edric's stomach, Vint removed the car keys with his right hand and opened the trunk. "Get in. Now!"

"All right. Keep calm. I'll do as you say."

Edric climbed into the trunk and Vint slammed it shut.

After driving to a deserted farmhouse, he saw along the way, Vint got out, opened the trunk and quickly stepped back with the razor in his pocket again. "OK, out of there."

Vint led him to the rear entrance of the old house and kicked the backdoor open. "Down those steps. Into the basement."

"Please don't shoot," Edric pleaded.

When they got down to the musty smelling basement, Vint spotted a piece of rope laying on the floor. "Back up against that pole. Hands behind your back."

"May I please have a drink first? I have a flask in my pocket."

"Hands in back of you, behind that pole!" Vint stepped behind Edric, wrapped the rope around his wrists individually, then tightly around both of them a few times and knotted it. He walked back in front of Edric. "You're going to do some talking now."

"Go ahead. Beat me. You'll get nothing."

"Beat you?" Vint laughed, then pulled out his razor and flipped it open. "I'm not going to beat you. I'm going to start cutting pieces off you till you admit the truth."

"I don't believe you. You don't have it in you."

Vint brought the razor close to Edric's face. "Because of you, I'm a suspect in a double homicide. If they pin it on me, I'll be sent up for the rest of my life."

"No ... please."

"Start talking or I start slicing." Vint waved the blade back and forth within an inch of Edric's face.

"I swear on all that's holy. You got this all wrong."

"I'm betting with your life that I'm right. I saw the snubnose I handled on the floor by the Krauses' bodies." Vint scraped the razor along Edric's cheek. "Tell me how you're profiting from setting me up."

"Vint, I beg of you. You're making a huge mistake."

"Which ear is your favorite?"

"W-what?"

"Pick an ear." Vint brought the blade to one side of Edric's head, then the other. "Which one's coming off first?"

"You wouldn't."

Vint grabbed Edric's right ear and began sliced it away from his scalp.

Edric screamed in fear and pain. When the skin was severed about a quarter-inch, he pleaded, "All right! All right! Stop!" He sobbed loudly. "I'll tell you everything."

Vint wiped blood from the razor onto the shoulder of the Englishman's suit. "No more lies. I'm running out of patience with you."

"The Krauses ... they could barely read. I had them sign some legal papers." He sniffed and continued in a wavering voice, "Most of it was standard legal fare. I slipped a couple of contracts in with the others ... one giving me power of attorney over their affairs and another making me beneficiary of their house, bakery and everything else they owned in the event of their death."

"So, you *did* kill them." Vint brought the razor to Edric's left eye. "Didn't you?"

"Oh, my God." Edric watched as blood dripped onto his suitcoat from his ear. "Yes ... yes. I shot them."

"And set me up to take the fall. I should cut your throat right now and let you bleed to death."

"Please. Have mercy. I don't want to die. I just wanted enough money to go back to England and clear my name."

"That why you kept putting the robbery off. You needed time to get all the paperwork filed."

"Yes." Edric whimpered and hung his head.

"I'm a hunted man because of you." Vint reached into Edric's pocket and pulled out his flask. "Why should I have mercy?" He unscrewed the lid of the container and took a gulp of gin.

"I'll make it up to you. I promise. Give me that chance."

"What've you got in mind?" Vint took another sip.

"After I sell off the Krauses' property, I'll send you a check, for half of everything I get." Between heavy breaths, Edric exclaimed, "I'll mail it to you. Where ever you want. You have my word."

"Your word's no good. How could I trust that you won't have the law waiting for me when I go to some post office or other address to get the check?"

"Well, I-I …"

"I got a better idea. You give my half to Lark Stookey, that little blonde who works at the diner. That kid deserves a break."

"Then you'll let me live? Of course. Anything you say."

"Tell her it's a going away present from me." Vint finished what was in the flask and let it drop to the floor. "I find out you welched, the world won't be big enough for you to hide in. I'll come over there to London and slice you up like a Sunday roast."

"I understand. Now, please release me."

Vint walked behind Edric. "As soon as I cut you free, I want you on your belly." He sliced through the rope. "Go on. Lie down. Count out loud to one-hundred."

Walking backward toward the stairs, Vint kept an eye on the prone Edric as he counted. He bound up the steps, two at a time and hurried to the Hudson. Pulling away he muttered, "Should have killed the bastard." Watching out for the marshal's car, he drove back to Adelle's.

Chapter 32

"Well, this is it. The big night." Adelle, dressed in a snug-fitting red dress and matching high heels, added a bit more twenty-four-year-old scotch to Vint's glass as they sat at the bar in her great room. "Fitting that it's Halloween."

"I didn't realize." Vint took a sip and stared into his glass. "All Hallow's Eve. Day of the dead."

"My favorite night of the year." She smiled slightly and raised one eyebrow.

He was quiet for a few minutes, nursing his drink and reading the final pages of *Hell Hath No Fury*. Feeling bedeviled, he tossed the book on the bar with an odd look on his face.

"Finally finish it?" She toyed with the diamond pendant that hung from her neck on a gold chain.

"Yeah. Things didn't work out too well for that guy." He brought his boot up to the rung of the chrome stool. "Not the way he expected."

Adelle picked up the paperback and inspected the cover. "Sounds like my kind of book. I'll have to read it."

"I think I'll take my money now." He reached his hand toward her.

"I'll pay you as soon as you produce results. Think I'm crazy? I'm going to put $5,000 in your hand and have you take off?"

"I want that cash, lady. I need to split as soon as that place is on fire."

"That's no good. What if the insurance investigators realize it wasn't an accident? Then I'm out the $5,000 and a business."

"Don't try changing the rules in the middle of the game." He poked a finger at her. "I want that money tonight or I'm not going through with this."

"How about this? If you wait until after I get the insurance money, I'll double your fee. I can mail you a check."

"Nothing doing, sweetheart." Vint's brow furrowed. "I want to see the cash now or I'm out of here for good."

"All right." Adelle left the room and returned a few minutes later. She held up a thick wad of banded bills.

Vint crooked a finger toward himself. "Let me count it."

"It's all here. I promise you." She put the money in her purse. "You're not touching it until you pull this off."

"You know I could just take it from you." He stood up.

Adelle backed up a step.

"Just kidding, lover doll," he said, staring into her eyes with a serious expression. "You leave that window unlocked like I told you?"

"Yes, yes, it's unlocked."

Vint glanced out the window of the great room. "It's dark enough. I'm heading over there. I'll meet you back here right after to collect."

"I think I should drop you off."

"Nothing doing, toots." He stood, pulled a handkerchief from his pocket, then wiped his fingerprints from his glass. "You shouldn't be seen anywhere near the mill. I'll walk there, follow along the river and stay off the streets."

"You can lay down on the backseat of my car. I'll drop you off close by in a dark area."

"Maybe you should just let me do this my way." Vint banged his glass down on the bar. "Don't you realize I'm watching out for you here?"

"Look, I'm the one paying you the $5,000. I want to make sure nothing happens to you along the way. Anything could go wrong. You could be spotted by Gilstrap or Anfield. This'll be faster."

"OK, damn it. Let's go."

* * *

"You never told me how you were going to do it." Adelle looked straight ahead as she drove.

Lying on the backseat, Vint answered back, "That's right."

"I'm the one in charge here. I have a right to know how I'm spending my money."

"You have a right to get good results. That's it."

Glancing back at him in the rearview mirror, she said, "I need to judge for myself whether or not your plan is sound."

"Shut up about it. You're driving me crazy. I'm doing it this way to protect you. When the insurance guys grill you, it's best that you're genuinely surprised."

"All right," she answered, with defeat in her voice.

Vint propped himself on one elbow. "Anywhere up here." As Adelle slowed to a stop, he added, "Turn your interior light off." He opened the backdoor and looked around before getting out.

With the sound of a distant coyote howling in the cool evening air, Vint crept along, keeping an eye out for anyone who might be walking about.

After safely making it to Hurst Lumber without being spotted, he slid the window up that was to the right of the main entrance. He climbed inside and called out, "Anybody here?" His voice echoed in the vast room. He yelled louder, "Anyone here?"

Going straight to the supply room, he grabbed a few cans of turpentine and brought them back to the large main room of the plant. Vint uncapped one, but accidently dropped it in a pile of wood shavings when he heard the main entrance door unlocking. He jumped behind a stack of planks.

"Vint … Vint, where are you?"

"What the hell are you doing here?" He yelled at Adelle. "I could have started the fire already."

"I looked through the window. It looked safe."

"I asked you, what are you doing in here?"

"I have to know how you plan to pull this off. If you don't tell me, the deal's off and you don't get a dime."

"Where's your car?"

"Just up the road." She put her key ring in her coat pocket. "I left it where it won't be spotted. Don't worry."

"Damn you." Vint stood glaring at her with his fists clenched.

"You're wasting time. Tell me."

Quickly weighing his options, he gave in. "I'm going to start the fire out back. I have the perfect spot to drop a lit cigarette. It'll start a fire in the dry leaves, they lead right up to the rear wall."

"That's it? A lit cigarette? That's what I'm paying you $5,000 for?"

"Trust me. I know what I'm doing. If the fire started anywhere inside the plant, it'd look suspicious. Doing it my way, the insurance company won't have any choice but pay you. Who can disprove that some bum didn't walk by and carelessly pitch a lit cigarette? I saved a long butt from an ashtray at Dewey's, wrapped it in a paper napkin and carried it around in my pocket so it would look like something a drifter would smoke."

"All right. I feel better now. I'll get out of here." Adelle removed an ornate silver flask from her purse. "A toast first. To me never setting foot in this hell hole again." She put the flask to her lips and tilted her head back. "And to you never robbing another bank or ever going back to prison." She handed it to Vint with a gleam in her eye.

Vint took a long sip of the scotch. "That's got a bite to it." He looked at the flask suspiciously. "Go on, get going."

Spitting and wiping her mouth with a lacy handkerchief, Adelle's demeanor changed. "Lover boy," she said in a mocking manner, "there's been a slight change of plans." She yelled out, "Come in!"

Vint watched Lark walk in with her pistol aimed at his chest. "Lark! What the … what are you doing here?"

"You like surprises, Vint?" Adelle greeted Lark with a passionate kiss. "I've got a great one for you. You're going to die in the fire."

"Put that gun away, Lark." He started to sweat. "You can't shoot me."

"You hurt me." Lark's hand trembled as she held her aim on him.

Adelle's laugh echoed in the vast room.

"Lark, you said you loved me." He felt dizzy.

"You never said it to me though, did you?" Lark answered back with watery eyes.

"I planned to contact you after things settled down." His breathing was labored. "The only reason I had anything to do with this witch is for the insurance money. You got to believe me, you never left my thoughts."

Adelle spoke up, "Was Lark on your mind the nights you left her alone and came over to screw me? He'd say anything right now to save himself."

"Listen to me." His eyes felt heavy. "I made a deal with Edric Randall. He's going to send you a check for a large amount of money."

"More lies, no doubt," Adelle stated loudly.

"Don't believe her. She doesn't know my plans included you." Vint dropped to his knees. "What did you give me?" Vint asked Adelle as he fought to keep his eyes open.

"I can't pronounce it, but it works fast. Doesn't it?"

"Don't ..." He tried to speak but the words wouldn't form. Everything was slowly going dark as he collapsed onto his side with Lark and Adelle in his line of vision.

Adelle grabbed the back of Vint's jacket, dragged him to a support beam, and pulled him into a sitting position. Reaching into his pocket, she removed his cigarettes and the silver cigarette lighter she had given him. She took out one of his Old Gold, lit it, and put it in his mouth. Slipping the lighter into her purse, then tossing the cigarette pack on the floor next to him, she said, "Now all we have to do is wait until his smoke burns down a little, then knock it out of his mouth and down onto his jacket. It'll look like he accidently fell asleep with a lit cigarette."

Lark stood whimpering, shaking her head side to side with the pistol aimed at Vint.

Adelle stood over him, smiling. "You're the perfect fall guy, an ex-con. Not only were you caught smoking in here before, you were caught sleeping here too." Her laughter became shrill.

With his last ounce of strength, Vint reached his hand to his mouth and tossed the cigarette over his shoulder and into the pile of turpentine soaked wood shavings.

"You bastard!" Adelle went to retrieve the lit cigarette but the shavings quickly caught fire. She backed away from the flames. "You ruined everything." Adelle kicked him in the face with her pointed shoe. Blood trickled down his cheek and his eyes closed again. She raised her heel and aimed it at his eye but the fire quickly spread and she backed away. "Let's get out of here," she yelled, turning to Lark.

"No! I can't go through with it!" Lark aimed her revolver at Adelle.

"What are you doing? We're almost there, honey." Adelle cautiously stepped toward her, reaching for the gun. "Lark! Don't be crazy!"

"I don't like being called crazy." Tears streamed down Lark's cheeks. "Good bye, Adelle." She pulled the trigger and the bullet tore into Adelle's chest.

Adelle's mouth dropped open. She made gurgling sounds, then coughed blood. Her eyes rolled back and she stumbled backward into the fire. Her clothing and hair went up in flames almost immediately. Staggering toward Lark ablaze with her eyes wide open, Adelle's arms flailed about. Lark fired again, putting a bullet through her forehead. Adelle reached out with one hand, then collapsed in the deadly inferno that engulfed her.

The sickening odor of Adelle's burning body and singed hair filled the air, choking Lark and Vint. She helped him to his feet and he vomited. She put his arm around her neck and walked him out of the burning structure. With the sound of the town's one firetruck blaring in the distance, his head began to clear.

"It's going to be me and you, forever, Vint. Me and you and our baby."

Vint pulled away from Lark with a shocked look on his pale, sweating face.

As he backed away from her, she cried out over the roaring flames and crackle of burning wood, "Me and you, always! Always!"

He staggered backward, trying to keep his balance.

"You're not going anywhere." She pointed the pistol at his chest. "Vinton!"

Vint coughed from the thick smoke filling the air, then turned and stumbled as he ran. He fell to the ground with a thud as a bullet whizzed by him. He got up and continued running.

Lark fired wildly as she ran after him, her bullets missing through the smoky haze.

Hearing the sound of a moving freight train, he continued running, his head aching and woozy from the drugs.

"Vinton!" She fired again. "I'm having your baby!"

Vint felt a searing pain in his left shoulder, knocking him to the ground. He scrambled to his feet and followed the sound of the freight train as it got closer in the dark. Through a clearing, he saw the train as it picked up speed along the straightaway.

"Don't run away!" she shrieked. "Stay with me! I love you!"

He ran as fast as he could, trying to grab hold of the metal ladder on the side of the boxcar. Reaching out and touching the cold steel bar with his fingertips, a bullet ricocheted off the side of the car, showering his face with splinters. Almost out of breath, trying to keep up with the train, he stretched his right hand out as his left arm dangled and flopped at his side. Finally getting a good grip on the side ladder and pulling himself closer, another shot rang out. Vint gasped as he felt a deep burning pain in his side.

"Please ... please." Vint held on tight with his right hand as his legs collapsed beneath him, his boots dragging in the stones. He felt his grip weaken as he muttered, "Please, God ... please help me."

Vint could no longer hang on. His sweating fingers slipped off the cold metal bar. He hit the ground hard and rolled a couple times on the stones, dangerously close to the tracks.

Over the squeal of metal to metal, inches from his face, from out of the darkness he heard Lark's desperate voice call out, "I love you! Don't make me kill you!"

Choking on air that was thick with the foul odor of oil-soaked railroad ties and burning lumber, he pushed himself to his feet with his uninjured arm, stumbled, then ran trying to keep up with the train. He saw a boxcar with an open door approaching and grabbed hold of the bottom handle, nearly sweeping him off his feet. Struggling to keep up and gasping for air, he kicked up off the ground and managed to get his left foot up and behind the opening. His vision started going dark, and with all the strength he had left, pulled himself up into the freight car.

He lay wheezing, his shoulder aching and his side feeling as though it was on fire. He looked up at treetops flying by as the train quickly picked up speed. The waning crescent moon was visible between scattered dark clouds and the stars shone brightly in the inky night sky. With a dry mouth and a tongue that felt like sandpaper, he slowly caught his breath. Just before passing out, Vint muttered, "If that's love, I can do without it."

THE END

If you enjoyed this book, please let others know by leaving a quick review on Amazon. Also, if you spot anything untoward in the paperback, get in touch. We strive for the best quality and appreciate reader feedback.

editor@thebookfolks.com

www.thebookfolks.com

Be sure to also read Lou Holly's fiction debut, SOUTHSIDE HUSTLE, a fast-paced crime thriller set in 1980s Chicago.

Available on Kindle and in paperback.